PUF...

by

KATE BENEDICT

CHIMERA

Puritan Passions first published in 2003 by
Chimera Publishing Ltd
PO Box 152
Waterlooville
Hants
PO8 9FS

Printed and bound in Great Britain by
Cox & Wyman Ltd, Reading.

PURITAN PASSIONS

Kate Benedict

This novel is fiction – in real life practice safe sex

He reached out again and seized her by the upper arm, flinging her facedown on the bed. As she struggled to rise he hauled her skirts above her waist, trapping her in the clinging folds. Grabbing her flailing hands at the wrist he wound his belt round them and fastened it to the bed-head so she was stretched out helplessly before him, naked from the waist down.

He ran his hand over her pert buttocks, enjoying the way her flesh cringed at his touch and feeling his manhood swell. 'Don't run away, sweetheart,' he panted. 'I shall be back, with a little surprise for you.'

She lay there frozen in the muffling darkness as his footsteps retreated, her heart pounding with horrified anticipation. What was he going to do?

In answer she heard him return. There was a moment's silence, a strange whistling sound, then she gasped as the world exploded into white-hot pain as a thin cane connected with her flesh. The soft globes of her bottom quivered beneath the blow, a fine red line appearing on the tender skin. She gritted her teeth. She would not scream... she would not scream...

'Mornin', Mistress Lucinda,' said Martha, depositing a mug of mulled ale on the small table beside the bed, and a copper can of hot water beside the basin and ewer, before going to pull back the heavy velvet curtains. Winter sunshine spilled into the room, but despite it, and the freshly laid fire crackling in the hearth, the air was still so cold that her breath came in white puffs. Lucy groaned and snuggled deeper under the covers.

'Come along now,' coaxed Martha. 'The weather's fine and the master's up and about already.' She looked round furtively and lowered her voice. 'And it's our Lord's birthday, too. A Merry Christmas to you, mistress.'

'What's merry about it when we're not even allowed to celebrate it?' Lucy muttered grumpily. Reluctantly she sat up in bed and allowed Martha to tuck her mother's old fur-lined cloak round her shoulders. 'Old Noll saw to that!'

Martha's hand flew to her mouth and she looked round furtively. 'Best not talk about Master Cromwell like that,' she hissed. 'You know what they say: "Walls have ears".'

'Don't be such a goose,' giggled Lucy. 'I doubt that even he has spies in my bedchamber! What crime would they discover? That I still wore ribbons in my shifts?'

'It's no laughing matter, mistress,' sniffed Martha. 'I did hear tell that down in London the soldiers go from house to house pullin' people's Christmas dinners from their very ovens!'

'Damned wart-faced old killjoy,' muttered Lucy. 'If he

5

had his way we'd do nothing but go about with long faces, praying forgiveness for our sins.' She giggled. 'But he's not here to watch us now, is he?' Reaching under her pillow she produced a tiny package wrapped in a scrap of linen, and handed it to Martha with a smile. 'A Merry Christmas – and to hell with Old Noll!'

'Oh mistress, you shouldn't have, you know it's forbidden!' exclaimed Martha in disapproval – but her eyes were bright and her fingers already scrabbling at the twine. The parcel fell open and a length of lace and several bright ribbons tumbled out. 'They're beautiful!' she gasped, holding them up and turning them this way and that in the sunshine to admire them – before coming back down to earth with a bump. 'But where did you find them? I haven't seen fripperies like this in years.'

'Old Martin at the October Fair,' smiled Lucy. 'He had them hidden beneath the counter of his stall.' Her smile vanished as she thought back. The fair, looked forward to by everyone in the county, both high and low, had been a shadow of its former self. No mummers. No gypsy fortune-tellers promising health and wealth and luck if you crossed their palms with silver. No jugglers or dog-baiting. Nothing but dull commerce.

Unless you knew where to look, that was. The English did not take kindly to being told what to do. Old Martin might have had nothing but needles, threads and other worthy and serviceable goods on display, but for his favoured customers there were always other things tucked away out of sight.

'You shouldn't have wasted your money,' scolded Martha. 'Lace and ribbons are banned. Where am I going to wear them?'

'Sew them on your shifts,' said Lucy, deliberately misunderstanding her servant's words. She grinned mischievously. 'Even Oliver Cromwell would think twice of looking under your petticoats – for fear of getting his ears boxed.'

'I'll box yours, you pert young madam!' chuckled Martha. 'Now get yourself up and dressed and down to the hall. Your father wishes to speak to you.'

'What about?' asked Lucy.

'I'm sure the master doesn't confide in me, Mistress Lucinda,' sniffed Martha. 'You'll have to wait till he tells you himself.' She folded the lace and ribbons back into their linen wrapping and tucked them between her ample breasts. 'Safe enough from Cromwell's spies there,' she winked. 'Now up with you, girl. The day's half over!' She bustled out, leaving Lucy smiling after her.

Once she had gone Lucy reluctantly swung her legs out of bed, shivering as the cold struck up through her bare feet. Pulling her mother's old fur-lined cloak tighter round her shoulders she walked to the window and stared out through the frost-ferned lattice. The whole world was still and white, and in the distance beyond the ha-ha she could see the deer cropping in the park. She felt like running down to the stables, mounting Beauty and riding until she dropped of exhaustion.

Instead she turned away, picked up the copper can of water, poured it into the washbowl, stuck a finger in it and pulled a face. Barely lukewarm. That would teach her to lie abed.

Gritting her teeth to stop them chattering she shrugged off the cloak, pulled her night rail over her head and began to scrub herself, anxious to get the ordeal over and done with as quickly as possible. No wonder some of the older tenants on the estate sewed themselves into their underthings at the beginning of winter and refused to take them off until spring!

7

Finished, she grabbed her furs up again, scurried across the room and threw herself down on her knees before the fire, sighing with relief as she held her hands out to the heat. The cloak fell open and the light of the flames reflected off her still-damp skin, casting a dancing pattern of light and shadow over her slender body. Sitting back on her heels she parted her legs to allowed the warmth to penetrate her, like the exploring fingers of an invisible lover.

She shivered again, this time with pleasure, and ran her hands down over her body, wondering what it would be like to have a man touch her. She trailed her fingers over her full breasts, feeling the hardness of her nipples and enjoying the strange tingling excitement in her lower belly. Closing her eyes she allowed her hands to drift lower still, down over the narrow curve of her waist and the swell of her hips to the secret place between her thighs.

Her breath shuddered in her throat as her caressing finger traced the soft slit, finding the nub of flesh at the apex. She stroked it gently, feeling it swell beneath her touch. She was wet now and the muscles in her thighs quivered as she parted the lips of her sex, inserted the tip of one tentative finger and...

'Good heavens, girl, not dressed yet?' demanded Martha, bustling in with an armful of clean linen.

Lucy's eye's flew open in shock and she jumped as if scalded, guilt turning her face scarlet. Her hands flew up and she tugged the cloak tightly round her. 'God's teeth, woman,' she snapped, 'can't you at least knock before you enter?'

'With my arms full?' chuckled Martha, depositing the linen on the end of the bed. 'That'd be a nice trick. Anyway,' she sniffed, 'don't you get on your high horse with me, young lady. You've got nothing I haven't seen before. Who d'ye think wiped your dirty bum and changed

8

your soiled napkins when you were a babby? Come along, girl, let's try and get you clad before the day's half over.'

Striding over to the garderobe, she examined the row of dresses. 'Now which gown would you wear today, mistress?'

'What does it matter?' grumbled Lucy, getting reluctantly to her feet. 'One's as dull as the other. Black, black and more black. You'd think the whole damned world was in mourning.'

'This one then,' said Martha, selecting a rich satin gown with discreet touches of lace at the neck and cuffs and laying it on the bed. 'Now, off with that cloak and we'll get you dressed.' Sulkily Lucy did as she was told, allowing Martha to lace her corset and help her into her petticoats, before sliding the dress down over her head and tugging its heavy folds into place.

'There now,' beamed Martha, 'that's better.' She picked up a comb. 'Now sit down before the mirror and I'll dress your hair.'

'Indeed you will not,' protested Lucy, ducking away from her. 'Last time you did it I was lucky to have a hair left on my head. The grooms have a lighter touch with the horses than you have with a comb! I'll do it myself.'

'Please yourself then, madam,' sniffed Martha, flinging down the comb in high dudgeon. 'But don't blame me if you end up looking as if you've been dragged through the hedgerows backwards.' She stalked out, banging the door behind her.

Lucy rolled her eyes and stuck out her tongue at the closed door, then sat down and undid her plait. Her long reddish-brown hair fell about her face, framing it, and Lucy stared critically at herself in the mirror. She could hardly be described as a great beauty, but she wasn't that bad, she supposed. Her eyes were clear, her skin free of

9

pocks and her teeth were good – though she wished she had a fuller mouth and that her hair was the fashionable blonde.

Wincing as the comb caught the tangles she set herself to taming her curls and pulling them back into a knot at the nape of her neck. Then she stood up, examined her reflection from all angles and heaved a sigh of discontentment.

It wasn't fair, she was sick to death of black! She'd been eleven when Oliver Cromwell came to power, and she could still remember the pretty things she'd had then. Dresses in all colours of the rainbow, their rich colours made even richer by beading and ornate stitching and froths of lace; tiny caps decorated with gold and silver; silk stockings embroidered at the ankle and shoes with jewelled buckles.

Now look at her; she could be mistaken for one of the servants!

And even worse, she was still a virgin. Tears of self-pity stung her eyes. She should have had her time at court then been married to James, as it had been arranged by their parents. As Lady Happington, she would have been a force to be reckoned with. She'd have had her own household and children by this time. Instead of which, James and her brother Roderick were off with the king somewhere in France or the Lowlands – and she was stuck at home in this dreary limbo, neither fish nor fowl nor good red meat. If she wasn't careful she'd end up an old maid, leading apes in hell. God damn Cromwell and all his followers!

Still sulking she flung her cloak back round her shoulders, gathered up her skirts and hurried out of her room and down to the hall for breakfast, before Martha could return to deliver yet another scolding. She smiled wryly as she hurried along the cold corridors. No doubt her father would be ready with one instead.

He wasn't. His anger was directed at the missive he held in his hand.

'Damned jumped-up little jackanapes!' he roared, flinging it down and banging his hand on the table so hard he made his tankard jump. 'Just who does he think he is?'

Used to such outbursts, Lucinda's mother, Lettice, barely glanced up from her embroidery frame. 'Calm yourself, Jeffrey my dear,' she said soothingly. 'What good will it do to put yourself in a fret?'

'Hell's teeth, woman!' he bellowed. 'How can I help it? Just listen to this!' He snatched up the letter again and read it out. '"I shall be pleased to dine with you this evening. Yours in God..." No word about whether we'd be pleased to have him! Not even so much as a "by your leave"!'

'Who, father?' asked Lucy, sliding into her seat and helping herself to ale and a hunk of bread and cheese.

'Our esteemed neighbour, Ezekiel Watkins, that's who,' spat her father. 'The man's had the temerity to invite himself into *my* home,' he snorted. 'No doubt to do a bit of spying on his master's behalf. See if we're celebrating behind his back. Putting up a sprig of mistletoe or a few bits of greenery.' He looked round the hall and smiled bleakly. 'Well, he'll be out of luck. This place is as bare as a pauper's arse.'

Lettice carefully tucked her needle into her sewing and gave her husband her full attention. 'Did he say why he was coming?' she asked.

'No doubt to complain about something, as usual,' snorted Sir Jeffrey. 'My cattle straying onto his land. My

11

tenants poaching his rabbits. God's bones! It would be just like the man to begrudge a couple of mouthfuls of grass or a potful of stew.'

'We must be polite to him, my dear,' pointed out Lettice. 'After all, he is our neighbour.'

If this was meant to calm Sir Jeffrey, it had the opposite effect. His normally rubicund face became almost purple with temper. 'Neighbour?' he exploded. 'He's no neighbour of mine! Rolly was my neighbour, and what's become of him? Dead, along with both his sons, while that whey-faced, Puritan bastard struts around his estates like a carrion crow round a corpse!'

He swallowed a mouthful of ale and returned to his subject with renewed venom. 'And how exactly did he get that estate, eh? Eh? I'll tell you! By being a traitor to his lawfully anointed king, that's how.' His lips twisted in a sneer. 'Puritan, eh? Not too pure to profit by another man's downfall though, was he? The fellow was nothing but a jumped-up tradesman before the war, and that's all he'd be now if he hadn't supported that treacherous bastard, Cromwell.'

'For pity's sake hold your tongue, Jeffrey,' said Lettice, white-faced. 'What if one of the servants should hear and report you? With Roderick off with the king our own position is none too safe as it is. Do you want to end up in the Tower, with your own estate confiscated while your wife and daughter are flung out to fend for themselves?'

Sir Jeffrey had the grace to look shamefaced. 'Sorry, m'dear,' he muttered. 'I wasn't thinking.'

'You never do,' Lettice said tartly, and pressed her advantage. 'So you will be polite when this man comes, won't you? For our sakes.'

'If I must,' he muttered. 'Though it's come to a pretty pass when a man can't even express his opinions in the privacy of his own home.'

Lucy breathed a sigh of relief that the storm was over, though it threatened to break out again at her mother's next words.

'Good,' said Lettice. She got to her feet. 'Now if you have done with breakfast we had better go and get ready for service.' Lucy and her father groaned in unison, and were quelled by a glare. 'We cannot afford not to attend,' Lettice pointed out sensibly. 'The less attention we call to ourselves, the better.'

Much later, Lucy sat wishing she'd claimed a bellyache and stayed in bed. Mr Oakley, the preacher, had been ranting for two hours, and showed no signs of stopping. Her fingers were numb with cold and her backside equally numb from sitting on the hard wooden bench. Around her the men folk of the parish sat nodding solemnly, while their po-faced wives sat dutifully beside them. Some of the more educated men of the congregation were even taking notes, though Lucy doubted if this was for their edification. She suspected it was more for either show or to refute the arguments later, should Mr Oakley ever give anyone else the chance to speak!

There wasn't even anything to look at to pass the time. The mural of Adam and Eve and the serpent that had once adorned the wall (and provided much innocent speculation on Lucy's part when she was a child) had been covered up with whitewash; the statues had been broken to pieces long ago and even the stained glass windows smashed and either bricked up or replaced with plain glass. It was like everything else in life: plain, dull and dreary.

Beside her, her father had crossed his arms, propped himself against the wall and was snoring gently. Her mother sat with her hands folded, a polite smile on her face, and was no doubt mentally rearranging the linen closets or deciding on which dishes to serve for dinner. With a sigh Lucy composed her features into an expression of dutiful attention and prayed – for the service to finish!

At long last it did and they finally wound their way back into the sunshine. Mr Oakley stood at the door, shaking hands and accepting compliments with the smug holiness of a man who had done a thorough job.

'Excellent service, Oakley,' boomed Sir Jeffrey. 'Most... er... enlightening.' Lucy earned herself several disapproving glances by failing to suppress the giggle provoked by that blatant lie. Mr Oakley could have been dancing naked in the pulpit for all her father knew! At the thought of his pot-belly and skinny shanks, she giggled even more and was promptly hustled off by her mother.

'What are you thinking of, girl,' she hissed, giving Lucy a sharp shake. 'Do you want to be branded a hussy and reported for un-Puritanical behaviour?' She glanced round, nodding and smiling at the onlookers through gritted teeth. 'Half the folk here would tattle on their own grandmothers if they thought it would bring them a few pennies from the fine. Now behave yourself.'

'Yes, mother,' said Lucy, chastened, following her mother out of the churchyard with her head down, all desire to laugh gone.

'Thank goodness that's over,' said Lettice, once they were safely home and sitting over a light repast of cold capon. 'I thought that boring little man was going to go on forever.' She looked at her husband. 'Now what shall we give this Watkins for dinner?' She paused thoughtfully. 'We had better err on the side of frugality, so I thought I would get cook to do venison in a cream and caper sauce,

14

followed by pears poached in wine and accompanied by some of the good claret from the cellar.'

Her husband threw down the capon leg he'd been chewing on and stared at her as if she'd suddenly announced she was the Queen of Sheba. 'Are you mad, woman?' he demanded. 'The fellow has the cheek to invite himself and you want to treat him as if he's an honoured guest? Frugality? I'll show him frugality! He'll have a good, honest Puritan dinner. Mutton and turnips washed down with plain ale – and if he's still hungry he can have a lump of cheese.'

'But…' began Lettice, then took a look at her husband's expression and sighed. Once he got like this there was no moving him. 'Yes, dear,' she agreed meekly. 'I'll go and tell cook now.'

'Was he at the service, father?' asked Lucy, curiosity overcoming her. Since Cromwell had begun his rule they seldom had visitors, so even a Puritan guest – and an uninvited one at that – was a novelty.

'No,' he grunted. 'He's been abed with the ague.' He grinned wickedly. 'Let's hope the mutton isn't too strong for his delicate stomach. T'would be a pity if our hospitality were to give him a relapse.' He wiped his hands on his breeches, belched and got to his feet. 'Now if you'll excuse me, m'dear, I'm off to see the groom about my hunter. See if his fetlock's recovered yet.' He waved a vague hand. 'Why don't you help your mother or something?'

She watched him stride out of the hall, humming cheerfully under his breath, and sighed. It was all right for men. They could always find something to pass the time. Even her mother would be quite happy spending the afternoon fussing in the kitchen and driving the cook mad or else returning to her embroidery, but for her there was nothing.

15

The bare hall depressed her even more. It was Christmas Day, she thought resentfully. It wasn't fair. It should have been crowded with friends and neighbours and family, ablaze with candles and decorated with swags of holly and ivy, with the Yule log burning in the hearth. There should have been music and laughter, good food and wine, dancing and song and kissing under the mistletoe, not this dreary emptiness.

She thought idly of taking a brisk walk to blow her megrims away, and then slumped again. Cromwell had taken even that small pleasure away, damn his eyes. It was unlawful to walk on a Sunday unless it was to church. It wasn't worth the risk of being seen and reported.

Pushing her plate away, she got to her feet and trailed miserably back to her room, where she lay on her bed and stared at the ceiling until she fell into a dull doze.

'Hell's teeth, girl, sleeping again?' demanded Martha, shaking her roughly by the shoulders. 'Your mother has been running mad this past half hour looking for you.' Lucy sat up yawning, and Martha glared at her, hands on hips. 'Master Watkins will be here any minute now,' she scolded, 'and just look at you. Your dress crumpled and your hair like a bird's nest! Up and get changed this minute, young lady. And you'd best wear your plainest gown too, lest you offend our guest.' She went to pull it from the garderobe.

Lucy's face was suddenly alive with mischief. 'Oh no I shan't,' she announced with glee. She pushed Martha aside and pulled out another dress. 'I shall wear this!'

'B-but you can't,' protested Martha. 'Master Watkins would have a fit!'

'Good,' said Lucy, grinning wickedly. 'Then we'd be rid of him. Now stop your blathering and help me into it.'

Reluctantly Martha did as she was told, and when the gown was on Lucy regarded her reflection and smiled. It was black, like the rest of them, but there the resemblance ended. It was cut low, to show the upper swell of her breasts, and it clung to her waist like a second skin, before falling into soft folds to just above her ankles. The full sleeves were gathered at her elbows in a froth of lace, and there was matching lace at the revealing neckline.

Sitting in front of her mirror she tugged her hair out of its tight knot and swiftly combed it into ringlets that fell softly round her face. That done, she rummaged round her jewel box and pulled out a pair of garnet ear-bobs and a matching necklace that she defiantly put on. Finally she bit her lips and pinched her cheeks to bring up the colour.

'There,' she said, turning to Martha with a smile of satisfaction. 'What do you think? Shall I meet with Master Watkins' approval?'

'You brazen little hussy!' gasped Martha, grinning despite herself. 'He'll probably choke on his turnip!'

'And hell mend him,' grinned Lucy. 'Now let us go down.' She lowered her eyes demurely. 'It would be remiss of me to keep our visitor waiting.'

He was already there, making stilted conversation with her parents. Lucy could tell by her father's glowering expression that he was barely keeping his temper, while her mother fluttered ineffectually around them, trying to keep things calm.

At Lucy's entrance they all turned to her and there was a stunned silence. Her mother's mouth fell open in shock and her hand flew to her breast, while her father regarded her with a mixture of surprise and amusement. But it was Master Watkins' reaction that pleased her most. He looked at her with stern disapproval, but behind it she could detect

17

a flicker of barely suppressed lust. What a hypocrite, she thought in disgust, but she kept her feelings to herself and gave him her most dazzling smile.

'Master Watkins,' she said huskily. 'How nice to meet you.' Then she dropped into a graceful curtsey, making sure her breasts were pushed into prominence.

'Humph, no need for that, mistress,' he said dourly. 'We are all equal in the eyes of God.' But despite his words she noticed his gaze lingered on the full swell of her bosom.

'But of course,' she agreed demurely. 'I was merely treating you with the respect one owes a guest.' She allowed her eyes to trail over him, and was pleased when she saw a flush spread across his narrow cheekbones. 'And such a welcome guest, too.'

Welcome guest? God, he was ugly! And old! He must be almost her father's age. Father had been right; with those spindly legs and baggy black breeches he *did* look like a carrion crow, and the effect was heightened by his thin lips and that huge beak of a nose.

Still, tormenting him would be entertaining. Perhaps this Christmas Day would not be entirely without amusement after all.

She flirted outrageously with him all evening: smiling at him from beneath lowered eyelashes; hanging on his every word; agreeing with his every opinion – and he had plenty of those; bending forward to give him the full benefit of her low-cut neckline; even accidentally brushing his leg beneath the table. By the end of the evening he was stumbling over his words like a green boy.

But unfortunately her father brought her little ploy to an end.

'Well, Master Watkins,' he said briskly. 'Now that the pleasantries are over, may I ask what brings you here? I'm sure your visit wasn't merely for the pleasure of our company.'

Master Watkins dabbed the corners of his mouth fastidiously with his napkin before answering. 'You're right, Sir Jeffrey,' he said with an unpleasantly ingratiating smile. 'I did have something I wished to ask you.'

'I knew it!' snapped Sir Jeffrey. 'Well, spit it out, man. What are you after? To graze your cattle on the lower meadow? The loan of a few men come the spring planting? What?'

Master Watkins' next words wiped the smile from Lucy's lips and froze her blood. She stared at him in horrified disbelief.

'I wish to ask for your daughter's hand in marriage.'

There was a long moment of silence as Lucy and her parents stared at their uninvited guest in disbelief. Her father was the first to recover. 'Is this some kind of jest, Master Watkins?' he demanded.

'No jest, I assure you, Sir Jeffrey,' Watkins said coldly. 'A good honest offer, and one I doubt you will better.' His thin lips twisted in a sneer. 'Not many men in my position would ally themselves to a family such as yours.'

'"A family such as ours"?' snarled Sir Jeffrey. 'How dare you! The Carstairs family have been loyal servants of the crown since time out of mind.'

'Aye,' smirked Watkins, 'and there's the rub. The Lord Protector rules this country now. There's no room for nests of treacherous vipers such as you. By the time he's finished he will have wiped you out like the poisonous vermin you are.'

Lucy looked at her father in dismay. His face was almost black with rage and there were flecks of foam on his lips.

'Treacherous?' he hissed. 'Treacherous? There is but one traitor in this room! And one who has profited well by it too!' He drew in a shuddering breath. 'You come here uninvited, abuse my hospitality, insult me to my face and expect me to seriously consider an offer of marriage to my daughter? You must be a madman as well as a traitor. I'd rather see her wed to a poxy beggar than married to scum like you. Why, if my son were here—'

'But he's not, is he?' sneered Watkins. 'He's off God knows where with that cur, Charles Stewart.' He got to his feet and threw down his napkin. 'I suggest you consider my offer, Sir Jeffrey, and consider it well.' He drew himself up to his full height. 'I am not the kind of man to cross lightly.'

'Get out!' roared Sir Jeffrey, flinging his tankard at Watkins, who taken by surprise gave a startled yelp and tucked his head in like a frightened snail withdrawing into its shell. A pewter plate, the contents of which splattered his breeches, followed the tankard. Scarlet with humiliation he abandoned his dignity, and scuttled from the hall to the sound of Sir Jeffrey's laughter.

'Well done, father,' said Lucy, clapping her hands gleefully. 'That sent him off with a flea in his ear! Did you see his face when you threw that tankard?' She giggled at the memory.

'Serves the bastard right,' chuckled Sir Jeffrey, good humour restored. 'Waste of good ale, though.' He noticed that his wife was silent. 'What's wrong, m'dear?' he enquired genially. 'It wasn't one of the best ones, was it?'

'That was *not* well done, Jeffrey,' she said, her fingers nervously pleating the linen of her napkin. 'You should have pleaded Lucy's prior betrothal to James instead of losing your temper like that. We have made an enemy tonight, and we can ill-afford enemies.'

'Come, come now, my dear,' he scoffed. 'You worry

yourself unnecessarily. We pay our taxes. We obey the rules and regulations. We go to service. And there's no law yet that says I must give my daughter to any jumped-up jackanapes who takes a fancy to her. What can he do to us? Nothing! We're safe enough.'

'I don't know,' fretted Lettice. 'He must have friends in high places to have acquired Rolly's estate. All it would take would be a word here, a word there, and...' she shuddered.

'Nonsense,' Sir Jeffrey reassured her. 'Do you think he'll be anxious to blab this evening's humiliation to anyone else, and become a laughing stock throughout the county for his pains? I think not. He'll keep his mouth shut and lick his wounds in private. No, no, my dear,' he went on confidently. 'If we keep our noses clean all will be well. You'll see.'

He clapped his hands to summon the servants. 'Now enough of cold mutton, turnips and sour ale,' he said, waving a hand at the barely touched meal. 'The man's gone. Let's forget him and have some decent food and wine to celebrate.' He winked. 'I warrant cook has something tucked away for Christmas Day, Oliver Cromwell or no Oliver Cromwell.'

He was right, and with bellies full of roast goose and sweetmeats, the unfortunate incident with Master Watkins was soon forgotten.

Until the small hours of the morning.

Lucy sat bolt upright in bed, heart pounding. What was that? The noise came again, the sound of pebbles against the windowpanes. A sudden fear washed over her that Master Watkins, having been thwarted in his proposal, was now resorting to abduction.

Cautiously she struck a light and lit her candle. Shivering

as the night cold struck through her she got out of bed, tiptoed across the room and pulled the heavy curtains aside as carefully as possible, trying to see without being seen.

Below in the darkness she could make out two shadowy figures, neither of which was tall and thin enough to be Master Watkins. Another shower of pebbles struck the window, making her jump with fright.

'Lucy!' hissed an impatient voice. 'For God's sake wake up! It's freezing out here!'

Joy swept through her and she flung open the window and leaned out, ignoring the cold. 'Roddy?' she gasped. 'Roddy, is that you?'

'Who else were you expecting?' demanded her brother's exasperated voice. 'Some rustic lover come a-wooing? Now get downstairs and open the backdoor before we die of cold.'

'I'll be down in a trice,' she called, then closing the window she flung on her cloak, grabbed the candle and hurried down the main staircase and along the narrow corridors to the oak door that barred the back entrance. Putting down the candle she grabbed the heavy bolts with both hands, tugged them aside and threw it open. Glancing over their shoulders both men hurried inside, dropping their saddlebags in a heap.

'Thank Christ!' exclaimed Roddy through chattering teeth. There was a dusting of frost on his shoulders and he brushed it off and bent to kiss Lucy with icy lips. 'A Merry Christmas, sister,' he grinned. 'And a damned cold one.'

'Come into the kitchens,' urged Lucy. 'I'll stir the fire and mull some ale to warm you up. There's cold mutton and goose, and there's some pottage I can put to heat.' She turned to lead the way and smiled shyly over her shoulder at the stranger standing behind Roddy. 'And bring your friend.'

'Friend?' he laughed, clapping his companion on the shoulder. 'Now there's a warm welcome from your betrothed, eh, Jamie? You can tell she's been heartbroken without you.'

Lucy stopped dead and spun round. 'Jamie?' she gasped.

'The kitchens, Lucy,' grinned Roddy, grabbing her by the shoulders, turning her round and swatting her backside to get her moving again. 'You can save your tender reunion till we've been fed and watered.'

Head whirling, she did as she was told. Bustling round the kitchen, stirring the fire and setting the poker to heat, she cast quick glances at Jamie when she thought he wasn't looking. No wonder she hadn't recognised him. The last time she'd seen him he was a gangly youth of fifteen, too interested in riding and hawking and hunting to be bothered with his eleven-year-old bride-to-be. Now he was a man. And a good-looking man at that!

She blushed and lowered her eyes as he caught her glance and smiled at her, his own eyes raking her slender body appreciatively. When he smiled his teeth were startlingly white against his dark beard, and even huddled over the fire in his filthy travel-stained cloaks, he still had an air of elegance.

'My Lord Happington,' she murmured, holding out a tankard of mulled ale. Her hand trembled as he took it, his strong fingers touching hers.

'Why so formal, sweetheart?' he said. 'You never called me that before.' His grin widened. 'If my memory serves me right, you were remarkably rude when I used to tug your hair. I seem to remember you calling me an "odious toad" on several occasions.'

'I was but a child then,' protested Lucy.

'Not any more,' he pondered, his eyes lingering on her breasts beneath the thin nightshift. 'You've turned into a woman in my absence, and a damned pretty one too.' He got to his feet. 'In fact, I have been remarkably remiss in greeting my betrothed.'

Before she knew what he intended he had grabbed her, lifted her off her feet and bussed her soundly on the lips, his mouth warm against hers, then he deposited her on her feet again. 'There, that's more like it,' he chuckled.

To hide her confusion, Lucy turned away and busied herself fetching the food. Once their attention was fixed on their plates she sat quietly beside the fire and allowed herself the pleasure of watching them undetected. Even covered in the dust of travel they were like two exotic birds compared to the drab Puritans she was used to. Their hair fell in tangled curls below their shoulders, and now they had discarded their concealing cloaks she could see their clothes glowed with colour: dark sea-green in Roddie's case, and a deep wine in Jamie's. Candlelight caught the rich gleam of satin and she hid a smile. No doubt they imagined this unduly sober, too.

'Ah, that was good,' sighed Roddy, putting down his empty plate. 'Thanks, Lucy. My stomach was beginning to think my throat was cut!' Jamie muttered in agreement, his mouth still crammed with cold goose.

'Some wine?' she asked, getting to her feet. They nodded enthusiastically.

She was halfway through pouring it when she froze at the sound of furtive footsteps. The door flew open and her father burst in, a pike clutched in his hands, with her mother close behind, holding a candle high. They stared at the occupants of the kitchen for a moment then Lettice gave a shriek, dropped the candlestick and flew across the floor.

'Roddy!' she cried, flinging herself into her son's arms and hanging onto him as if she'd never let him go. 'Is it really you?' Jamie got to his feet, and received almost the same treatment.

'Good God, woman,' grumbled Sir Jeffrey, bending to retrieve the candle as an excuse to hide his emotions. 'Have a care. You could have burnt the house down.' He slapped Roddy on the back. 'Welcome home, boy,' he said gruffly. 'And you too, lad,' he went on, turning to Jamie. 'It's grand to see you both again.'

Her first astonished delight over, Lettice rounded on her daughter. 'How could you, Lucy?' she demanded. 'Roddy home and you didn't even think to come and tell us? Your father and I thought that thieves had broken in. He could have run your brother through with his pike!'

Lucy flushed. She had been too concerned with her own tumultuous emotions to consider anyone else's. 'I'm sorry, mother...' she began.

'No, *I'm* sorry, mother,' grinned Roddy, slipping his arm round her waist and kissing her cheek. He winked at his sister. 'It's not Lucy's fault. We kept her so busy dancing attendance on us she didn't have a chance to fetch you.' He shuddered dramatically. 'When we arrived we were frozen stiff and on the point of eating our own horses.'

Distracted, Lettice forgot all about Lucy's scolding. 'And are you warm enough now, dearest?' she demanded. 'Have you had enough to eat? Are your clothes dry? Shall I fetch some of your father's to change into?'

'We're fine, mother,' sighed Roddy, rolling his eyes. He yawned prodigiously. 'Though a soft bed would not come amiss. We have been riding hard since we landed at Dover.'

Sir Jeffrey regarded his son and Jamie shrewdly. 'And what brings you here?' he asked. 'I doubt you both risked capture for the sake of sharing Christmas with us.'

'True,' said Roddy ruefully. 'Though I have brought gifts. Wait here while I fetch the saddlebags.' He disappeared for a moment and came back bearing them, then dropping them on the long deal table he unfastened the buckles and began to rummage inside.

'For you, mother,' he said, presenting Lettice with a badly wrapped bundle.

'Oh, Roddy, thank you, darling!' she exclaimed, shaking out a length of delicate lace. 'It's lovely!'

'And so it should be,' grinned Roddy. 'If the French know anything, they know how to charge for their wares.' He produced a smaller package and handed it to Sir Jeffrey. 'Brandewijn,' he explained as his father looked at the flask with interest. 'From the Lowlands. The Dutch may be a stolid race, but their drink is fiery enough to make up for it.'

By this time Lucy was on tenterhooks of expectation, and by the time Roddy made a great show of looking for her present and being unable to find it, she was practically hopping from foot to foot. Finally he produced a small box and handed it over with a flourish.

She opened it eagerly and her eyes widened. 'Oh, Roddy!' she gasped, staring at the gold pendant. The emerald in the centre, surrounded by tiny pearls, glittered in the firelight. 'It's beautiful. I've never had anything so costly.' She looked stricken. 'But you shouldn't have spent so much money on me.'

'I didn't,' he said. 'I won it in a card game.'

'Even so,' she frowned. 'You could have sold it. I know how hard things must be for you.'

'Giving my little sister such pleasure was worth a few

supper-less evenings,' he said, then lifting the pendant from the box he fastened it gently round her neck. 'Wear it in good health, Lucy.'

The sound of Jamie ostentatiously clearing his throat made him grin again. 'Oh dear, I think your future husband is becoming a trifle impatient. I believe he has something for you as well.' He winked. 'Though his luck at cards is notoriously bad. He was forced to buy his.'

Jamie gave him a mock glare then stepped forward and took Lucy's hand. 'This is for you,' he said, smiling down at her as he slipped a ring on her finger. 'As a token of our betrothal.' He kissed her formally and stepped back.

For a few moments she was speechless as she held out her hand, turning it this way and that as she admired the ring. He must have searched long and hard to find one that matched the pendant so well. The setting was slightly less ornate, but the emerald and pearls were the same.

'Oh, Jamie,' she gasped. 'It's exquisite!'

'But not half as beautiful as the girl who wears it,' he said gallantly, and she blushed scarlet with pleasure.

'Harrumph!' said Sir Jeffrey gruffly. 'All these pretty speeches are well enough,' he glared at his son, 'but you still haven't answered my question, boy. What brings you both back here, eh? You didn't risk your lives for the glimpse of a pair of pretty eyes and all this romantic folderol, I warrant.'

'You're right, sir,' sighed Roddy. 'I am afraid I come a-begging on behalf of the king.' He rummaged in his saddlebags again and produced a tattered piece of parchment, greasy and creased from much handling. Laying it on the table he flattened it out with the palm of his hand. 'Read that.'

Sitting down, Sir Jeffrey picked it up and peered short-sightedly at the stained letter. It was brief and to the point:

27

a request for money for food and supplies. It was signed 'Charles Rex', and beneath that were the signatures of all those who had already contributed. Roddy stared at his father anxiously.

'Of course we'll give,' said Sir Jeffrey simply. 'Did you doubt it?'

'Your loyalty will be well rewarded when his majesty comes back into his own, sir,' said Jamie.

'I do not think of gain,' snorted Sir Jeffrey. 'He is the king. It is nothing but our bounden duty.' He frowned. 'But we have little enough to spare. I only wish we could give more.'

'There is always the silver,' Lettice pointed out eagerly. 'We buried it at the beginning of the war. It could be dug up and pawned.'

'Excellent, my dear,' beamed Sir Jeffrey. 'I had forgotten that.'

Lucy sighed as duty warred with the desire to keep her pretty new things. It wasn't fair. Why get them at all if they had to be taken away again? 'My presents could be pawned, too,' she pointed out reluctantly.

'His majesty is not reduced to stealing jewels from pretty young women, quite yet,' said Jamie, and he nodded to Sir Jeffrey. 'Though the offer of your family silver will be much appreciated, sir. If I remember it correctly, it should bring a fair price in one of the pawnshops in Europe.'

'God's bones,' snorted Roddy. 'Sometimes I think the pawnbrokers are the only ones to profit from all this.' He smiled at his father and stifled another yawn. 'But I thank you, sir.'

'That's settled, then,' said Sir Jeffrey, waving a hand to indicate the subject was closed. 'Enough of this.' He picked up the flask Roddy had given him. 'We'll toast his majesty in a glass of this Brandewijn and then it's bed for the pair of you.'

'Yes,' fretted Lettice, looking anxiously at her son and his friend. 'You are white in the face with exhaustion. I still think you should both have a dose of physick.'

'Nonsense, mother,' said Roddy. 'We shall sleep, safely out of sight, all day tomorrow.'

Lettice's hand flew to her mouth. 'The beds, they still have to be made up!' She waved an imperious hand at her daughter. 'Come, Lucy, we dare not wake the servants so you must help me fetch clean sheets. The best, mind you, none of the patched ones. Hurry up, girl!'

Bobbing a mock curtsey, Lucy left the men to their drink and followed her mother as she bustled out of the hall.

By the time all had been arranged to her mother's satisfaction – finally! – the first faint streaks of dawn were showing in the sky. Returning to the kitchens they found the men half asleep over their empty glasses. 'Bed!' scolded Lettice, briskly clearing the table of all evidence. 'The servants will be stirring soon and they must not find you here. Off you go, and take your saddlebags with you.' Her hand flew to her mouth again. 'But what about the horses?'

'Fear not, mother,' yawned Roddy, getting to his feet. 'We woke the groom as we rode in. Old Seth hates the Puritans as much as we do. He's got the nags fed, watered and tucked away at the back of the stables along with the others.'

'Good,' said Lettice, sighing with relief. 'Be off with you, then. I shall wake you this evening when the servants are abed again.' She ushered them out like a housewife shooing chickens before her. 'You too, Lucy,' she said, turning back to her daughter. 'And remember, not a word to anyone about this. Not even Martha.'

'Of course not, mother,' Lucy said crossly. 'I am not some light-tongued village gossip.'

'I know, sweetheart,' sighed Lettice. 'I'm sorry. It's just that one must be so careful these days.'

'Don't worry, mother,' smiled Lucy, kissing her cheek. 'All will be well. Now you must go to bed too. You look exhausted.' After a final glance round to check they had left no signs of their unexpected visitors, they went wearily up the great staircase to their bedchambers.

Despite her exhaustion Lucy was unable to sleep. Her bed was cold and the exciting events of the night played over and over in her head. Her thoughts kept returning to Jamie and how much he had changed. Her fingers strayed unconsciously to her lips where she could still feel the ghost of his kiss, and a quiver of excitement went through her belly.

The vague thoughts of how it would feel to have a man touch her were vague no longer. Now she thought of Jamie. She knew what his lips felt like on hers, now she imagined how it would feel to have his hands explore her eager body. To have him take her and bend her to his will...

The stealthy creaking of her bedroom door interrupted her thoughts and she sat up in alarm as it swung slowly open. What now? She pulled the covers to her breast as a shadowy figure crept towards the bed. 'Wh-who is it?' she quavered. 'Roddy? Is that you?'

'Shh, sweetheart, it is only I,' said a voice, and she felt the bed give as he sat down.

'Jamie!' she gasped, staring at him in the half-light of dawn. 'What are you doing?' A bolt of excitement ran through her, but she suppressed it firmly. He must not think her light. 'You should not be here,' she protested. 'It is not seemly.'

'What harm is there?' he smiled, moving towards her and taking her hand. 'We are to be married, after all. Surely you do not begrudge your betrothed one last kiss to take away with him?'

She knew perfectly well she should send him packing with a flea in his ear, but the touch of his hand had undermined her already wavering good judgement. 'Well, perhaps just one,' she said weakly.

His mouth came down on hers, demanding, his tongue pushing against her lips. She kept them tightly closed, then with a sigh gave herself up to his touch and opened them. For a long moment she allowed herself to enjoy the strange new feelings he aroused, then she pushed him away.

'We must not,' she protested.

'Why not, sweetheart?' he coaxed. 'Tomorrow I must leave, and who knows when we will meet again? If ever.'

'What do you mean?' she gasped, fear gripping her.

He shrugged. 'Who knows what might happen?' he said. 'We could be captured by Cromwell's men and put to death, for all we know.' He stroked her cheek and gazed into her eyes. 'Could you not find it in your heart to give me one last sweet memory to take with me?' he pleaded, kissing her again. 'Give me tonight and I could die happy on the morrow.' His hand found her breast and cupped it, his thumb gently stroking the nipple. She shivered as it hardened beneath his touch, pushing against the linen of her nightshift. 'Please?' he murmured against her mouth.

The soft sigh that escaped her was answer enough. Smiling, he stood and pulled his shirt and breeches off, dropping them where they fell. She stared up at him wide-eyed, taking in the breadth of his shoulders, the thin scar across his chest, and his narrow waist. As her eyes fell lower she gasped in shock; his member was fully erect, jutting proudly from the base of his belly like a thick stave. The skin was stretched tight and glistening over the swollen tip. How could that great thing fit inside her? It was impossible!

Before she could change her mind he had thrown the covers back and was slipping off her nightshift, leaving her naked and defenceless. 'Beautiful,' he murmured, running his hands over her quivering body, then he was beside her and she could feel the hard length of him pressed against her belly. She cringed away.

'Shh... shhhh,' he whispered, pulling her back into his embrace. He stroked her back with one hand, speaking gently as if soothing a skittish horse.

Gradually she relaxed and he grew bolder, his other hand finding her breasts again. Her breath came faster as he fondled them, kissing her as he caressed her nipples into hardness, rolling them between his thumb and finger until they stood stiff and swollen. Then she gasped as he lowered his head and took first one then the other into his mouth, his tongue flickering over them until she thought she would die with pleasure.

His fingers were busy elsewhere now. His hand drifted down over the sweet curve of her belly to that secret part of her that had been untouched – until now. She clenched herself, but he gently parted her legs and stroked the silken skin of her inner thighs, until the muscles loosened to allow him access to her.

He ran his fingers up and down her virginal cunny with tantalising slowness, teasing the soft curls until he felt her juices begin to flow, then he parted the soft lips and delicately slid one exploring finger inside her.

32

It was his turn to gasp at the hot wetness that engulfed him. With a groan he lifted his head from her breasts, took her hand and placed it on his cock, wrapping her fingers around his swollen length.

Lucy tried to pull away, then instinct took over and she began to move her fist, her own excitement mounting as she stroked the silky hardness, feeling him swell even further beneath her touch. His fingers were moving inside her and she whimpered with pleasure.

'No more, sweetheart,' he groaned as she caressed his shaft. 'I must have you now before I explode.' Rolling over he knelt between her open thighs, pushing the head of his manhood between the lips of her sex. She whimpered as it thrust against her, meeting the resistance of her maidenhead – then whimpered in pain as that gave. Gradually pain became pleasure as the full length of him slid inside her, inch by exquisite inch, and she gave herself up to the delicious sensations pulsing through her.

He began to move, withdrawing then thrusting in again, slowly at first then faster and faster. She wrapped her legs around his waist, lifting her hips to meet him until they were but a single writhing body. He moaned aloud and she felt him swell and judder, his hot seed spurting inside her, and she shrieked her own release.

'Thank you, my love,' he sighed, when they had recovered enough to speak again. 'Cromwell can do his worst while I still have this to remember.' He glanced at the window and sat up. 'But I must be away before your parents rise. See, it is almost full daylight.' With a final kiss he leapt from bed, pulled on his clothes and was gone, leaving Lucy to sigh dreamily as she fell into a sated sleep, the secret place between her thighs still throbbing with a delicious mixture of pain and pleasure.

Martha was bustling around her room, bristling with disapproval when she woke. 'What time is it?' she yawned, stretching contentedly.

'Almost ten in the evening,' snorted Martha. 'Your mother said you had a megrim and were to be left in peace.' She sniffed. 'Though a bit of fresh air would soon have blown that way.' She stamped around noisily as she hung up Lucy's gown. 'But you're to go down to the hall if you feel up to it. As for me, I'm for my bed. We can't all lie around doing nothing all day.'

Waiting till she was gone, Lucy threw on her cloak and hurried down to the hall, and then her heart sank. Roddy and Jamie were there, but they were spurred and booted and ready to go.

'Why couldn't you have woken me earlier?' she wailed.

'No point,' said Roddy. 'We were sleeping ourselves.' He nodded at Jamie. 'In fact, I thought he was never going to wake.' Jamie winked at her and she turned scarlet. 'Anyway, we must be off. We have a hard night's riding in front of us.'

He kissed Lucy then his mother, and shook hands with his father. 'Let's hope the next time we meet it will be under happier circumstances, when the king has come back into his own. Come on, Jamie.'

Huddled together against the cold, Lucy and her parents watched them ride off into the night, and the last thing she saw before they disappeared into the darkness was Jamie blowing her a kiss.

The next morning Lucy woke late, feeling dull and heavy. The megrim her mother had claimed for her the day before had become unpleasant reality and her head ached unbearably. Only the thought of Martha's nagging forced her from her bed.

Looking out of the window she sighed. The frost had finally broken and now she could barely see the deer park for the skeins of rain blowing past. The panes rattled as fitful gusts of wind hit the window, splattering more raindrops against it. Damn! Even if she had wanted to, it was no day for riding. Miserably she turned away and began to dress.

Down in the hall her mother was pacing back and forth, eyeing the dark sky anxiously. 'I hope Roddy and Jamie are safe,' she said, biting her lip. 'This is no weather to be abroad in, let alone to be at sea.'

'They'll be fine, mother,' said Lucy, with the confidence of youth in its own immortality. ''Tis but a short crossing to France, and if the sea is too high to set out, no doubt the captain will pull in to some cove to ride out the storm. Now sit by the fire and I will go to the kitchens and get cook to make you a posset to hearten you.'

She was returning with it when the hall doors opened and her father stomped in. 'Damn lower meadow's flooded again,' he growled, shaking himself like a wet dog. 'Had to move the cattle to higher ground.'

'Couldn't the men have done that?' protested Lettice.

'Had to oversee 'em, didn't I?' he grunted, flinging himself down and stretching out with his boots towards the fire. Steam rose from the wet leather and the aroma of cow dung began to permeate the hall.

'Really, Jeffrey,' complained Lettice, waving her hand daintily before her face. 'Sometimes I think you're worse than the tenants.'

'Good honest muck, m'dear,' he grinned. 'You'll be singing a different tune when the money comes in from the spring fair. There'll be no complaints then, eh?'

The sharp sound of boot heels ringing against the stone

floor of the corridor leading to the hall interrupted him. It was followed by angry voices and the sound of a scuffle immediately outside the door. Sir Jeffrey rolled his eyes in exasperation. 'Hell's teeth!' he grumbled, getting to his feet again. 'What's to do now? Can't a man get any peace? Don't tell me the damned beasts have got loose again!'

They hadn't. The hall doors burst open and Ezekiel Watkins stalked in with one of the manservants vainly attempting to hold him back. 'I tried to stop 'im, Sir Jeffrey,' he panted. 'But 'e wouldn't take no for an answer.'

'Leave him be, Carter,' said Sir Jeffrey, waving his hand. He gave Watkins a grim smile. 'I warrant he'll be leaving again soon enough.' With a bow to Lucy and her mother the man disappeared, closing the doors behind him. Sir Jeffrey took his place beside the fire again without offering Watkins a seat.

'So, Master Watkins,' he drawled. 'To what do we owe the honour of this visit? Didn't I make myself clear enough the last time? You are not welcome in this house.'

Ignoring the insult, Master Watkins continued to brush his sleeve, ostentatiously wiping away the touch of the servant's hands. When the silence had become almost unbearable he finally condescended to speak.

'Oh, I think you will soon change your mind, Sir Jeffrey,' he smirked. 'I *shall* be welcome. Not only as your guest, but as your son-in-law.'

Sir Jeffrey gawped at the man's effrontery. 'God's bones!' he snarled. 'Are your wits addled? Why the hell should I change my mind?'

Watkins pulled himself up a chair, sat down uninvited and leaned towards Sir Jeffrey. 'Because if you do not,' he smiled, 'your traitor's head will be adorning a spike on London Bridge and your wife and daughter will be begging

36

on the streets.'

'What are you talking about?' demanded Sir Jeffrey. 'I am no traitor.'

'I think Master Cromwell might view that differently,' smirked Watkins. His eyes narrowed. 'According to my reports, you had guests these past two nights; guests who came under cover of darkness, and left under cover of darkness. Hardly the actions of honest men.'

Lucy gawped at him too. Who had betrayed them? The new stable lad? The whey-faced maid who helped Martha change the beds? Fear gripped her guts. It did not matter who had betrayed them. It only mattered that they were undone.

Lettice's hand had flown to her mouth, but Sir Jeffrey quelled her with a glance. 'So what if I did?' he blustered. 'A man's entitled to have who he likes in his own home.' He snorted. 'I had guests, certainly. I do not deny it. They were merely distant relatives come to visit.'

'Hah!' Watkins gave a bark of humourless laughter. 'They were distant relatives indeed, Sir Jeffrey. France and the Lowlands are distant enough.' His thin lips twisted in a sneer. 'Do not prevaricate with me, sirrah,' he hissed. 'I know exactly who they were. Your son, Roderick, and his friend James Happington.' He leaned back, folded his arms and gave Sir Jeffrey a smile of malicious triumph.

There was a moment of stunned silence before Sir Jeffrey recovered himself.

'Prove it!' he spat.

'Oh, I shall,' smirked Watkins. He reached into the pocket of his voluminous black coat and produced a worn piece of parchment. Smiling, he unfolded it and held it just out of reach. 'Recognise this, Sir Jeffrey?'

All colour drained from Sir Jeffrey's normally rubicund face, leaving it white and gaunt. Staring at him in dismay,

Lucy thought that just as he would look when he lay upon his deathbed.

'H-how did you get that?' he stammered.

'I have my methods,' smiled Watkins, regarding the parchment with satisfaction. 'It makes interesting reading, does it not? Signed by the arch-traitor Charles Stuart himself, not to mention all those who sent him aid. Now,' he went on, 'if I were to hand this over to Master Cromwell, you would find your head – and those of your friends – on the block before you had time to say your prayers.'

Sir Jeffrey swallowed. 'You said "if",' he muttered. 'What do you mean? Surely if you are loyal to Cromwell you have no choice.'

'Ah yes,' purred Watkins, 'but loyalties change.' His voice became insinuating. 'Now if I were to marry your daughter, my loyalties would lie with you, would they not? I would hardly wish to see my father-in-law dangling from the end of a gibbet.'

Sir Jeffrey stared at him in disgust. 'I'd rather die than give my daughter to a treacherous blackguard like you!' he snarled, and closed his eyes against the thought. If he was lucky he would be beheaded. If he was not – hung, drawn and quartered. His bowels clenched at the very thought. Hung till he was half-dead, then cut down, castrated and disembowelled – his guts burnt before his eyes. Dear Christ!

Watkins heaved a sigh of mock regret. 'As you please, Sir Jeffrey,' he said, folding the parchment and putting it away. He got to his feet and smiled down at them. 'Good day, Ladies. Good day, Sir Jeffrey. No doubt you will be receiving a visit from Master Cromwell's men soon. I trust you will enjoy it.' He bowed briefly, and then turned towards the door.

'No, wait!' cried Lucy. 'Please, Master Watkins.'

'Yes, Mistress Lucinda?' he said politely, but the malice dancing in his eyes belied his words.

'I'll do it,' she gasped.

'No, Lucy, you can't…' began her father, but she glared at him and turned back to Watkins.

'I will marry you, Master Watkins,' she said, forcing herself to smile. 'Provided you give me that parchment as my wedding gift.'

'But of course, my dear,' he purred. 'You shall have it on our wedding night. You have my word upon it.' He smiled at her in admiration. 'I can see you are a young lady of sense as well as beauty. But first, a token of our betrothal.' He seized her and forced his thin lips against hers, thrusting his slimy tongue into her mouth until she thought she must vomit. Finished, he set her on her feet again and strode from the hall, laughing.

She stared after him, shuddering in horror as she wiped her mouth in a vain attempt to remove the loathsome taste and feel of him. Dear God in heaven! What had she let herself in for?

The day of her wedding dawned bright and clear, sunshine glittering on the early morning frost. The irony of it was not lost on Lucy as she stared out of her chamber window for the last time. It was the kind of wedding day any girl would pray for – the traditional omen of good fortune. 'Happy the bride on whom the sun shines', went the old saw.

Lucy smiled bitterly. Hah! If the weather were to reflect how she truly felt, the skies would be black with roiling thunderclouds and lightening would be splitting the trees!

Her wooden chest lay open in the corner, packed to the brim with the things she would be taking to her new home.

She averted her eyes and looked into her mirror instead, staring at her reflection in dismay. She had tossed and turned sleeplessly for half the night, and it showed. Her face was pale and drawn with dark circles beneath her eyes. She pulled a face. She looked more like a corpse than a blushing bride.

There was a tap at the door and Martha came in with a dress over her arm. She stared at Lucy in surprise. 'Good morrow, mistress,' she said. 'I came to wake you, but I see there is no need.'

'I was too happy to sleep,' said Lucy dryly. 'It is my wedding day, after all.'

Martha's cheerful face quivered into lines of misery. 'That I should live to see this day!' she wailed. 'My pretty girl married off to that ugly old lecher – and he a Puritan and as common as muck into the bargain.' Her bottom lip trembled and tears welled from her eyes. 'I had hoped to dress you for your wedding to Sir James, not this, this...'

'Bastard?' Lucy suggested flippantly.

'Bastard's too good for the likes of him,' said Martha hotly. 'Spawn of Satan more like.' She shuddered. 'Those cold fish eyes of his! And to think of you bedding him! I can't bear it. It makes my skin crawl.'

It made Lucy's skin crawl, too, but rather than dwell on it, she pointed to the dress hanging over Martha's arm. 'What's this?' she asked. 'I thought there was no time to have anything new made.'

'Master Jenkins sent it,' said Martha, with distaste. 'You are to wear it for the marriage ceremony.'

'Am I indeed?' said Lucy. 'And what does he think suitable for such an auspicious occasion?'

Martha shook it out and held it up, the cheap stuff drooping from her hands. Lucy stared at it in horror. The dress was plain black, with long narrow sleeves, a high neck and not even a hint of adornment. The rough cloth was as dull, coarse and lifeless as the wing of a dead crow. 'Good God!' exclaimed Lucy. 'I am to be married, not buried!' She tossed her head defiantly. 'Well, he is not my husband yet. I shall wear what I please.' She pointed to her chest. 'Fetch me the dress I wore when he invited himself to dinner.'

'Are you sure, mistress?' said Martha. She lowered her voice. 'He might not take it kindly.'

'He can take it how he will,' said Lucy stubbornly. 'I am no meek Puritan mouse to be ordered about as the whim takes him. I shall go to my wedding as *I* choose.'

A sudden thought hit her and she began to laugh. 'But I shall do something to satisfy my new husband.' Running across to her chest she began to rummage through it. She dragged out her pretty nightshifts, made of lawn so fine they were practically transparent, and threw them on the floor.

'What are you doing?' gasped Martha.

'Getting rid of these,' she said. 'It would not do to offend his sensibilities on our wedding night, now would it? Do you have any old ones, Martha?'

'There's a couple I'd put past to make cleaning rags,' said Martha in bewilderment. 'But they're coarse things, stained and patched beyond repair, and anyway,' she looked from her own ample figure to her young mistress's slender one, 'they'd be far too big. You'd be lost in them.'

'Good,' said Lucy in satisfaction, lowering her eyes in mock modesty. 'I would not wish to place wicked thoughts in the mind of such a godly man.' She grinned at her maidservant. 'Well, don't just stand there, woman. Go and fetch them.'

Giggling, Martha did as she was told, reappearing five minutes later with the voluminous garments. 'Excellent!'

41

Lucy squealed mischievously, holding them up. They were yellow with age, smelt horribly fusty from having been stored away for so long, and were as appealing as a shroud. 'I am sure my new husband will be delighted with my thoughtfulness in sparing him the temptations of the flesh.'

'Be careful though, mistress,' warned Martha, anxious despite her laughter. 'I wouldn't push him too far.'

'Fiddlesticks!' said Lucy blithely. 'What can he do to me? I might be his wife, but I am still the daughter of Sir Jeffrey Carstairs, and once I get the...' she cut herself off. No one was to know about the damning parchment. She smiled. But once it was in her hands and safely burned, Master Watkins could go hang himself! She would leave him so fast his head would spin and there wouldn't be a damned thing he could do about it.

Her humour much improved by the prospect, she turned her attention back to her wedding preparations. After Martha helped her to slip on her gown she sat down in front of her mirror to allow her to dress her hair. As Martha began to drag it back into a knot, she tugged herself free and shook it loose again. 'Not like that,' she protested. 'God's blood, Martha, I am not his wife yet. Time enough for plainness when I am. Now stick the curling tongs in the coals and do it properly.'

Half an hour later she regarded herself with satisfaction. Her hair had been pulled back into a mass of tiny ringlets that cascaded down her neck. 'Much better,' she smiled. 'And now for my jewels.'

Defiantly she clasped the emerald pendant Roddy had given her around her neck, the heavy stone nestling between her breasts – but her courage almost failed her when she picked up Jamie's ring. He should be the one slipping a wedding band on her finger today, not the loathsome Ezekiel Watkins. But at least she could wear this token of his love. She put it on, admiring the cold fire trapped at the heart of the stone. So should she be. She might be trapped, but nothing could touch or dim the love she held inside.

Leaning forward she pinched her pale cheeks to bring colour to them and bit her lips to redden them. There, that would have to do. 'I am ready,' she announced, getting to her feet.

'You look beautiful,' said Martha, swallowing the lump in her throat and hugging her. 'And don't you worry your pretty little head, my love. Remember, I'm coming with you. You'll have me there to see he treats you right and proper.'

'Thank God,' Lucy said fervently, kissing Martha's wrinkled cheek. 'At least I'll have one friend in the enemy camp. Now come along; mother and father will be waiting below.'

In the great hall Lettice was sitting, shoulders slumped, while Sir Jeffrey paced up and down before the fire. Lucy could see from her mother's reddened eyes that she had been weeping. At the sight of her daughter she rushed to hug her, fresh tears coursing down her cheeks.

'I cannot bear it,' she sobbed. 'My poor girl! To be wed to that brute.'

'Come now, mother,' said Lucy, with a lightness she did not feel. 'You will bring me ill-luck weeping on my wedding morn. I am not the first to marry a man she does not love.'

'You need not do this, Lucy,' her father said heavily. 'Let Watkins hand the parchment to whomsoever he wills. I am prepared to take my chances.'

'But I am not,' said Lucy firmly. 'I have already lost a brother and a lover. I am not prepared to lose a father as well. Besides,' she went on, 'once I have destroyed it we shall all be safe.' She smiled slyly. 'And women have left their husbands before now, too. Who knows? If all goes well this may be the shortest marriage in history.'

'Are you sure?' asked her father anxiously, and she nodded.

'Now, we had better call the carriage,' she said. 'It would not do to keep the bridegroom waiting.'

For all her fine words her stomach was churning as they drew up outside the meeting house. Her mother gave her one last kiss and hurried in to take her place, while she stood with her father at the door. Taking a deep breath she laid her hand on his arm and nodded to show she was ready, and together they walked inside.

There was not even a flower or a note of music to greet her. The meeting house was as bare and unwelcoming as a pauper's larder. Even worse, there was a gasp of disapproval as the congregation took in Lucy's low-cut gown and glittering jewels. Scowling faces met her wherever she looked and she suppressed an hysterical giggle. It was like being married in front of a murder of crows! Defiantly she tossed her head. Let them think what they liked of her.

Watkins was standing in front of the table at the head of the meeting house, and turned at the sound. Lucy faltered at the thunderous expression that crossed his face as he realised she was not wearing the drab gown he had sent. But it vanished, and was replaced with an even more frightening one of lechery as his eyes lingered on the swell of her bosom… then that too disappeared and he was all prim piety again.

She took her place beside him and Master Oakley cleared his throat. 'We are gathered here today to witness the marriage of Master Ezekiel Watson and Mistress Lucinda Carstairs,' he said. 'But before I join these two in Holy matrimony, it behoves me to say a few words…'

Oh, Lucy thought rebelliously as he launched forth on a sermon, it would! Hell's teeth, even at a wedding the man could not resist the sound of his own voice! Still, at least it postponed the marriage a little longer.

'…As the disciple Paul said: "It is better to marry than burn",' he began pompously.

Two hours later he was still droning on and Lucy was fidgeting with boredom.

Even so, it was still too soon for her when he finally stopped pontificating and began the service proper, and when it came to, 'Do you take this man to be your lawful wedded husband?' her mouth was so dry with nerves she could barely mumble, 'I do.'

Behind her she could hear her mother sobbing again as Watkins slipped the thin gold band on her finger.

'I now pronounce you man and wife,' concluded Master Oakley. 'You may kiss the bride.' Lucy shuddered as Watkins' cold lips touched hers in a brief peck.

As he placed her hand on his scrawny arm and turned to lead her out, a wave of sheer panic ran through her. She was no longer Lucy Carstairs. She was Mistress Ezekiel Watkins.

And his to do with as he pleased!

Outside again, Lucy blinked, the sunlight dazzling her after the gloom of the meeting house. Her new husband stood beside her while members of the congregation expressed their good wishes for the future, though she noticed these were directed to him rather than her.

'Enough of this,' said Sir Jeffrey, eventually losing

patience. ''Tis a cold day and the graveyard is an ill place to celebrate. Come now, the wedding breakfast is waiting back at the Hall.' He beamed round at the solemn faces with forced jollity. 'And all are welcome.'

Lucy smiled at her father gratefully. At least the marriage feast would put off the evil hour when she must go to her new home for just a little longer, and a few glasses of wine would dull her senses when her husband claimed his marital rights.

Master Watkins regarded Sir Jeffrey coldly. 'There will be no marriage feast,' he said. 'I do not approve of indulgence.'

Sir Jeffrey stared at him, flabbergasted. 'What?' he spluttered. 'No feast? Good God, man, our Lord turned water into wine at the marriage at Canae. I'm sure he wouldn't begrudge us a little now.' He forced himself to hang on to his temper. 'Besides, it is already prepared,' he went on reasonably. 'And surely waste is just as great a sin.'

'You may give it to the poor,' said Master Watkins, with a self-righteous smirk. 'For I will have none of it.'

'Oh, please, Master Watkins… Ezekiel…' begged Lucy, laying her hand on his sleeve. 'It is our wedding day.' She forced herself to dimple up at him. 'Would you not do this one small thing – to please me?'

He smiled. 'But of course, my dear,' he said. She breathed a sigh of relief and opened her mouth to thank him, then stopped as he went on coldly. 'In the same way you chose to please me by wearing the wedding gown I sent you.' She stared at him in dismay, bitterly regretting her defiance.

'This is outrageous!' fumed Sir Jeffrey, his face almost apoplectic with rage. 'Is my daughter's wedding to be some hole-in-corner affair, as if she were hiding her shame like some baggage six months gone with child? I won't have it, I tell you. You can't do this.'

Watkins smiled again, revelling in his power over this man who despised him. 'Oh, yes I can,' he sneered. 'I have the whip hand now, Sir Jeffrey. She is Mistress Watkins and she must obey *me*.' He clicked his fingers at Lucy as if she were a dog. 'Come, wife,' he snapped. 'I do not wish to remain here arguing. We are going home.'

Without a backward glance he strode off towards the carriage that waited at the gates, and Lucy could do nothing but follow him. Bundling her inside he ordered the coachman to drive off, and the last thing she saw as it clattered away was her mother weeping in her father's arms as he stared after them in impotent fury.

In the carriage she sat as far away from him as possible, her eyes on her hands as she clasped them tightly in her lap to stop them trembling. But there was little comfort there; the cheap wedding ring glinted on her finger, reminding her that there was no way out.

Plucking up her courage, she cast a sideways glance at Master Watkins – she still could not think of him as her husband – but he was staring straight ahead with a stony expression on his face. In profile he looked more like some carrion bird than ever, and she shivered and returned to contemplating her hands.

It was but a short journey to Sir Roland's estate – she still could not think of that as Master Watkins' either – yet it seemed to last forever. Finally they turned between the gateposts and up the long drive towards the house. Its mullioned windows glittering in the winter sunlight, it looked exactly as it always had and Lucy felt as if she were trapped in some strange dream. She had been coming here all her life: visits with her mother when she was young; dinners with the whole family; balls when she became old enough; and she still half-expected the two boys to come galloping alongside the carriage to escort it up the drive to the steps where Sir Roland and his wife Lady Mary would be waiting to greet her.

She shook herself. She was being ridiculous. Lady Mary had died of the flux before the Civil War had even started – a blessing in disguise, since it saved her the heartbreak of knowing her two beloved sons had been killed. Sir Roland had lingered on, a broken man, before he too followed his wife and sons to the grave.

She gasped with shock as she saw figures in front of the house. For one horrible moment it seemed as if the dead had indeed risen to meet her, then she giggled nervously at her own lurid imagination. Master Watkins had obviously left orders that someone keep a lookout for their return and it was merely the household staff gathered to greet their new mistress.

This was so. As the carriage drew up, one of the under-coachmen hurried to open the carriage door and lower the step. Master Watkins descended and held out his hand to help her down. She shivered at the clasp of his bony fingers, but stuck a smile on her face as he led her towards the waiting servants.

As she walked along the line, nodding graciously as they bobbed or bowed, she searched the faces for someone – anyone – she might recognise. But in vain. The household was Puritan to a man. There were no Toms or Harrys amongst the male servants. They were all Obadiahs and Zebadiahs and Jeremiahs. Despite this she suppressed a giggle, for there was even one unfortunate Jonah! As for the female staff, they were all Prudences and Faiths and Hopes. Good God, she thought, the Old Testament must be empty today, for they were all here instead!

Finally they reached the head of the line, where an unsmiling woman stood. She was in her early thirties and her face was as stiff and cold as if it had been carved out of marble.

'This is Mistress Charity Blackstock, my housekeeper,' said Master Watkins. The woman's curtsey was insolently brief and as she looked into her new mistress's eyes, Lucy could have sworn she saw a flash of pure hatred – then she lowered her eyelids demurely, leaving Lucy wondering if it had been merely a figment of her own vivid imagination.

The introductions to her household servants over, Master Watkins led her up the steps to her new home. Inside she looked round in amazement. If the house looked the same from outside, the same could not be said of its interior. Gone were the old comfortable furnishings, worn with age and use. They had been replaced and her eyes widened, for even buying the cheapest he could find, it must still have cost a fortune!

Master Watkins saw her expression, mistook it for awe and smiled for the first time. 'I had it all torn down or flung out,' he announced proudly. 'Every yard of material and stick of furniture is new.'

She could see that. The whole place looked raw and vulgar, like a stately old dowager forced into the newest fashions from France. The comfortable old pieces had fitted their surroundings, the new ones merely looked cheap and gimcrack.

He was waiting expectantly for her to compliment his good taste, and for a moment she was tempted to tell the truth, then thought the better of it. She had already been punished once today for defying him over the wedding dress, and no doubt any ill-considered remarks made now would have to be paid for too.

'It is… um… most impressive, Master Watkins,' she said. 'Most impressive, indeed.'

His chest swelled with pride and he insisted on escorting her from room to room, pointing out his favourite acquisitions, until she grew weary of murmuring words of false praise. Finally they returned to the main hall and he stopped in front of a huge portrait hanging above the fireplace. 'There, what do you think of that?' he demanded, pointing at it proudly.

She stared at it. The man in the portrait was a handsome subject for any artist, his manly bearing matched by classic features and a noble brow, and his expression one of keen intelligence, tempered by wit and humour. She smiled. 'An excellent painting, Master Watkins,' she acknowledged. 'Who is it?'

His proud smile vanished and he looked at her as if she was mad. 'It is myself, of course,' he said.

She looked from him to the portrait incredulously. Did he really imagine he looked like that? He must have paid the painter well to overlook that nose of his! A giggle welled up inside her and she fought it down. 'Of course it is, sir,' she said smoothly. 'I meant, who is the artist?'

It was too late. 'I know exactly what you meant, madam,' he said stiffly. 'So do not try and cozen me with sweet words now.' He clicked his fingers and his housekeeper appeared at his elbow, smiling obsequiously. 'Take your new mistress to the bedchamber,' he ordered. 'So that she may change for dinner.'

'Certainly, sir,' said the woman. 'This way, madam.'

'B-but I can't change,' protested Lucy. 'I have nothing to change into. My chest has not yet come from home and all my clothes are in it. And what about my maid, Martha?' she went on. 'She has not yet come either.'

'Nor will she,' said Master Watkins, with a sneer. 'I

want no blowsy old trollop in my house, preaching sedition under my very nose. Mistress Blackstock and the maids here can attend you.' Turning on his heel he stalked off, leaving Lucy staring after him in dismay.

'If you will follow me, madam,' said the housekeeper. Lucy turned back to her, and this time there was no mistaking the expression on the woman's face. It was one of vindictive pleasure at Lucy's discomfiture – and she made no effort to hide it. 'This way, if you please,' she smirked, turning towards the stairs, and without a word Lucy trailed after her.

Master Watkins' renovations had been limited to the public part of the house. Upstairs was as shabby as she remembered it. She followed Mistress Blackstock along the corridors until she flung open the door of the bedchamber. Once inside she averted her eyes from the huge four-poster bed and turned to face the woman again.

'And what, pray, am I to wear?' she demanded.

Mistress Blackstock walked across the room and opened the garderobe. 'One of these,' she said, revealing the four black gowns that hung inside. She smiled maliciously. 'You may take your choice.'

Lucy stared at them. There was no choice. They were all exactly the same as the one he had sent for her to wear for their wedding. 'And if I refuse?' she said defiantly.

'In that case, the master has given orders that we are to "help" you dress, madam,' smiled the woman. Her arms hung loosely at her sides, but her fingers curled into claws and Lucy could tell she was just itching for an excuse to lay hands upon her.

'Why do you hate me so?' she asked plaintively. 'What have I ever done to you?'

The housekeeper stepped closer, thrusting her face into

Lucy's. 'This should have been *my* wedding day,' she hissed. 'He would have married me if you had not flaunted yourself at him, tempting him with your low-cut gowns and your loose ways.'

Lucy gawped at her. The woman was mad. The idea that she had deliberately set her cap at Watkins was ludicrous.

'You are mistaken, Mistress Blackstock,' she said coldly. 'You could have had him and welcome, for all of me! I had no desire to marry the man.'

'Don't lie to me, you brazen little hussy!' snarled the housekeeper, her eyes blazing with fury. '*I* should have been Mistress Watkins, not you!'

The sound of the slap rang round the room like a pistol shot and the woman fell back, clasping her hand to her face, her mouth an 'O' of shock. 'But you are not mistress here,' said Lucy, with a calmness she did not feel. '*I* am – and if you ever dare speak to me like that again I shall have you turned off to seek your fortunes elsewhere.'

'Yes, mistress,' said the housekeeper dully. Her face was stark white apart from the scarlet imprint of Lucy's hand and her eyes were lowered, but Lucy did not make the mistake of thinking she had bested the woman. This was just the opening skirmish in the battle.

'You may go now,' she said, pressing home her small victory. 'I shall change and be down to join my husband for dinner shortly.' The housekeeper left, head still bent, closing the door behind her with a quietness that was more ominous than if she had banged it shut.

As soon as she had gone Lucy collapsed on the edge of the bed, her stomach quivering with nausea. She had made an enemy, and one who would do everything in her power to see her brought low. It made it even more imperative that she get the parchment and leave this accursed place

52

as soon as possible.

And to that end she must do all in her power to please him – at least for the moment. She would wear one of the gowns he had chosen and be as mim and coy as any Puritan maiden. Once he had his way with her – se shuddered involuntarily at the thought – and she had the precious parchment, she could laugh in her fist at him as she walked away. Then Mistress Blackstock could have him, and welcome!

Getting to her feet she walked across, took down one of the drab black things and laid it on the bed. Slipping off her own gown she slid the new one over her head. The cheap material was harsh against her skin after the soft satin, and the high neck made her feel as if she was being throttled. Looking round she was surprised to see there was a mirror in the room. She thought he would have disposed of anything like that as being frivolous. But one glance in it revealed why he hadn't; it was mottled with age and the distorted reflection was hardly an encouragement to vanity.

She groaned inwardly, for even without that she looked hideous. The gown hung on her like a sack and drained every speck of colour from her complexion. Her ringlets looked as out of place as a bunch of ribbons on a corpse. With a sigh she unloosed her hair, picked up the bone comb that lay beside the mirror and began to drag out the curls.

When she had finished and her hair was tied in a tight knot at the nape of her neck, all traces of Lucinda Carstairs were gone and Mistress Ezekiel Watkins stared back at her. Or almost all traces. Roddy's pendant still glowed with green fire on her breast and Jamie's ring still glinted on her finger, eclipsing the narrow wedding band. Heaving another sigh she reached back to undo the clasp – then stopped.

God's bones, she'd be damned if she gave up everything! Instead she pulled the material away from her neck and tucked the pendant underneath. She could feel the comforting weight of it nestling between her breasts, but the baggy gown concealed any signs of it. Then she turned Jamie's ring round so that the stone was pressed against her palm and only the shank showed.

Regarding her reflection she smiled for the first time since she'd entered the house. There, she might be Mistress Watkins on the surface but she was still Lucy Carstairs underneath! Head held high, she turned towards the door.

Dinner was appalling. Instead of having it in one of the smaller rooms, Master Watkins had obviously set out to impress, with ludicrous results. They sat stiffly at each end of the long dining table in the main hall, so far apart that conversation was almost out of the question unless one was prepared to bellow. Lucy was not, so the meal passed in stony silence.

The food was what he no doubt referred to as 'good, plain fare'. It would have been had it been cooked properly. Unfortunately the roast beef was tough and stringy, the winter vegetables boiled to mush and the wine – his one concession to festivity – was thin and sour. Lucy pushed the cold, unappetising food round her plate, but forced as much of the wine down her throat as she could, in an attempt to anaesthetise herself for what was to come. It was useless. For all the effect it had, she might as well have been drinking water.

When the last plate had been taken away he cleared his throat. 'Well, madam,' he announced loudly, 'it is time to retire.'

'Already?' she said desperately. 'But it is early yet. Perhaps we could sit before the fire a while? Enjoy a game of cards and another glass of this excellent wine?'

He stared at her as if she were mad. 'Cards, madam?' he thundered. 'Cards are the Devil's picture books. I'll have none of your evil ways in this house. Now get to bed. I shall be up shortly.' Stomach churning, she did as she was told.

Back in the bedchamber Mistress Blackstock had been about her duties. A dull fire glowed in the grate, candles were lit and the bed was turned back. At the foot lay a voluminous nightgown, and despite her fears, Lucy smiled wryly as she held it up. It was almost as bad as the old one of Martha's she'd intended wearing. No doubt the housekeeper had gloated over her cleverness in making her rival as unappealing as possible, not realising she had actually done her a favour.

Shivering despite the fire, Lucy undressed and slipped the thick garment over her head. Her emerald pendant was still about her throat, and she was just about to unclasp it when the door swung open. She whirled round, her hands still at the nape of her neck.

Master Watkins stood on the threshold, his eyes focused on the jewel. 'What frippery is this, madam?' he snarled. He strode across the chamber, reached out and tore it from her throat, making her gasp with pain. Her hands flew to her neck, then she remembered the ring and attempted to hide them behind her, but he was too quick. Seizing her wrists he pulled them back. 'So what else are you hiding?' he snarled, found Jamie's ring and wrenched it from her finger. His eyes glinted with greed as the jewels gleamed in the palm of his hand. 'A fine dowry, madam,' he gloated. 'These will bring a good price when I sell them.'

'And bring the Sheriff too, if you dare,' spat Lucy, her lips curled in a sneer. ''T'would be a fine thing were the saintly Master Watkins to be taken up for a common thief.

'What do you mean?' he demanded.

'They are not mine,' Lucy lied. 'They are my mother's. She lent them to me for my wedding day.'

'See that they are returned to her, then,' he snapped, flinging them down beside the mirror. 'And get into bed.' He stalked into the adjoining dressing room, leaving her to slip between the cold sheets. Biting her lip, she lay there rigidly, dreading what was to come.

He did not take long, and when he returned her eyes widened at the sight of him in his nightshirt. She fought back an hysterical giggle at the sight of his hairy shanks, but it died in her throat as he climbed in beside her.

Turning towards her he dragged her thick nightgown up to her neck and began pawing at her. He groped her breasts, twisting her nipples until she whimpered with pain, while his mouth came down on hers and his tongue thrust its slimy way into her mouth, making her gag. His breathing became heavier and she could feel his swollen manhood pressing against her through his nightshirt.

Worse was to come. Pulling her legs roughly apart he knelt between them, lifted his nightshirt and pushed clumsily against her. She groaned as he thrust his cock roughly inside her, his scrawny buttocks clenching as he forced himself on her. At her groan he jerked convulsively and was done. He rolled off her and lay there, mouth open, gasping like a stranded fish.

Lucy sighed in relief that, thankfully, it was all over. It had been extremely unpleasant, but mercifully brief – just as she had expected.

But she had not expected what came next.

Instead of falling into a satiated slumber, he got out of bed, threw back the covers and stared down, his face turning black with fury. Then before she could lift a hand to protect herself he leaned over and slapped her face so hard her head rocked.

'Wh-why did you do that?' she gasped, holding her cheek, and in answer he dragged her from the bed, seized her by the neck and thrust her face towards the sheets.

'What do you see there?' he hissed.

'N-nothing!' she stammered in bewilderment.

'Exactly!' he snarled. 'Slut! You were no virgin when you came to my bed!' He shook her like a rat. 'Who had you first, eh? The stable boy? One of the servants? Some drunken traitor?'

'My betrothed!' she spat back, shaking free and glaring at him. 'And he's twice the man you'll ever be!'

'You'll pay for that, you little whore,' he hissed. His hand snaked out, caught the neck of her nightgown and tore it from her body, leaving her naked and defenceless. He caught her by the hair and dragged her down over his knee, and then there was the harsh sound of flesh meeting flesh as his hand swept down.

She went rigid with shock and humiliation as the soft flesh of her buttocks quivered beneath the blow. His handprint stood out red against her white skin and he licked his lips lasciviously. Savouring her helplessness he lifted his hand again.

The second made her gasp and jerk, the pain more intense as he connected with already spanked flesh – and by the third and fourth she was shrieking and writhing with the pain. Her bottom was scarlet now, but it was nothing to the white-hot pain that seemed to radiate through her entire lower body. Tears poured down her cheeks yet still he continued to beat her relentlessly, his breath coming shorter with each blow.

Worse still, she could feel his rigid member sticking into her belly. Her struggles to break free had aroused him again!

But the worst humiliation of all was her own reaction. As the heat spread through her belly the pain transformed into something much more insidious. She fought against it, but she could feel herself moisten and the throbbing in her bottom transferred itself to her vulva, making her ache with the need to satisfy it. She moaned again, but this time it was a moan of need.

He pushed her from his lap and she fell to the floor, still moaning, but he had not finished with her yet. Seizing her by the shoulders he pulled her onto her knees. 'Pray for forgiveness for your sins,' he thundered, and whimpering she knelt against the bed, hiding her face in her hands to conceal the disgust she felt at her body's treacherous reaction.

He looked down at her in satisfaction. Naked and sobbing, with her head bent in shame, she didn't look quite so proud now. His eyes lingered on the full curves of her buttocks, scarlet from his beating, and lust overwhelmed him again. Pulling off his nightshirt he flung himself down behind her.

She gasped as one hand snaked round her body to fondle her breasts, pinching and kneading her nipples until they rose hard and firm against his touch. The other plundered roughly between her thighs, finding the hot wetness there. He thrust his fingers inside, making her whimpered again.

'Bitch!' he panted against her neck as he pushed the lips of her sex apart and rubbed the hard head of his prick between them. 'Whore! Slut! You want this, don't you?'

'Yes,' she moaned, despite her loathing of the man. 'Yes... yes!'

In answer he thrust inside her again. This time he slid in easily and she took the whole length of him, pushing back to force him even deeper. She rocked back and forth, impaling herself on his sturdy cock as he withdrew then thrust again and again, faster and faster until he exploded inside her, triggering her own release.

Then he pulled himself free, got to his feet and looked down at her with contempt. 'Lady indeed,' he sneered. 'You're no better than a tavern whore. And to think I made you my wife.'

She raised her head and mustered what little defiance she could. 'I didn't ask you to marry me,' she countered. 'You got what you wanted. Now keep your side of the bargain. Give me the parchment.'

He threw back his head and laughed in genuine amusement. 'You stupid little trollop,' he scoffed. 'Did you really think I would give it up?' Ignoring her horrified look he stooped, picked up his nightshirt and pulled it on. 'Now make yourself decent and come to bed, *wife*. We must be up early for morning prayers.' He climbed into bed and was snoring in moments.

Shivering, Lucy got to her feet. Pulling the remnants of her torn nightgown about her she slid into bed and lay as far away from him as possible. Her spanked body throbbed and she stared into the darkness in shame and humiliation. She was tied to a man she hated, and it had all been for nothing!

A rough hand shook Lucy by the shoulder. 'Let me alone, Martha,' she mumbled, pulling away and snuggling deeper into her pillow. ''Tis far too early to rise yet.'

Then her eyes flew open as the covers were wrenched away and cold air shocked her into wakefulness.

She found herself staring up into Master Watkins'

sneering face and the events of the previous night rushed back into her consciousness. She closed her eyes trying to blot them out, but the vision of her moaning with lust as she gave herself to him played over and over in her brain. Sickness washed over her and she barely had time to pull the chamber pot from beneath the bed before she vomited.

He leapt back with a curse and looked down at her in alarm. 'God's bones, bitch,' he snarled. 'If you are with child...' His voice trailed off, but his clenched fists showed what fate she would meet if she were.

She raised her head. 'I am not,' she said bitterly. 'But, by God, I wish I were! At least that way you would not be able to plant *your* foul whelp in my belly.'

He lifted his hand to slap her, but she glared at him defiantly and he let it fall again, smiling coldly. No, he would not give her the satisfaction of flaunting the marks of his anger and playing the martyr. There were other ways – infinitely more pleasurable ways – of breaking the high-flown little madam. He remembered her tears and humiliation of the night before and licked his lips. By the time he'd finished with her she would grovel at his feet like a beaten bitch, licking the hand that whipped it.

'Get dressed, madam,' he said calmly. 'We do not lie abed here. I shall expect you at breakfast.' Turning he walked out of the door, leaving her staring after him in surprise.

Once he had gone she swung her legs out of bed and stood up, suppressing a whimper of pain. Her bottom throbbed from the beating he had inflicted and between her thighs still ached from the savagery of his lust.

Walking gingerly she crossed the room to where a basin and ewer stood on a stand. The water was icy cold, but she was grateful for its numbing touch on her tender body. As she sponged herself, she winced. Tiny bruises marked the insides of her thighs: the imprints of his fingers on her soft white flesh. Gritting her teeth she scrubbed them viciously, as if she could somehow wash both them – and him – away.

When finished she put on the hated black dress, pulled her hair back into a tight knot and made her way slowly downstairs. She could feel the servants' avid eyes on her and almost hear the titters behind her back. She flushed with rage. God rot the lot of them! She'd be damned if she provided more fuel for their kitchen gossip!

Straightening her back she ignored the pain between her legs, walked swiftly into the hall and took her place opposite Master Watkins, helping herself to bread and cheese and ale as casually as if they were a perfectly ordinary married couple, instead of sworn enemies.

'So, husband,' she said, forcing herself to smile at him, 'shall I have the pleasure of your company today? Or have you business that you must be about?'

He looked at her in surprise, then his lips set again. Whatever her little game was, it wasn't going to work. 'I have farm accounts I must attend to with my bailiff,' he informed her. 'Then I must ride into town to oversee a new shipment of stock for the shop.' His eyes narrowed. 'Why?'

'No reason,' she said casually, 'but if you were not using the carriage, I thought I might take it and visit my parents.'

'I think not,' he said coldly. 'You are my wife now. Your place is here. I warrant there are plenty of housewifely duties you can find to occupy yourself with, instead of gallivanting around the countryside.'

'Visiting my parents is hardly gallivanting,' she snapped,

all pretence of pleasantness gone. 'And what exactly is there for me to do? I have no doubt that Mistress Blackstock has the household well in hand.'

He got to his feet and glared down at her. 'I neither know, nor care,' he snarled. 'But if you think I shall allow you to go running back to your mother and father carrying tales, then you are very much mistaken, wife.' His expression became pious for a moment. '"The Devil finds work for idle hands",' he quoted sanctimoniously. 'So you will remain here and find something useful to do, or I shall know the reason why. Good morrow to you, madam.' Slamming his tall black hat on his head he marched out, leaving her fuming.

'Shall I clear away, mistress?' said an oily voice, and Lucy looked up, into the smirking face of Mistress Blackstock.

'Do what you damned well like,' she snapped, flouncing out.

The pleasure of putting the woman in her place did not last. She could not sit sulking in her chamber forever. After half an hour of staring at the four walls she was bored, bored, bored.

So making up her mind, she decided to explore the rest of the house and grounds and see what other changes her parvenu husband had made.

She began with the library. It was obvious that Master Watkins seldom used it, for it was much as she remembered. It was cold, too. The grate was full of ashes and the tops of the books were layered in dust. She looked at them with disfavour. It was hardly surprising they had lain untouched for so long. She had hoped to find something to while away the weary hours, but there was nothing but ancient histories, books on husbandry and tomes of dry sermons.

She had almost given up when she noticed that one shelf of books tucked away in an alcove by the fireplace was free of dust. That was odd. Why had they been singled out? What was so special about them? She went across to investigate.

At first glance there was nothing out of the ordinary about them. They were no different from any of the others in the library – then she peered more closely and saw that they were set out slightly from the shelf. Excitement ran through her. There was something hidden behind them! Perhaps even the precious parchment!

Going across to the library door, she stuck her head out and looked in both directions along the corridor. There wasn't a servant in sight, but just to be on the safe side she closed the door and turned the key in the lock. If someone were to come along it would give her warning, and time to put whatever she discovered back in its hiding place.

Ears pricked for the sound of footsteps she carefully began to remove books, one by one, until she could see behind them. Her face fell. There was no hidden treasure after all. No parchment. Nothing but more books. Perhaps they'd fallen down behind the others, or there simply hadn't been enough room left on the shelves.

Pulling up her sleeve to avoid spiders, she reached carefully into the dark space and took one out. The leather binding was worn and soft to the touch, so it had obviously been well handled. She looked at the title, *Historiae Romanae*, and sighed. Another damned history book, and in Latin as well. How exciting.

As she went to put it back the corner caught on the edge of the shelf, and the book slipped from her fingers and fell open on the floor. She bent to pick it up and stopped short, her mouth falling open with shocked surprise. Recovering herself she lifted the book and flicked through it, her cheeks turning scarlet.

It was a history book all right – a history of perversion! Page after page of beautiful pen and ink drawings of every sexual position she had ever heard of – and some she hadn't! She read a few words and blushed. The text was as graphic as the illustrations. And what illustrations! She stared at one of a woman in congress with three men at once and hastily turned the page, only to find herself gawping at another of two young men busily engaged in sucking each other's... she gasped and banged the book shut, her face flaming.

So this was how Master Watkins improved the shining hour. Not in contemplation of God but in contemplation of this filth! Then for a moment it seemed so incongruous that she thought she might have misjudged him. Perhaps these had been lying forgotten in their hiding place for fifty years or more? Then she remembered their dust-free condition, and his bestial behaviour the night before, and her lips tightened. Oh no, they were his all right.

Laying the first book down, she reached into the dark space again and again until she had retrieved the rest of his hoard. There were five books in all, each more obscene than the last. She stared from one to the other, the germ of a plan forming in her head. She put them back and replaced the concealing volumes carefully in their former positions, and when she unlocked the door and left the library, her fertile brain was busy mulling over how she could use this new information to her advantage.

In the corridor she paused, wondering what to do next. It was almost noon but the very thought of eating sickened her after what she had just seen. What she needed was not food but some good clean air to clear her head. She

64

ran swiftly up the oak stairs to her chamber, flung on her cloak and hurried down again. She hesitated at the foot. If she were to go out the main door she was sure to be seen from one of the upper windows, but if she used the back entrance she could leave unnoticed through the kitchen gardens.

Holding her breath she tiptoed by the kitchens, where loud voices and laughter told her that the servants were already at their meal. Luckily they were too engrossed in their own concerns to notice the shadowy figure as it passed. Reaching the heavy back door she pulled it open a crack and slipped outside.

Cold winter sunlight washed over her and the icy air was delightfully refreshing after the mustiness of the library. It was a relief to get out of the claustrophobic confines of the house and away from the constant feeling of being watched and judged. Unpinning her hair, she shook it loose and allowed it to fall over her shoulders, revelling in her brief moment of freedom. To hell with Master Watkins!

A pile of frosted turnips in the corner of the kitchen garden caught her eye. Picking up a small one she chopped it into pieces with the rusty knife that lay nearby, and hurried off in the direction of the stable. When she reached it she checked that the yard was empty – marking the fact for future reference – then went in.

It was cosier there. The bales of hay acted as insulation and the animals' body heat warmed the winter air. There were four horses in the stable and a soft chorus of whickering greeted her arrival as they regarded their unexpected visitor with interest. She walked up to the first and stroked its smooth neck, laughing as it nudged at her hopefully.

'All right, greedy-guts,' she smiled, producing a chunk

of turnip and offering it on her outstretched hand. It snuffled at it disdainfully and she laughed again. 'Make the best of it, my lad,' she advised. 'That's all I have today.' Finally it condescended to accept her offering and she patted the soft nose as it chewed. 'Next time I'll raid the store loft for apples,' she promised. Disgruntled snorts came from the others, who were resentful of the attention being paid to their stable mate, making her laugh again. She made her way to each of them in turn, stroking their warm hides and murmuring endearments as she dispensed the last of her largess.

Once she had finished she explored the rest of the stable, her mind busy with possibilities. In the tack room she discovered the saddletree and smiled again. There were several saddles of different sizes, including one that looked as if it could have been made for her.

She smiled wistfully, remembering the way her mother had scolded her for hanging around their own stables when she was younger – but thank goodness she'd been such a tomboy. She'd taken a perverse pride in the fact that she could saddle a horse as well as any of the stable boys. And it would stand her in good stead now.

The sound of voices and footsteps on the cobbles brought her back to the present. Pulling her cloak tightly round her she darted into the shadows and crouched down, hardly daring to breathe. 'Saddle up they mares, boy,' ordered a voice. 'Best get 'em exercised 'fore maister gets back.'

'Wouldn't mind saddling yon new mare of his'n,' said a younger voice. There was a lewd chuckle. 'I warrant she'd give you a ride to remember!' Lucy turned scarlet with fury as she realised he was talking about *her*!

'Show a little respect, boy,' grumbled the older man. 'Less'n you want yer ears boxed. She ain't for the likes of you. Just you keep your cock in your breeches and get on with yer work.'

Fury turned to fear as a shadow fell across the door of the tack room. She crouched lower, heart pounding as the stable lad passed by, so close she could have reached out and touched his legs. Thankfully he remained oblivious of her presence and went back the way he'd come, carrying a saddle and whistling cheerfully, then making two more trips for the other saddle and the tack.

It seemed to take forever for them to saddle up, but finally she heard the clatter of hooves on the cobbles as they left the yard. She stood up shakily, wincing in pain as the muscles in her legs screamed in protest at being cramped for so long. She lifted her skirts and rubbed her calves until the pain had gone, then scurried back the way she had come, slipping back in the rear door. Closing it, she leaned against it and breathed a sigh of relief.

Which was short-lived.

'Where have you been?' demanded a cold voice. 'I took a tray of food up to your chamber, but you were not there.'

Lucy looked at Mistress Blackstock in disbelief. How dare the jumped-up bitch spy on her? She glared at the woman until her gaze fell. 'I was not aware that I had to give an account of myself to the servants,' she said sarcastically. 'And in future, kindly remember to call me "mistress" when you speak.' She tossed her head. 'But if you must know, I had a headache and took a walk about the grounds to clear it. I trust that meets with your satisfaction?'

'Yes, m'm,' muttered the housekeeper.

'Good,' said Lucy, stalking past her. 'Now, fetch me some fresh food from the kitchen. I shall take it in the hall.'

When Master Watkins returned from his business Lucy was sitting before the fire, stitching industriously. At his entrance she tucked her needle neatly into the material and looked up at him. 'I trust your day went well, sir?' she said, forcing a smile.

'Well enough,' he muttered, flinging himself down and looking at her sourly. 'What tomfoolery is this?' he demanded, waving a hand at her embroidery.

''Tis a half done tapestry,' she informed him. 'It must have belonged to Lady Mary. I found it pushed away into a dark corner of the hall and forgotten, so I thought I would finish it.' She lowered her lashes. 'As you so kindly pointed out, sir, "The devil finds work for idle hands".'

'Pah!' he grunted. 'There is plenty of good honest mending to be done instead of this useless frippery.'

'True,' she agreed. 'And perhaps when I have finished darning the servants' stockings you would like me to sweep the floors and scrub the stool room?' She smiled sweetly. 'Or would you prefer me to muck out the stables?'

'Hah, very amusing,' he snarled. 'Now pour me some wine. I am chilled to the marrow.'

She got up and did as she was told, hanging onto her smile. 'Will there be anything else?' she enquired sarcastically. It was a mistake. An unpleasant smile crossed his face.

'Yes,' he said, leaning back and stretching out his legs. 'You may help me off with my boots.' She looked at them in dismay. They were wet and covered with mud – or something worse. 'Well?' he demanded. 'Are you going to stand there gawping at them all night?'

Biting her lip, she bent, seized the right one and tugged. Nothing happened. 'Useless bitch,' he snarled. 'Not like that. Put your back into it.' Gritting her teeth she turned her back to him, straddled his leg and hauled on the boot again. Smirking, he put his other foot on her backside, pushed, and both Lucy and boot went flying to land in an undignified heap on the floor.

She got to her feet again. 'Now the left one,' he ordered, not even bothering to conceal his amusement. Without a word she straddled his other leg, but this time when he planted his foot on her bottom and pushed she was ready for him. She staggered a few paces but did not fall. Ignoring his smirk she placed both boots neatly in front of the fire, where they began to steam gently, filling the hall with the stench of drying dung. She wiped her hands on her skirts, leaving wet brown stains.

'Faugh,' she said with a grimace. 'I am going to my chamber to wash my hands and change my gown.'

'Too much of a lady to put up with a little honest dirt, are you?' he sneered. 'Well, while you are about it, make yourself useful and tell the servants to bring dinner. My belly thinks my throat's been cut. I could eat a scabby horse – raw.'

'I'll see if they have one, then,' she said, turning on her heel and marching out with as much dignity as the two muddy boot prints on her rear would allow.

Dinner, when it came, was almost as appetising: lumps of fatty mutton congealing in its own grease, along with the inevitable turnip. Lucy pushed her plate away and made do with a wrinkled apple and a chunk of dry cheese. Master Watkins had no such compunction and shovelled his food in with gusto, chewing the stringy meat with his mouth open and washing it down with copious amounts of wine.

Lucy watched him, wrinkling her nose in disgust. Apparently his Puritanism did not mean denying himself. Still, the more he drank, the better it might be for her. If he fell into a drunken stupor at least he would not be forcing his attentions on her.

When they retired from the table, to sit before the fire, she continued to ply him with wine, making sure his glass was never empty, and eventually she was rewarded. His eyes drooped, his head fell back, his jaw dropped and he began to snore like a pig. She waited until it was obvious he would not wake, and then tiptoed off to her chamber, praying he would remain asleep and leave her unmolested.

He did.

Several times she started awake in a sweat, convinced he was looming over her, but it was merely a bad dream. There was no one in the bedchamber but her – and the mice that scuttled behind the wainscot. Sighing with relief she closed her eyes again and eventually drifted off into deeper slumber, and when she woke again the morning sun was shining through the casement, casting a pattern of diamond shadows on the counterpane.

Smiling, she swung her legs out of bed and padded barefoot across to her basin and ewer. They were empty, but there was a timid tap on the door and one of the Faiths or Prudences stood on the threshold carrying a copper can of water – hot for once, judging by the tendrils of steam curling from beneath the lid.

Lucy nodded graciously to the girl. 'Thank you…?'

'Hope, mistress,' said the girl, blushing and trying to curtsey without spilling the hot water. Lucy hid a smile. She'd been close.

'Thank you, Hope,' said Lucy. 'You may put the hot water on my washstand.' Obediently the little maid trotted across the room and deposited her burden. 'Will there be anything else, mistress?' she asked shyly.

Lucy smiled. The girl looked harmless enough, and it would be pleasant to be waited upon again. 'Take that to be washed and mended,' she said, indicating the torn nightshift lying in the corner. 'And sponge the stains from yesterday's gown as well. When you have done that, you may return and help me dress.'

The maidservant bobbed again, poked the fire back into life then gathered up the clothes and was gone as quietly as she had come. Humming to herself, Lucy tipped the hot water into the basin and set about making her toilet.

She was in her petticoats when Hope returned. 'Which gown do you wish to wear today, mistress?' she asked.

'Mmmm,' smiled Lucy. 'Which one shall I choose? The black, perhaps?'

Hope stared at her uncomprehendingly. 'But they're all black, ma'am,' she said in bewilderment.

Lucy's shoulders slumped. 'I know,' she sighed. ''Twas merely a jest.' She waved a hand. 'Whichever one is nearest.' Relieved, the little maid fetched it and helped her mistress slip it on. Then she was in the middle of brushing Lucy's hair when the door burst open.

'You – out!' ordered Master Watkins, glaring at the girl. Hope took one look at her master's furious face, dropped the comb and fled.

'And a good morrow to you, too, husband,' said Lucy sweetly. 'I trust I find you well?'

'Very witty,' he snarled. His face was stubbled and his bloodshot eyes scowled unpleasantly. 'And a most cunning ploy last night, too.'

'I don't know what you're talking about,' she said, sticking her chin in the air. 'What am I supposed to have done now?'

'A man and wife should share their bed,' he snapped.

'So?' she said, her lip curling in disdain. 'It's hardly my fault if you can't hold your drink. What was I supposed to do, carry you upstairs on my back?'

71

'We had a bargain—'

'Which if I remember rightly, you did not see fit to keep,' she snapped. 'So kindly do not come prating to me about how ill-used you have been.' Her eyes flashed. 'If it had not been for this damned Civil War you would not even have dared look upon me, let alone take me as a wife.'

'So what does that make you?' he sneered. 'A Civil Whore?' He grinned at his own wit, and then his smile vanished as she lashed out and slapped his face.

'I take it back,' he said, rubbing his face. 'You are a whore all right, but a most *uncivil* one. You will regret that, madam, indeed you will.'

'Oh yes?' she goaded. 'And what do you intend to do about it?'

'This!' he said, and reaching out with one hand he gripped the collar of her dress and pulled. For a moment the rough material resisted, then the buttons gave and the top of her gown fell about her waist. She backed away, gathering it against her heaving breasts, her flesh a shocking white against the harsh black. He licked his lips and advanced on her, unfastening his belt as he came. She looked about wildly for some escape – but there was none.

He reached out again and seized her by the upper arm, flinging her facedown on the bed. As she struggled to rise he hauled her skirts above her waist, trapping her in the clinging folds. Grabbing her flailing hands at the wrist he wound his belt round them and fastened it to the bedhead so she was stretched out helplessly before him, naked from the waist down.

He ran his hand over her pert buttocks, enjoying the way her flesh cringed at his touch and feeling his manhood swell. 'Don't run away, sweetheart,' he panted. 'I shall be back, with a little surprise for you.'

She lay there frozen in the muffling darkness as his footsteps retreated, her heart pounding with horrified anticipation. What was he going to do?

In answer she heard him return. There was a moment's silence, a strange whistling sound, then she gasped as the world exploded into white-hot pain as a thin cane connected with her flesh. The soft globes of her bottom quivered beneath the blow, a fine red line appearing on the tender skin. She gritted her teeth. She would not scream… she would not scream… she would not—

She shrieked as another blow descended, then another, her muscles jumping as the cane bit again and again. He grinned down as she writhed against the counterpane in a vain attempt to escape his attack, her white skin now a fiery red.

He was erect now, his cock pressing against his constraining breeches. He fumbled at his crotch, releasing his swollen member. As the cane rose and fell he stroked himself in time to her shrieks, until it felt as if the bulbous purple tip of his prick would explode. His teeth showed in a cruel smile. Oh no, she didn't get off that easily. He laid down the cane.

Muffled helplessly in darkness, Lucy gasped as he gripped her hips and shoved the pillow beneath her belly, raising her buttocks. The slightest touch on her bruised skin brought fresh pain, and even worse, the dreadful, sick pleasure she had felt on her wedding night. She could feel her own juices trickling between her thighs and the heat that pounded through her groin. She loathed him – yet longed for him to take her.

She groaned as he thrust his fingers roughly into her hot wetness, trying to shut out the feelings they aroused, then froze as he withdrew and she felt him explore the tightness of her anus. Oh no, he couldn't mean to…

She screamed as she felt the tip of his finger force its way into the tight pucker of flesh.

'So,' he said, leering wolfishly, 'still a virgin in some ways, eh?'

She tried to wriggle away from the unwanted invasion, but he pushed harder and she whimpered as he penetrated her further, and then gasped in relief as he withdrew.

But it was a short-lived relief. Kneeling behind her he coated his cock with her juices, then put the tip of it against the soft pink pucker of flesh, and thrust. She screamed as resistance gave and the swollen head of his prick disappeared slowly into her rear passage – then felt the whole length of him slide in and heard him groan in pleasure as her flesh gripped him. She whimpered as he began to thrust harder and faster. She whined in a terrible mixture of pain and desire as he pushed deeper and deeper into the sweet forbidden place between her beaten buttocks. Each movement pressed the bud of her clitoris against the pillow, sending delicious sensations through her, while the harsh material of her gown rubbed against the sensitive tips of her breasts like a coarse tongue.

He gave one last massive thrust and exploded, his hot seed splattering inside her, triggering her own release – then she felt him collapse and withdraw.

Humiliated beyond belief she buried her scarlet face in the muffling folds of her skirts, thankful that they hid her shame. Even when he untied her hands and she heard him stalk from the room she continued to lay there, tears of shame trickling down her cheeks.

She *must* put her plan into action, and she must do it soon.

There was to be no chance to do so for several weeks; weeks that seemed to drag on forever. The frosty weather broke and an onslaught of winter rain turned the roads into muddy rutted channels where even a light carriage ran the risk of being bogged down or toppling over into a ditch. Even with all the fires blazing the house stank of dampness, and mildew blossomed in dark corners.

Master Watkins strayed no further than the estate, with the result that Lucy's days were filled with excruciating boredom. That was bad enough, but the nights! She shuddered. The nights were best forgotten about. She was coming to dread the moment each evening when he yawned, stretched and announced that it was time for bed. Even on the few occasions when he did not use her for his pleasure, she lay sleepless and rigid trying desperately to keep her body from touching his, lest he wake and reach for her with those dreadful, clutching, bony fingers.

On the last morning of February she woke and lay for a few moments, wondering what was different... then it dawned on her. The constant beating of rain against the casements had stopped. She glanced sideways, but Master Watkins was still asleep, his mouth gaping open in a snore. Careful not to disturb him she slipped out of bed, padded across the room and eased the window open.

It was still damp and cold, but light from a watery sun was finally breaking through the clouds and glinting off the puddles. There was a hint of green on the skeletal trees and Lucy felt her spirits rise a little. It was not yet spring, but the faint promise of the season hung in the air.

It was another two days before the roads were clear enough to pass, and the first she knew of it was when a mud-stained carriage came trundling up the driveway towards the house. As it drew up Lucy stared with her mouth open – then rushed to greet its occupants.

'Mother, father!' she gasped, hugging them in turn.

'Oh, my dear, I have missed you,' said her mother, holding Lucy away and looking at her disapprovingly. 'But you are so thin and pale. Are you eating enough?' Her expression became anxious. 'You haven't been ill, have you?' She tutted. 'This dreadful weather! Half the servants have been ill of the ague and your father has been driving me mad, pacing up and down like a caged bear.'

'I am fine,' protested Lucy, 'and all the better for seeing you. Come in!' Ignoring Master Watkins, glowering in the background, she clapped her hands and ordered the servants to bring wine and cakes, then led her parents to the fire, chattering nineteen to the dozen. 'How are you?' she demanded. 'How is Martha? Still as bossy as ever?'

'You know Martha,' smiled Lettice. 'She never changes.' She frowned slightly. 'But what of you? We have heard nothing from you since your wedding. Not a message. Not a scrape of a pen.' She looked at her daughter reproachfully. 'Why, you could have been dead for all we knew.'

Lucy opened her mouth to make some feeble excuse, but she did not get the chance to answer for herself.

'My wife,' he said the words pompously, laying emphasis on his possession, 'has had no time for such trivial matters. She has been busy acquainting herself with her new duties.'

'I hardly think her duties so heavy that she could not find time to send a few words to her own parents,' grumbled Sir Jeffrey. For a few moments the men glared at one another, then Lettice broke in with a nervous laugh.

'Come now, let us not squabble like children. 'Tis done with. We are here now.' She looked at Master Watkins. 'How are you, Ezekiel?' She smiled. 'I may call you that now, may I not? Now that I am your mother by marriage?'

His grim expression softened a little. 'You may,' he agreed. 'And I am well, thank you.'

Much to Lucy's dismay, her mother's charm had worked too well. He joined them round the fire, helping himself to a glass of wine, and thanks to his presence the conversation became stilted. There was no chance to ask if they had heard anything from Roddy and Jamie. No chance to tell them that Master Watkins had reneged on his promise to hand over the parchment.

As for anything else, it was out of the question. Even if she had the opportunity, she could not have told her parents about the horror of her nights. It was bad enough that they lived with the guilt of seeing their only daughter forced into a loveless marriage, but the knowledge that she was the prey of a monster of sexual depravity would have been too much to bear. Her father would kill him – and then what?

So she smiled and prattled on about inconsequential matters. The changes Master Watkins had made in the house. The difficulty of keeping the floors clean in such dreadful weather. How hard it was to produce decent meals at this time of year. Anything at all to keep the conversation light and innocuous.

By the time her parents rose to take their leave she was exhausted by the strain of putting on the appearance of a happy newly wed. Her only consolation was that Master Watkins was smiling approvingly. Then as they rose to go Lucy remembered something. 'Oh, mother, I must not forget to return the jewels you lent me for my wedding day,' she said, and as Lettice stared at her blankly and opened her mouth to ask what her daughter was talking about, Lucy's foot came down hard on her instep, making her wince. 'The emerald ring and pendant. Remember?'

smiled Lucy, willing her mother to understand.

There was a long moment before she caught on, then she smiled. 'Good heavens,' she said. 'I had quite forgot them. Thank you, my dear.'

'I'll fetch them now,' said Lucy, smiling in relief. She lifted her skirts and ran from the hall up the long oaken staircase. Two minutes later she returned, panting, with the precious tokens, and handed them over to her mother. It hurt to part with them, but at least she knew they were safe now, and, God willing, the time would come when she could reclaim them.

'Oh dear, what happened to the chain?' asked Lettice, holding it up. 'The links have snapped.'

Lucy cast a frightened glance at Master Watkins, her hand lifting unconsciously to her throat as she remembered the cruel way he had wrenched the pendant from her. He glared back, defying her to tell the truth.

'I'm so sorry, mother, it was all my fault,' she said anxiously. 'I was leaning over my embroidery and caught it on the frame.'

'Never mind, my dear,' smiled Lettice, tucking them away. 'Least said, soonest mended. I will take it to the goldsmith. By the time he's finished it will look as good as new.' She glanced at her husband and smiled. 'Well, we had best be off,' she said. 'I can see your father is champing at the bit. He is thinking of buying a new horse, so we are calling to look at it on the way home.'

She kissed Lucy and held her at arms' length. 'You will eat properly, my dear, won't you?' she said, her anxiety returning at the sight of her daughter's pale face. Putting her hand on Master Watkins' arm, she gave him a beseeching look. 'And you will take care of my little girl, Ezekiel?' He nodded brusquely and she smiled. 'Thank you.' She turned to her husband. 'Well, my dear, I suppose we must be off and look at that horse of yours. Come along.'

Sir Jeffrey kissed Lucy, grunted a grudging goodbye to Master Watkins and took his wife's arm. Together they walked out to their carriage, with Lucy and Master Watkins following behind. As the carriage disappeared down the long drive Lucy felt a lump in her throat. It had been such a pleasure to see them and feel cared for again, but their loving presence had simply underlined the bleakness of her life now.

She bit her lip to keep back the tears. Still, the visit had gone well. She smiled wryly. At least her father and Master Watkins had not come to blows this time!

She turned to smile gratefully at her husband, and was horrified to find him glaring at her, his lips white with suppressed fury. 'Wh-what is wrong?' she stammered.

'I'll tell you what's wrong,' he sneered, gripping her by the arms and shaking her. 'How dare they come into my house and look down their highbred noses at me?'

'B-but they didn't!' protested Lucy.

'Don't lie to me, you whore,' he snarled, flecks of spittle spraying her cheeks. '"You will look after my little girl, won't you, Ezekiel?",' he said in a high-pitched parody of her mother. 'Condescending bitch!' He let her go, then reached out again and pinched her left nipple viciously, his eyes glinting with twisted amusement as she flinched.

'I wonder how proud she'd be if she could see her "little girl" sprawled naked on my bed with her legs spread, panting for it like a bitch in heat?' he leered, then stalked off, leaving her to stare after him, shivering, as she rubbed her bruised breast and the tops of her arms where his fingers had dug in.

She thought with dread about the night to come when he would make her pay for his imagined slights. Oh, dear

God! Please, please let the chance to put her plan into action come soon!

That opportunity did come, three days later.

'I am going into town today,' he announced over breakfast. 'With this damned weather it has been far too long since I attended to business,' he grumbled. 'My servants could be robbing me blind, for all I know.'

'Yes, Ezekiel,' she murmured demurely, hiding her excitement. 'What time shall I expect you back?'

He glared at her suspiciously. 'Why do you want to know?' he demanded. 'So you may entertain some lover in my absence?'

She forced a laugh and made herself pat his hand. 'Of course not. I merely wished to have your meal ready and waiting on your return. As a good wife should,' she added.

'I am glad to see you are learning your place at last,' he said, mollified. 'If the roads are clear I should be back by seven.'

She lowered her eyes to hide her exultation. That would give her plenty of time.

After he had gone she spent the morning sewing dutifully at her mending, counting the slow hours as they passed. When midday approached she laid down her needle and made her way to Mistress Blackstock's room, off the kitchens.

'The master will be returning at seven,' she informed the woman coldly. 'See that his meal is ready for him.' She rubbed her temples and sighed. 'I do not wish anything to eat just now. I have a megrim, so I shall go and lie down in my room until it clears.'

'Yes, ma'am,' Mistress Blackstock said sullenly. 'Will there be anything else?'

'Yes,' said Lucy. 'I do not wish any of the servants clattering around upstairs and making it worse, so see that I remain undisturbed.' The woman bobbed a reluctant curtsy and Lucy made her way slowly upstairs, clutching the banister with one hand, the other to her 'aching' head.

As soon as she was inside her chamber her demeanour changed. Flinging off the pretence of being ill, she hurried across the room and tugged the hangings across the window to shut out the light. That done, she went to the bed and pulled down the coverlet. Laying the pillows down the middle of the bed she tugged the coverlet back into place, and regarded her handiwork with satisfaction. Even if someone did look in to the room, in the dim light it would look as if she were lying there, sleeping.

To be on the safe side she allowed another half hour to drag past, listening to the voices of the outdoor servants as they made their way across the courtyard to the kitchens for their midday meal. Then when all had fallen silent she made her move.

First she made her way to the library, tiptoeing slowly and carefully along the corridors and easing the door slowly open. It was deserted, the shelf beside the fire as undisturbed as she had left it. Leaning over, she swiftly removed two books from the front until she could reach in and retrieve one of those hidden behind, before putting them back in place. A brief flick through confirmed her first impression of the nature of Master Watkins' depraved tastes. She smiled wryly; with evidence like this, who would dare disbelieve her accusations?

Clutching it to her bosom she fled silently back the way she had come. As she neared the kitchens she stopped short and pressed herself against the wall as the door swung open and a figure stamped out. It was the older man in charge of the stables. Fear of discovery made her heart pound so loudly she was convinced he would hear it, but he was too busy fumbling with his breeches to notice her. Thank God! He was only paying a visit to the privy! Trembling, she stood frozen until he returned and the kitchen door swung shut behind him, then she grabbed a cloak from the pegs at the door and scurried across the courtyard to the stables.

Ignoring the whickers of curiosity from the horses, she hurried through to the tack room, pulled the smallest saddle from the tree and staggered back through with it. Laying it down on the cobbles she opened the gate of the stall, led out the roan mare and tethered it while she saddled up, her nervous fingers fumbling with the straps and buckles.

At last it was done. Mounting, she tugged the reins and the roan cantered out of the gates, head tossing. As soon as they were clear Lucy dug her heels into its flanks and the mare took off as if the devil himself were after her, hooves biting into the damp sward. Lucy laughed in sheer exhilaration at the feel of the cool spring air streaming past her fevered cheeks. Her hair tumbled free from its tight knot and flew like a banner behind her.

Oh, they'd find out soon enough that she'd gone, but they would have no way of knowing where – and by then she would be out of reach anyway. She thought of the panic the discovery of her escape would cause. They would be running around like headless chickens! She laughed again. Hell mend the lot of them! For the moment she was free.

She felt the comforting weight of the book tucked against her waist. And if all went according to her plan, she would be free of Master Watkins' disgusting attentions as well!

The ride took longer than she expected, and she had been out of the saddle for too long, with the result that she was beginning to tire when she finally reached Master Oakley's house. Master Oakley's *new* house.

She shook her head. Before he had been nothing but a common tanner, his tumbledown tenement abutting his business, and his puritan rantings confined to what free moments he could snatch from his work. Like so many others – her husband included – he had profited well from the war and gone up in the world. Now he was a respected landowner whose congregation hung on his every word as if it came straight from the lips of the Lord God Almighty Himself.

She pulled her horse to a stop and regarded the house critically. Despite the raw newness of the timbers, it was an imposing edifice, obviously modelled on the manor houses of the gentry, and far enough away from town that Master Oakley's newly sensitive nostrils would not be assailed by the stench from his own tanning vats. Her lip curled in contempt at the sheer hypocrisy of the Puritans. How ironic that, in coming into money, their first move was to emulate the class they affected to despise!

But she shook her head and smiled ruefully. Considering she was flinging herself on the mercy of the man, she had better keep that little opinion to herself.

Wincing at the ache in her thighs, she slid down out of the saddle and tethered the mare to a tree, checking that it could graze comfortably. Patting its nose, she straightened her shoulders, walked up to the imposing front door and lifted her fist.

The sound of her knocking echoed through the front hall and there was a long moment before she heard footsteps inside. At last the door swung open, and her jaw dropped as she found herself staring into the face of Charity Blackstock!

'Yes?' snapped the housekeeper, and Lucy realised her mistake. This woman was years older, her face set in uncompromising lines and her hair more grey than black. The similarity was there, though, like two peas in a pod – or two serpents hatched from the same egg, more like. This must be some older sister or cousin.

'I wish to see Master Oakley,' Lucy announced.

'Master Oakley is busy,' said the woman, looking her over contemptuously. Under her gaze, Lucy suddenly became aware that her hair was as tangled as a bird's nest from her wild ride; that her dress was travel-stained and that the cloak she had 'borrowed' from the servants' hall was long past its best. The woman's next words confirmed it. 'Besides,' she went on. 'He disapproves of beggars.'

'How very Christian of him,' said Lucy through gritted teeth. 'Then it is a blessing indeed that I am not one.' She glared at the woman. 'I am Lady Lucinda Carst…' she caught her mistake and corrected herself. 'I am Mistress Ezekiel Watkins,' she said haughtily. 'And I wish to speak to Master Oakley immediately.'

'What about?' demanded the woman.

None of your damned business! thought Lucy, but she was far too sensible to say so. She hadn't ridden this far to have the door slammed in her face. Instead she forced herself to smile politely. 'I am afraid that is a private matter, mistress…?'

'Blackstock,' said the woman, confirming Lucy's earlier suspicions. Dear God, how many of the bitches were there? 'Wait here,' she went on brusquely. 'I will see if Master Oakley wishes to see you.' She half shut the door and disappeared, skirts swishing, leaving Lucy to stand shivering on the doorstep.

When she returned her manner had changed completely. 'Do come in, madam,' she said, ushering Lucy inside. 'Please come this way.' She led Lucy to a room off the hall, and ushered her to a seat beside the fire. 'May I fetch you some refreshment while you are waiting?' she enquired obsequiously.

'Thank you, that would be kind,' smiled Lucy.

The housekeeper bustled off again, then returned bearing a small tray containing a bottle of wine, two glasses and a small plate of sweetmeats. She placed this on a table at Lucy's elbow, then curtsied briefly and disappeared, leaving Lucy to her own devices.

Pouring herself a glass of wine, Lucy looked round with interest. This was obviously where Master Oakley dealt with members of his congregation, since the furniture was comfortable but almost stark in its plainness. A desk in the corner held a large bible – prominently displayed – an equally large inkwell, half a dozen goose-feather quills and several pages of a half-scrawled sermon.

Dominating the room was a huge portrait of Master Oakley that hung above the fireplace. He was standing at his pulpit, one hand on the open bible in front of him, his other raised in stern but loving admonition and his eyes cast piously up to heaven.

Lucy recognised the style immediately and bit back a grin. The same artist who'd painted Master Watkins – the one who possessed the wonderful gift of blindness when it came to his clients' flaws – had obviously done it. Judging by the painting, Master Oakley's paunch had mysteriously vanished; his narrow shoulders had broadened and he seemed to have grown at least six inches in height!

She started as the door opened and the subject of the

painting walked in. Master Oakley cast a smug glance upwards and smiled. 'I see you are admiring my portrait,' he smirked. 'An excellent likeness, is it not?'

'It is indeed,' Lucy agreed solemnly. 'Almost miraculous in its portrayal.' It was not a lie; anything that rendered those unprepossessing features tolerable definitely deserved the title of 'miracle'!

His expression became even smugger at the perceived compliment. He took a seat behind his desk, indicated that she should take the one opposite and smiled at her genially. 'So how may I help you, mistress?' he enquired.

'I have come about my husband,' she said.

He leaned back, folded his hands across his paunch and nodded. 'Ah, yes, Ezekiel,' he beamed. 'A fine man and a good Christian.'

'He is neither,' snapped Lucy. 'He is a brute who has treated me shamefully!'

Master Oakley, whose own meek wife had dutifully borne him nine children then died, still uncomplaining, could not have been more shocked had the bible on his desk suddenly grown teeth and bitten him! He sat bolt upright and stared at her with his mouth hanging open.

'I beg your pardon?' he spluttered, scarcely believing his own ears.

'You heard me,' said Lucy grimly. 'The man is a beast. He has beaten me regularly since the day we were married.'

Master Oakley regained his composure. He was on safer ground here. 'Women are poor, frail vessels,' he said pompously. 'And it has fallen to men to guide them in the paths of righteousness. I am sure that any gentle chastisement your husband has provided has been for your own good.'

'Balderdash!' spat Lucy. 'It has been for his own perverted pleasure! He has used and abused me in ways that no decent man would even think of.'

'What do you mean?' he demanded indignantly.

Lucy turned scarlet but refused to back down. 'He has inserted his member in forbidden places,' she said primly. Master Oakley continued to gape at her blankly and she felt her temper begin to fray. Did she have to draw the idiot a picture? 'He takes me up the arse!' she blurted. 'Is that clear enough?'

Master Oakley drew in his breath as if he'd been kicked in the stomach by a horse. 'I don't believe you!' he gasped.

'Believe this then,' snapped Lucy, reaching into the folds of her gown and producing the book she'd taken from the library. She flung it on his desk and it fell open at a well-thumbed page.

There was a shocked silence, and then he reached for it and began to flick gingerly through it. His face flushed and beads of sweat broke out on his brow. 'How did you come by this… this… this filth?' he demanded.

'I found it in my precious husband's library,' she informed him. 'Cunningly concealed – and it was not the only one, either. He has more.' She smiled triumphantly. 'So what do you have to say about your "fine, Christian gentleman" now, sir?'

'This is indeed shameful,' he said, his breath unsteady. He opened his desk drawer and slid the book inside with a shaky hand. Then once it was safely concealed, he recovered himself somewhat. 'I shall keep this foul pamphlet and pray for guidance,' he informed her piously. 'Once the Lord has spoken to me, I shall know how to act upon it.'

'I trust the Lord will not take too long about it,' said Lucy tartly. His look of outrage told her that she had gone too far and she lowered her eyes. If she wanted his help she had best keep on the right side of him. 'I am sorry,' she apologised. 'I should not have spoken so. 'Twas the thought of my sufferings that made me forget myself.'

He decided to be magnanimous. 'That is understandable, my dear,' he said, reaching over and patting her hand. 'But rest assured that I shall deal with your... er... difficulties... shortly.' He leaned back again. 'Now, is there anything else I may help you with?'

Realising the interview was over, Lucy shook her head and got to her feet. 'Thank you, no,' she replied. 'I must be on my way before darkness falls.' She looked at him. 'I trust this will remain between us?'

'But of course, my dear,' he said. He tapped the side of his nose. 'It shall be our little secret.' She cringed inwardly at his coy expression, but forced herself to thank him yet again. He tugged the bell rope and the housekeeper materialised to usher her to the door.

Outside she took a deep breath of fresh air and felt the weight of worry fall from her shoulders at last. Thank God the whole sordid business was over and done with. No doubt he would have a private word with her husband and that would be that. Master Watkins would hardly dare defy the instructions of his own pastor.

Untethering the mare, she cantered slowly through the darkening evening, savouring the last iota of freedom before she had to enter her hated prison again. She smiled ruefully. No doubt there would be hell to pay on her return, but it would be worth it.

As she rode back into the stable yard she was surprised to find it deserted. It looked as if she hadn't even been missed. Thanking God for small mercies she stripped the saddle from the mare; replaced it where she'd found it; fed the animal some oats and made her way back into the house.

Even the kitchen was empty and she began to wonder what was wrong. Had some plague wiped out everyone in her absence? Hanging up the cloak she'd borrowed, she tiptoed along the corridor to the foot of the stairs.

As she reached it she heard Master Watkins speaking in the hall. There was a pause, followed by the murmuring of many other voices. He must be addressing the entire household. She frowned. What was going on?

The sound of movement sent her scuttling upstairs to her chamber, where she washed herself quickly, ran a comb through her tangled hair and changed into a clean gown before hurrying back down again – just as the servants were going slowly back about their business, talking in solemn undertones.

Ignoring them she walked into the hall, where Master Watkins was staring gloomily into the fire. 'Good heavens, Ezekiel,' she said, with a nervous laugh. 'From the expression on your face one would think the world was coming to an end.'

He turned to look at her, his face stony. 'The Lord Protector is ill,' he informed her coldly. 'Oh, my,' she said flippantly. 'I was right. The world is indeed coming to an end. How should we manage without him?'

The slap almost knocked her off her feet. 'Bitch!' he hissed. 'Get to your chamber! Now! On your knees and pray for his recovery, or I shall know the reason why.'

Clutching her face she stumbled from the hall, then kneeling beside her bed, head bent, she prayed for Master Cromwell, all right – that the bastard died, writhing in agony, and all the devils in hell came to carry off his blackened soul.

Unfortunately her prayers remained unanswered. Word came barely three weeks later that he had recovered. Not only that, but he had not been at death's door at all. It had merely been a bad attack of the ague, combined with the gout that normally plagued him. Lucy cursed the rumours that had raised her hopes, only to dash them again.

But she brightened; at least one good thing had come of it. Master Watkins had been so worried about the situation that he barely glanced in her direction, let alone laid a finger on her.

Her lips curved in a malicious smile. And well he might fret. If the Lord Protector died then the Protectorate died with him. Oh, he had a son, Richard, but he was nothing but an amiable buffoon who could never take his father's place. No, once he was gone it was just a matter of time before the king returned, and when he did, where would Master Watkins' fine estate be then? He had bought it for a pittance from Cromwell's government, but if that government were declared illegal? He might well find himself out on his ear, and kicking at the end of a rope for treason into the bargain. She laughed. No wonder his member had wilted and he spent his nights pacing the floor. Long might it continue!

But it didn't.

News of his master's recovery put fresh vigour in his blood and he celebrated that night by pleasuring himself upon her till every muscle in her body ached. She laid there, teeth clenched, enduring the pain as he pounded his cock into her, her only consolation that he was in such a good mood he didn't beat her first.

The next few days were a torment of disappointment, as she looked expectantly out of the window every half hour, hoping against hope to see Master Oakley riding up. But he never did.

Surely he had not forgotten his promise to take her

husband to task? He had heard her out. He had seen the proof. What more did he need to act? Surely he did not intend to ignore it. As a so-called 'Man of God', he was duty bound to keep his word.

A week passed and she had almost given up hope when he finally appeared in the late afternoon. He made an amusing sight. Unused to riding, he was clutching his high black hat like grim death as his ancient horse ambled up the drive. She suppressed a giggle. He was an unlikely knight in shining armour, but he would have to do. Smiling, she went and sat before the fire, arranging her skirts sedately as she waited for the housekeeper to usher him in.

'Ah, Master Oakley, you are most welcome,' she said, getting to her feet as he came in. 'Do take a seat. You must stay for dinner, and in the meantime, Mistress Blackstock,' she smiled, '*our* Mistress Blackstock, will fetch us some refreshments.' She nodded to the woman, who smiled at Master Oakley and glowered at her mistress before going to do as she was told.

As soon as she had gone Lucy lowered her voice. 'Thank you for coming,' she said. 'I am sure that a few stern words from you will curb my husband's unnatural desires.'

He nodded uncomfortably, but was saved from answering by the return of the housekeeper with cakes and ale. Lucy raised her voice again.

'And after dinner you must stay the night,' she smiled, and then turned to the housekeeper. 'See that a room is prepared for Master Oakley, and make sure a fire is lit. The nights are cold yet.'

'I am not sure…' he demurred.

'Nonsense,' she said briskly. 'I will not hear another

word upon the matter. You cannot possibly ride home again until tomorrow. It is a long journey in the dark and I am sure you and my husband will have much to discuss.'

'Well, if you insist,' he murmured, giving in.

'I do,' she said firmly. 'Now, let me fill your tankard – and you must try one of these cakes.' She heard footsteps and turned with a bright smile to greet Master Watkins. 'Look, husband,' she trilled. 'Just see who has honoured us with a visit. Why do you not sit and take a tankard with him while I go and oversee dinner?'

He looked startled by her effusive greeting, but nodded at Master Oakley in genuine pleasure. 'You are most welcome,' he said, and when she left to go to the kitchens they were already deep in conversation about Master Cromwell's illness.

Over dinner she smiled and nodded, barely aware of what was being said. The meal seemed to drag on forever, and even afterwards she had to sit dutifully for another hour before she could make her excuses and go to bed.

Finally she laid down her mending and yawned prodigiously. 'Heavens, you must forgive me,' she apologised, 'but I am exhausted.' She rose. 'If you will excuse me, I am for my bed.' She cast a meaningful glance at Master Oakley. 'I shall leave you two gentlemen to your talk. Goodnight.'

As she took a candle and climbed the stairs to her chamber, a smile of triumph played about her lips. After tonight her troubles would be over!

'What was that?' she gasped, sitting bolt upright. Fumbling for the tinderbox she lit the candle beside her bed with shaking fingers and peered around the shadowy room. She had no idea of how long she had been asleep – or of what had awakened her – but it was still pitch-black outside. It must be well after midnight, or even later.

She turned apprehensively to see if the noise had woken Master Watkins, then sighed with relief. The bed beside her was empty. No doubt Master Oakley was still wrestling so save his soul. She smiled wryly. If his sermons were anything to go by, then it would probably be daylight before her errant husband came crawling to bed with his tail between his legs.

There had been no more inexplicable noises, and she was just about to blow out the candle and lie down again, secure in the comforting thought that she had simply been awakened by one of the usual creaks and groans that old houses were prone to, when it came again.

She shivered in the cold, straining her ears to make out what had caused it. It came again, and this time, despite the muffling effect of the thick oaken door, she recognised it as the sound of furtive movement. As if someone were creeping along the corridor to her chamber. Her hand flew to her throat. Had some thief broken in? Surely not. If they had, then her husband and Master Oakley would have apprehended them.

She froze as the handle of the chamber door turned slowly and it began to creak open, to reveal the sight of her husband on the threshold. She relaxed – better the devil you knew than the devil you didn't – though she could not understand why he had taken the trouble to be so quiet. He had shown mighty little consideration for her till now. Usually he cared nothing for waking her when he came late to bed.

'For Heaven's sake, husband,' she said crossly. 'You well nigh scared the wits from me. I thought thieves had broken in and were about to rob us.'

He ignored her words. 'How touching,' he sneered, staring down at her. 'The little bride. And still awake to greet her husband. What devotion.'

An icy finger ran down her spine as she looked at him properly. He was swaying slightly and the wine-flush was high in his cheeks. He took a step towards her and she cringed back, clutching the coverlet to her chest.

'Not devoted enough to keep her mouth shut, though,' he went on. 'Oh no! Not devoted enough not to go running off and telling a pack of foul lies to anyone who'd listen to them.'

Her anger overpowered her fear. 'I am no liar!' she protested. 'You are. Your entire life is a lie! Puritan, rubbish! There's little enough purity in your little collection of picture books, is there? What's wrong?' she asked in contempt. 'Frightened that your neighbours would despise you if they knew what you are really like?' Her face wrinkled in disgust. 'Faugh! You cannot even be an honest lecher. You must hide your filth behind a mask of prudery. You make me sick.'

He glared at her, speechless with drink-fuelled fury, but she was too angry herself to take notice of the warning signs.

'And what does Master Oakley think of you now, then?' she taunted. 'Now he knows what you're really like?'

Master Watkins gave an evil smile. 'Why don't you ask him yourself, my dear?' He stepped back and Master Oakley stumbled into the bedchamber. She stared at him in horror. He was as drunk as a lord!

'M-Master Oakley,' she gasped.

He drew himself up and leered at her, his eyes lingering on the partly hidden swell of her bosom. 'Mistress Watkins,' he mumbled, attempting to bow and almost falling over in the process.

'My dear wife would like to know what you think of me now,' said Master Watkins, raising an eyebrow. 'Would you care to enlighten her?'

Oakley peered at him owlishly, then turned his attention back to Lucy. 'I was shocked,' he announced, enunciating his words with the studied clarity of the very inebriated. 'Shocked and distressed.' He hiccupped. 'It was sinful. Sinful indeed.'

Lucy began to relax – until his next words.

'That a wife should tell such monstrous lies about her husband,' he went on, wagging a finger at her. 'It beggars belief.'

'B-but… but I did not lie,' stammered Lucy. 'How can you say that when you have seen the evidence with your own eyes?'

'Ezekiel has explained it all, to my complete satisfaction,' he announced, slurring his words slightly. 'And I was horrified.' He shook his head sadly. 'Utterly horrified to find that such a sweet face could hide such dreadful depravity.'

She gawped at him, stunned. 'Wh-what do you mean?' she gasped.

'Do not try and play the innocent with me, madam,' he said sternly. 'Your husband has told me it all. How he discovered this filth concealed at the bottom of your chest, and how he took it and hid it away to try and save you from yourself.'

Lucy looked from his red, sweating face to that of her smirking husband, who was leaning against the mantle-shelf watching the entire scene with barely concealed amusement. 'And you believed him?' she demanded in utter disbelief.

'Of course I believed him,' said Master Oakley indignantly. 'Why should he lie?'

'Because he is a heartless brute without a shred of conscience,' Lucy said bitterly. She glared at Master

Oakley. 'And you, sir, are an even bigger damned fool than you look!'

She cursed the words as soon as they were out of her mouth. If Master Oakley had a shred of pity for her, her hasty jibe destroyed it, and Master Watkins took full advantage of her stupidity.

'You see what I am faced with, Master Oakley?' he said, shaking his head in mock sadness. 'Even when her wickedness is revealed, she still refuses to repent.'

'I do, indeed,' agreed Master Oakley. 'Shameless! Utterly shameless!' His indignation might have been more impressive had he not slurred his words and belched halfway through them.

Master Watkins ignored this minor interruption. 'So what do you suggest we do?' he asked solemnly. 'Should she be allowed to carry on in her evil ways, or should she be punished that we might lead her feet back to the paths of righteousness?'

Lucy stared at him in dismay. The cunning bastard! The way he had phrased his question, there was only one logical answer...

And Master Oakley promptly made it.

'Spare the rod and spoil the child,' he mumbled. His eyes focused on her breasts again and he licked his lips. 'Though, by God, she is no child,' he muttered, and then looked horrified at the words that had popped unbidden from his mouth.

'Then much though it pains me, I shall bow to your superior wisdom,' sighed Master Watkins, with mock humility. Oakley swayed suddenly and Master Watkins grabbed his arm and led him to the chair in front of the mirror, where he slumped down. 'Pray, rest yourself a moment,' he said. 'I shall be back.' With a triumphant glance at Lucy he hurried from the room, her eyes following him with apprehension. She had no doubt he had gone to fetch some vile instrument of punishment.

Left to his own devices, Master Oakley began to nod off into a drunken sleep. As his head fell lower and lower on his chest Lucy watched for the moment when she could make her escape. If she could only make it to one of the other chambers, she could lock the door and, even drunk as they were, she doubted they would risk raising the entire household trying to break it down.

When a faint snore escaped his lips she pulled back the covers and swung her feet lightly to the floor. Moving as stealthily as a cat, she tiptoed towards the door.

Unfortunately she had underestimated him. Years of dealing with unruly apprentices at the tannery had honed his reflexes. He was awake and across the room in a flash, seizing her and dragging her backwards so that they stumbled and fell across the bed. Whimpering in fear she rolled away from him and attempted to get to her feet, but he grabbed her again, his hand closing over her breast. Then the door swung open and he immediately let her go and sat up, guilt suffusing his heavy features.

'Er... she tried to get away,' he muttered, avoiding Master Watkins' eyes. 'I was merely trying to restrain her.'

'But of course,' said Master Watkins smoothly. He held out a bottle of wine. 'Perhaps a little more of this to soothe your nerves,' he said, and Master Oakley seized the bottle gratefully and drank from the neck. When he put it down almost a third of the contents were gone, along with the last tattered remnants of his sobriety. His eyes were glazed and there was a mindless grin on his lips.

'And now to business,' said Master Watkins. From behind his back he produced a small, wicked-looking whip. He flicked his wrist and the thin lash uncurled as quick and deadly as a snake's tongue. Lucy stared at it in fascinated horror.

'If you would be so kind?' said Master Watkins. Oakley looked at him blankly, and he sighed in exasperation. 'Here, hold this,' he ordered, shoving the whip into the other man's limp hand.

Then advancing on the cringing girl, he reached for her. She scrambled to her feet and made one last, futile attempt to flee, but he grabbed her nightgown and ripped the flimsy garment from neck to hem. She moaned and tried to hold the shredded cloth to hide herself, but it was no use. Laughing, he tore the torn remains away, leaving her naked and unprotected.

Master Oakley's eyes opened wide as he took in the shapely body cowering against the wall. Lucy's vain attempts to cover herself merely served to draw attention to her quivering bosom, and the neat triangle of tight curls that hid the forbidden place between her thighs. He licked his lips. The feel of her soft breast was imprinted on his palm and he could feel a stirring in his loins.

As he watched avidly Master Watkins reached out, gripped her arm and with one swift movement flung her facedown on the bed, presenting him with a view of a bottom, as round and delectable as a ripe peach. As she tried to struggle to her knees he caught an even more tantalising glimpse of the dark cleft between her slender thighs, and the stirring in his loins became more insistent.

'Don't just stand there,' snapped Master Watkins. 'She must be taught the error of her ways. For her own good, the evil must be beaten out of her.' Oakley nodded, barely hearing the words, his eyes fixed on the curve of her hips and the pert buttocks, and he licked his lips in anticipation.

'Grab her wrists,' ordered Watkins, exasperated by the other man's slow response. 'Hold the bitch down while I dispense her punishment.'

Master Oakley dragged his gaze reluctantly from the naked girl and looked blankly at Watkins. 'Eh, what…?' he muttered.

'I said, hold her,' repeated Watkins, gritting his teeth to bite back the words 'you fool', for even at this stage of drunkenness Oakley might come belatedly to his senses and realise what he was doing, and that would be most inconvenient. He was still smarting from the pompous idiot's sanctimonious lecture on morality – before he'd convinced him those damned books were Lucy's, that was – but once this night was over, he'd have the man in his pocket forever. There would be no more preaching from Master Oakley, and there were several disputes over land in which the man would come in extremely useful. He looked at him contemptuously. God's bones! He was salivating over the girl like a starving dog over a bone!

'Erm… yes, hold her,' mumbled Master Oakley, reaching gingerly for Lucy's wrists, but she reared up, hissing between her teeth, her fingers curving as she clawed for his eyes. He lurched backwards in alarm, but then his lips set in drunken stubbornness. 'Hold her, indeed,' he muttered. 'For the devil is in her and no mistake.'

Lunging at her he caught her flailing arms and jerked hard, giggling as she toppled forward again. She squealed in pain as his fingers bit into her wrists, grinding the delicate bones together, but he merely tightened his grip, rendering her immobile – and completely at the mercy of Master Watkins.

'Well done, Oakley,' said the latter approvingly. 'Now hold her fast. The Devil will give her the strength of ten once we begin to beat him out of her.'

'I will,' panted Oakley, biting back another excited giggle. It had been a long time since he'd been so close to a woman, even one as dangerously possessed as this. Mistress Oakley had been a good and loyal wife, but she never permitted him to see her naked. Their couplings had been brief and carried out under the covering of darkness – a joyless fulfilling of her marital duties – and latterly, after so many years of childbearing, he felt little or no desire for her flabby body. But this! This was different. Mouth dry with excitement he knelt beside the bed, watching as Master Watkins raised the whip and brought it down across the girl's trembling buttocks.

Lucy jerked and screamed as the lash bit into her delicate skin, leaving a thin red line across the pale flesh of her bottom. It felt as if a thin tongue of flame had licked her, and she writhed in a vain attempt to escape the pain.

'What's wrong, my dear?' asked Master Watkins. 'Am I being too harsh?' She shuddered as he allowed the tip of the lash to trail teasingly down her smooth back and between the cheeks of her bottom.

Lifting her head she spat in defiance, then screamed again as he flicked his wrist and the lash bit sharply once more. The muscles of her buttocks spasmed in agony as another thin red line crisscrossed the first – and then another and another, the plump globes jerking at each blow. Every snap of whip against flesh was followed by a shriek of pain, until Lucy could scream no more and lay there, whimpering.

Grinning, he leant forward and ran his hand over her smooth bottom, relishing the heat that radiated from her beaten flesh. The creamy skin was scarlet now, the whip marks so close they merged into one another. He kneaded her buttocks and she groaned beneath his touch. Her rear throbbed like a rotten tooth, each pounding beat of her heart sending the hot blood coursing to the source of the agony. Every inch of her skin seemed sensitive, her senses heightened by the pain.

Worse still was the heat growing between her thighs. The throbbing in her bottom was spreading to her belly. She writhed against the coverlet, trying to escape the fever growing in her blood, but that merely served to inflame it more. The tips of her breasts were hard and swollen and every movement made the rough material chafe against them, exciting her even further. She groaned again, this time with humiliation as her body betrayed her.

'You see what we are up against, Master Oakley,' said Watkins, shaking his head. 'Even a whipping is not enough to quell her insatiable lusts.' With one swift movement he rolled Lucy onto her back, revealing her shameful arousal. Before she could even attempt to close her legs he knelt between them, parted the lips of her sex and slid a finger inside her. When he took it out it was glistening with her juices. 'See,' he crowed in triumph. 'Incontrovertible proof of her devilish lechery.'

At the sight Master Oakley felt his member swell and throb, pressing against the coarse material of his breeches. He wriggled uncomfortably. He had gazed in fascination as Master Watkins beat his wife, fighting back his own evil desires, but this was too much for him. Still gripping Lucy's wrists in one hand, he reached for the wine bottle and gulped down the last of its contents, barely pausing for breath.

Its comforting warmth spread through him, the alcohol washing away the last vestiges of his conscience. He put the bottle down, then leaned forward and used his free hand to fondle each of Lucy's breasts in turn, pinching and tweaking her nipples, relishing the way they hardened at his touch. She whimpered, trying to squirm away from the tormenting sensation, but she was trapped. All her futile struggles did was inflame her attackers more, and

101

send the pain from her beaten bottom spiralling through her once again, triggering another wave of lust. She groaned once more, this time in shame at her own response, then froze as she realised Master Watkins was unbuttoning his breeches. Dear God, surely he did not intend to take her in front of another man?

But he did.

Grinning wolfishly, he undid the final button and allowed his organ to spring forth. It was swollen with lust, the skin so tightly stretched over the bulbous purple tip it looked as if it might split. She closed her eyes against the sight.

Master Oakley, on the other hand, stared in fascination as Watkins reinserted his fingers into the girl's wet sex, sliding them in and out until she whined with wicked pleasure. Removing them he coated his rampant prick with her juices, then knocking her legs apart with his knees until she was fully exposed, he ran the tip up and down between the glistening lips before plunging into her.

Master Oakley licked his dry lips as he watched the girl writhing in pleasure as his friend's long cock rammed in and out, faster and faster. With each thrust her pale flesh quivered and her breasts jounced beneath his hand, the hard tip of her nipple rubbing against his palm. He let it go as if it was red-hot, but his own prick was throbbing in response. Almost unaware of what he was doing, he reached for the buttons of his own breeches and fumbled himself free, groaning in relief. Lucy had gone beyond all shame. She tossed her head from side to side, aware of nothing but the wild pleasure coursing through her with each thrust of Master Watkins' cock. Raising her hips she matched each thrust with her own, grinding against him as she tried to get the hard maleness even deeper inside her. Finally she felt him give one last mighty thrust and his hot seed exploded inside her, sending her over the edge into her own shuddering climax.

Tears leaked from beneath her closed eyelids as consciousness returned and she realised the depths to which she had fallen. It was bad enough that she had given herself up to her husband's evil desires – but that her shame should be witnessed! Please, God, please. Let them go now and leave her to her shame.

A sharp slap on her naked flank made her eyes fly open in shock. Her husband was grinning maliciously down at her. 'You enjoyed that, didn't you, bitch?' he said mockingly. 'Well, there's more to come.' He turned to the pastor. 'Would you care to sample the whore's wares, Oakley?'

For a moment Oakley stared at him uncomprehendingly, then a drunken grin spread across his ruddy face. He got to his feet and stood there swaying, buttons undone and his rigid cock grasped in his fist. 'My pleishure,' he slurred, and Lucy stared at him in horror. Dear heavens, no! Not him too!

'You can't do this, Master Oakley,' she protested. 'You are a man of God.'

'Man first,' he muttered. 'And it's a long time since I've had a woman.' He giggled and made an obscene pumping movement with his erection. ''Cept for Mishtress Palm and her five lovely daughters.'

'So what can we tempt you to, Master Oakley?' asked Watkins, as casually as if he was offering the man a drink or a meal. 'A nice tight arsehole between a pair of fine plump buttocks? A warm wet cunt?' Lucy gazed at him in horror as he itemised her like a carcase hanging in a butcher's shop.

Oakley ran his eyes over her naked body, and then he

focused on her mouth and a drunken leer spread across his face. 'I want her to suck me off,' he announced with a hiccup.

It was Lucy's turn to gaze blankly. What did he mean? She found out soon enough.

Tugging off his breeches he flung himself onto the bed, straddling her chest and pinning her arms down with his knees. He leant forward and his cock bobbed, scant inches above her horrified face. At last guessing his vile intentions she set her lips tight and turned her head away in disgust.

'Do you want another beating?' asked her husband, and she cringed at the thought of the whip sweeping down on her already bruised and beaten flesh. 'Then I suggest you do as you're told,' he grinned evilly, watching as she reluctantly parted her lips, gagging as Master Oakley thrust the swollen head of his cock between them, almost choking her.

Gingerly she licked the tip of it with her tongue, feeling him shudder with pleasure at her touch. Steeling herself, she ran her tongue around the rim of his stalk and sucking gently, praying it would be over soon.

And it was. After all he had seen already, the feel of her suckling wet mouth was too much for him. With a groan he reared up, pulling his cock from her mouth. It twitched and jerked, sending molten seed splattering over her face to run dripping from her chin, then he toppled over sideways like a dead tree and lay sprawled on the bed, snoring in a drink-sodden stupor.

Master Watkins let out a stream of oaths at the curtailing of his amusement. Damn the man. They had only just begun! Now he would have to cart his drunken carcass back to his room before the servants started to rise.

Still swearing, he picked Master Oakley's breeches from the floor and dragged them back on over his flaccid buttocks, then heaved his unconscious body over his shoulders.

At the door he paused and stared menacingly back at Lucy. 'And you'd better not tell anyone about this, my dear,' he advised.

As soon as he'd gone Lucy wrapped a blanket round her naked body and fled for the safety of one of the unused bedrooms. Locking the door behind her she leaned against it, staring hopelessly into the dusty darkness. Who could she tell? With Master Oakley's drunken betrayal her last hope was gone!

When day broke it found her curled up, shivering, on the unmade bed. Master Watkins' much vaunted restoration had not reached this far and dust and cobwebs coated everything. There had been no fire in the hearth for many a year and the air in the chamber was chill and damp.

With a shudder she stretched her aching limbs and put her feet to the icy floor. Much though she would have liked to keep the world at bay, she could not huddle here, naked save for a single blanket. She would die of cold and hunger, if Master Watkins did not simply break the door down and haul her ignominiously out. Pulling the cover tighter round her, she tiptoed to the door and unlocked it.

The corridor was silent. The servants were up and about, no doubt, but their duties kept them below stairs at this time of day. So taking her courage in both hands she scurried back to her own chamber. With any luck her husband would still be deep in a drunken slumber and she could dress and be gone before he stirred.

Cautiously she pushed the door open, then let out her breath in a gusty sigh of relief. After all that, the room was empty! But nausea swept over her as she caught

105

sight of the bed, the tangled sheets mute witness to the vile activities of the night before. She turned her eyes away.

There was cold water in the ewer and she washed herself roughly, grateful for its icy touch as she tried to scrub away the memory of the two men's sweaty hands mauling her body.

That done, she flung on the first gown that came to hand, grabbed her cloak and went quietly down the oak stairs, past the servants hall and towards the stable. She had escaped once, she could do it again, only this time she would not be coming back!

The stable was deserted and she hurried past the stalls towards the tack room. She was just about to lift down the saddle when a shadowy figure loomed out of the dusty darkness and a hand closed on her arm and spun her round.

'Not so fast, milady,' came a gloating voice, and she found herself staring up into the grinning face of the younger stableman; the one she'd overheard making lewd remarks about her.

'Get your filthy hands off me, you oaf,' she squealed, struggling to break free of his grasp.

His grin vanished. 'Think you're so much better than I, do 'ee, mistress?' he sneered. 'Well you b'aint. For all your fancy airs and graces you'm nothing but a wench – and a Royalist wench at that.' His grin returned, but this time there was an unpleasant edge to it. 'And we all knows what they're like. Hoors, the lot of 'em.'

Before she knew what he was about he wrapped both her wrists in one meaty paw, and began to fumble at her breasts with the other, his breath coming faster as he felt the soft flesh beneath the rough material. 'Mind you, you'm a damned pretty wench, for all that,' he muttered, tweaking a nipple.

With a strength she didn't know she had, Lucy managed to free one hand and brought it round in a swinging blow to the side of his head, and beneath the impressive impact he recoiled, his hand leaving her bosom to cradle his throbbing ear.

'The master shall hear of this,' she hissed.

'Tell him and be damned,' he said defiantly. ''Twas the master hisself set me here, to make sure you didn't try and run off again.' He smirked. 'So who do ye think he's going to believe, his faithless trollop of a wife or his true and loyal servant?'

Lucy's face whitened as the truth of his words sank in. He could see it, too. 'Course, if you was to be nice to me,' the grin became a leer and he nodded suggestively towards the heap of straw in the corner. 'I wouldn't 'ave to tell him, now would I?'

With a sigh Lucy bent her head in defeat, and taking her silence as assent he renewed his assault on her breasts, molesting them eagerly. His mouth came down on hers, his thick tongue thrusting between her unwilling lips. Grunting with pleasure he scrabbled her skirts up and forced his hand between her thighs, his thick fingers parting the lips of her sex and plunging in. After a few moments' rough thrusting he withdrew and unlaced his breeches, his swollen cock springing free.

He put her hand on it and rubbed it up and down. 'Thisun's a damned sight better than the master's shrivelled old prick, I'll warrant,' he panted. 'You just wait, my girl. This'll be the best fuck you ever had.'

Lucy stroked his stout member, feeling it swell even further beneath her ministrations. 'That's the way, my beauty,' he gasped, moaning in pleasure again as her hand slid lower, cradling his heavy balls in her palm – then she sank her nails into them and twisted as hard as she could!

The groan of pleasure turned into a high-pitched shriek as he pushed her away and doubled over to protect his injured privates. As his head came down Lucy's knee came up – and smashed him square in the face. She felt the crack as his nose broke and blood gushed everywhere. With a moan he toppled over and lay writhing in the straw, trying to clutch his nose and his balls at once. So she kicked him in the kidneys for good measure.

'Tell *that* to the master, too, you ill-begotten whoreson!' she cursed, then picked up her skirts and fled.

Safe in the walled garden, she laughed gleefully. The bastard wouldn't dare tell anyone. Beaten and bloodied by a mere 'wench'? If his fellow servants ever found out he'd never live it down!

But her smile vanished, her brief moment of triumph over, and she slumped down on the marble bench against the wall. Where did she think she was going to run to anyway? If she fled home to her parents, Master Watkins would merely follow her and drag her back again. He was her husband. By law, short of murdering her, he could do with her as he damned well pleased.

Even if she managed to flee the county and lose herself in some town, what good would that do? She had no money and nowhere to stay. Who would take in a woman who turned up out of nowhere, without references and without skills? She gave a bitter laugh. The only employment open to her would be that of a whore, and by God, she was that already!

Her unpleasant thoughts were interrupted by the sound of someone clearing his throat, and she raised her head to find herself looking at Master Oakley. A white-faced and red-eyed Master Oakley. His normally snowy neckpiece was crumpled and askew, and his hands shook. He looked exactly what he was, a man paying for the sins of his own overindulgence. As she watched beads of sweat began to form on his balding pate.

'Good morrow, Mistress Watkins,' he muttered. 'I apologise for disturbing you, but I felt a trifle unwell and thought some fresh air might clear my megrim.' He smiled ingratiatingly. 'I trust I find you well?'

She stared at him in disbelief. The hypocritical bastard! Was he going to pretend that the previous night had never happened? That he hadn't watched her ravished by her own husband, then taken his own turn to use her?

It seemed she was wrong.

'I must apologise for my behaviour of last night, as well,' he went on nervously, and she gawped at him. Good God! Was he actually going to say he was sorry? For what? For forcing his filthy cock into her mouth? For making her suck him till his seed splattered over her face?

Wrong again.

'I am unused to wine,' he confessed, avoiding her eyes. 'I fear I may have drunk too much and fallen asleep by the fire.' He mopped his sweaty forehead. 'It was ill-done to repay your hospitality so.'

For a few moments she was uncertain. Perhaps he really believed what he was saying? After all, he *had* been very drunk. But then she caught his eye before he could look away and saw the truth lurking behind the façade of innocence. He knew exactly what he had done. Guilt was written all over him.

Her stomach twisted with loathing. She'd been right the first time; he had no intention of facing up to his actions. He was going to pretend that nothing had happened, and no doubt after telling himself a few times that he had simply overindulged and fallen asleep, he would actually come to believe his own lies.

She smiled cynically. And why not? That way he could continue to sit in judgement on his flock, secure in the knowledge of his own righteousness and moral superiority. 'Do not give it a moment's thought, Master Oakley,' she said, her voice heavy with sarcasm. 'I am sure we have all had one glass of wine too many and done things we regret – and falling asleep is hardly a sin.' She had the pleasure of watching him squirm, his face flushed an even deeper red. 'I trust you will feel much better after a good night's sleep,' she went on. 'After all, there's nothing like a clear conscience to aid one's rest, is there not?'

'Er... yes, indeed,' he muttered, running a finger round his neckpiece. 'Now if you will excuse me, I shall bid you farewell. I must say my goodbyes to your husband and be about my business.'

'But of course,' she said. 'Do not let me keep you. No doubt you have a sermon to write.' She smiled ironically. 'It would not do to fail in your duties when there is so much wickedness in the world.'

'Er... quite,' he muttered again, and with a brief bow he turned and scuttled away as fast as his skinny legs would carry him.

Good riddance to bad rubbish, she thought viciously. If there were any God in heaven, his horse would baulk on the way home and he would break his scrawny neck – but she very much doubted it. The devil looked after his own.

With a heavy heart she got to her feet and trudged wearily back towards the house.

She managed to avoid Master Watkins as best she could for the rest of the week: waiting till he had gone out about his business before leaving her chamber; leaving the room when he entered and busying herself elsewhere; retiring early and pretending to be asleep when he came to bed. Thankfully, with the onset of spring, he was preoccupied with the business of running the estate, and the night with Master Oakley seemed to have sated his vile appetites. For the moment, at least.

The following Sunday morning she was in the library, seated at a small escritoire, scribbling a brief letter to her mother. She longed to see her parents again and hear Martha's comforting scolding, but after their last visit she had written asking them not to come again, saying that it had made her too homesick. Since then she had written every week instead. Brief notes filled with comfortable chitchat about the servants or whose wife had had their sixth child. Arguing about the best way to cure a ham, or asking for remedies for the ague that plagued everyone at this time of the year. Anything at all, rather than speak of the hell her life had become since her marriage.

She was wracking her brains to find something light and cheerful to talk about when Master Watkins stamped in with a face like thunder.

'What are you doing here?' he demanded. 'Why are you not ready?'

She stared at his furious face. 'Ready for what?' she asked.

He looked at her as if she had gone mad. 'To go to meeting, of course,' he snarled. 'It is the Lord's Day. Had you forgotten?' He glared at her. 'You should be thinking of your immortal soul, not sitting here engaged in worldly pursuits. Now go and fetch your cloak.'

'I shall not,' she said defiantly. 'I have no intention of attending your damned meeting. After what happened, do you think I could sit and listen to that mealy-mouthed whoreson spouting his bloody platitudes? Go yourself if you have a mind to. I'm staying here.'

'Oh no you're not!' he said, and reaching down he snatched her unfinished letter, tore it into tiny pieces and cast them in the fire. 'Now fetch your cloak,' he grated. 'Or it will be the worse for you.'

She looked at his clenched fists and his face, suffused with anger, and decided that discretion was the better part of valour. Lord's Day or no Lord's Day, he would have no compunction about beating her into submission – and enjoying every moment of it. Resentfully she got to her feet and went to do as she was told. As slowly as possible.

Much to his fury, they were late. The sermon had already begun by the time they reached the meeting house. She could hear Master Oakley's bellowing voice even before they entered. 'And I say unto ye, that the sins of the flesh shall be punished tenfold!' he was snarling. There was the sound of his fist banging against the pulpit. 'Yeah, as ye burn with lust now, so shall your impure flesh burn in the everlasting flames of Hell!'

As they entered his finger was stabbing the air as he pointed from one frightened face to another. 'You! And you! And you!'

He turned to chastise the latecomers, caught sight of Lucy and faltered in mid-rant. The colour drained from his face and his arm fell weakly to his side. Beads of sweat stood out on his brow and he wiped them away with a trembling hand. 'Er... y-yes...' he stammered. 'The... the... the sins of the f-flesh...'

Lucy smiled. Perhaps today's sermon would be more amusing than she had expected. Seating herself in a prominent position she fixed her eyes on Master Oakley and looked demurely up at him. His expression became hunted and much to her amusement, his shaking hands sent the pages of his sermon flying in all directions.

By the time he had gathered them together again, all his fire had died out. He mumbled his way through the rest of the sermon, barely daring to look up from his papers, and the meeting ended far earlier than usual.

'Not much of a sermon today,' grumbled one woman as they filed out. 'Poor man must've been took sick. He were as white in the face as a baker's horse.'

Lucy hid a smile. Oh, he had been taken sick, all right – sick of a bad conscience. Well, hell mend the bastard. He deserved everything he got.

As they passed him at the door of the meeting house, she bobbed a curtsey and smiled innocently at him. 'An excellent sermon, Master Oakley,' she said politely, and holding his eye she ran her tongue round her lips. 'Though I am sure you yourself have had no experience of such wickedness.'

His face, already white, blenched even further – and then turned scarlet. Pleased with the effect of her barbed words, Lucy sauntered back to the carriage. That would give him something to think about when he was writing his next sermon, she thought venomously.

Next Sunday, much to Master Watkins' surprise, she was up bright and early, and ready to go to meeting even before he was. He nodded at her approvingly.

'I am pleased to see you are taking your religious duties seriously for a change,' he said pompously.

'But of course, husband,' she said, lowering her eyes demurely. 'I have learnt the error of my ways. I would not miss Master Oakley's sermon for the world.'

In the meeting house she compounded his surprise by insisting on sitting immediately in front of the pulpit, so she could 'better hear Master Oakley's words of wisdom.'

They had to wait for them, though. For the first time since his elevation Master Oakley was late to service, and when he did arrive, Lucy was shocked by the change in his appearance. Shocked – and delighted.

His neckpiece, normally pristine white and starched, was crumpled and grey, and the rest of his clothing was equally grubby, stained with food and what looked like wine.

But it was the man himself who had changed most. His normally round face was gaunt and haggard and there were dark circles beneath his eyes. His paunch had vanished and his clothes hung as loosely on him as if made for a larger man.

Lucy smiled to herself. Apparently he found it more difficult to lie to himself about his behaviour than she had thought.

When he began to speak she fixed him with her eyes and was amused to see him stumble and stammer his way through his sermon, particularly when she nibbled provocatively on the tip of her gloved forefinger.

He spoke only briefly, and there were more mutterings from the congregation when the sermon ended almost before it had started.

Thus began her silent campaign of revenge. Each Sunday found her in the same place, staring up at him in unspoken accusation, and each Sunday he deteriorated further.

'I could swear he were flown with drink today,' said one shocked woman, after the third week. 'He were swaying back and forrit in that pulpit like a tree in the wind. Disgraceful, that's what it be.'

'What does the damned fool think he's playing at?' grated Master Watkins, as he hustled Lucy away before she could hear any more. 'Much more of this and he'll be useless to me. Who's going to take the advice of a drunkard over that damned land?'

He needn't have worried. No one was going to take Master Oakley's advice ever again. The Sunday following that episode, he did not appear at all. As time marched on the congregation grew more and more restless. When the door finally burst open all eyes turned – but it wasn't Master Oakley, drunk or otherwise, who entered. It was one of his servants.

'It… it's the maister,' he gasped. 'He's dead!'

'Don't be ridiculous, man,' snapped Watkins. 'He can't be. I rode over to speak to him just last night. He was fine then.'

'He is,' wailed the servant. ''Twas me as found him this morning, dead as a doornail.' He wrung his hands. 'He… he's hanged hisself!'

There was a stunned silence, followed by uproar. Exclamations of shock and disbelief echoed around the meeting house and juicy snippets of speculation were passed from mouth to mouth. What in the name of all that was holy could possess such a man to take his life?

Lucy knew. For a moment a pang of remorse ran through her – then it vanished as quickly as it had come. He had shown no mercy to her when he vented his foul lusts on her helpless body. Why should she care now whether his black soul burned in hell? A feeling of bitter triumph washed over her. Perhaps there was a God, after all.

The journey home passed in ominous silence. From the corner of her eye, Lucy could see the veins in his temples throbbing as he gritted his teeth in impotent fury. His rage, contained for the moment, radiated from him like dull heat from a banked fire. She held her tongue, lest one word sent it flaring.

The carriage had barely drawn up in front of the house before he flung himself down and stalked inside. When she caught up with him he was pacing back and forth in front of the fireplace in the great hall, one curled fist slamming into his other hand.

'Fool!' he snarled. 'Damned, cowardly ineffectual fool! Between us we had this county in the palms of our hands. To hang himself! And for what? A few hours' entertainment with a slut.'

Lucy closed her eyes and shuddered. Was that all he saw her physical and moral degradation as? Nothing but 'a few hours' entertainment'? He paused in his pacing to spit into the fire and watch as the drops of spittle danced away to nothing on the fiery coals. 'Thus may his lily-livered soul sizzle in the flames of hell!' he muttered.

She cringed back as he turned on her, eyes glinting. 'This is all your fault,' he hissed. 'If you hadn't tempted him with your wicked flesh he would still be alive now.' He accompanied his words with a vicious slap that sent her reeling, but the unexpected pain made her lose control and her temper flared to match his own.

'My fault?' she countered, fear forgotten. 'I think not. Who poured drink down his throat then brought him to my bedroom? Who threw me to him like a bone to a dog, to do with as he pleased? Who watched as he sated his vile lusts on my body?

'What a shame he turned out to have a conscience,' she sneered. 'How very inconvenient for you. But do not try to pin his death on me. You have no one to blame but your—'

Her words choked in her throat as his bony fingers closed round it, cutting off her breath. She beat fruitlessly at his hands, trying desperately to drag air into her lungs.

116

'Do not tempt me, madam,' he hissed, pushing his face into hers. 'It would take so little effort to be rid of you.' He shook her as a cat shakes a mouse, and then flung her onto the settle.

'You would not dare,' she challenged, breathing in tortured gasps as she rubbed her bruised throat. 'England is not yet so far gone that you may murder with impunity. If you killed me you would hang as surely as Oakley did.'

'But I would not need to murder you,' he smiled cunningly. 'That would be far too easy, wouldn't it? Just one brief moment of pain and it would all be over.' His smile widened. 'If I wanted rid of you, my dear, I have a much more amusing way of doing it.'

She stared at him apprehensively. 'What… what is that?' she croaked fearfully.

'Why, by accusing you of witchcraft!' he smirked.

'What?' she gasped, looking over her shoulder automatically, even the words enough to strike terror into the heart. She had seen a harmless old woman accused of witchcraft once, and she would never forget it. The baying crowd watching as she was ducked in the village pond; her half-drowned body dragged out again, stripped and searched for so-called 'witches teats'; and finally her despairing shrieks as the flames licked around her feet as she stood at the stake in the village square. The greasy stink of burning meat had hung on the air for days afterwards.

It was as if he'd read her mind.

'You'd make a much better show than old Annie,' he smiled. 'I'm sure the village yokels would enjoy the sight of your naked body much more than that of that raddled old bitch.' He laughed unpleasantly. 'Not that it would be much to look at after the flames had been at it.'

She licked her dry lips. It was all too possible. She had

not endeared herself to the Puritan community and there would be no shortage of volunteers to bear witness against her. 'Y-you wouldn't…' she quavered, but she knew he would.

'Try me and see,' he taunted, relishing the fear in her eyes, and going by the ominous bulge in his breeches, the idea had obviously excited him. He fumbled at their fastenings, his breath coming faster as he undid them, releasing his monstrous member. It jutted forth semi-erect, and he gripped it, massaging it into full hardness.

With a gasp of revulsion she leapt to her feet and attempted to flee, but he grabbed her and dragged her back. Bending her over the back of the settle he flung her skirts up and shoved his knee between her legs, pushing them apart to reveal her plump buttocks and the dark cleft of her sex. Spitting on his hand he wet the head of his cock and thrust it brutally inside her, ignoring her muffled cries of pain. His hands gripped her hips, his fingers leaving bruises as he pounded himself into her, groaning his pleasure aloud as his balls tightened and he spattered his viscous seed.

Thankfully it was over almost as soon as it had begun. Smirking, he straightened up and tucked his wilting organ way, while Lucy pulled herself upright, dragged her skirts down and collapsed on the settle, whimpering at the pain that knifed between her thighs.

At least it had restored his good humour. 'Perhaps I shall not get rid of you quite yet,' he mused. ''T'would be a shame to see that smooth white flesh blackened and blistered by the flames.' He gave a self-satisfied smirk. 'Besides Oakley's untimely death may not have thwarted my plans after all. I have another idea.' He winked at her. 'Do not run away, my dear. I may have a use for you yet.'

Humming under his breath he walked from the hall, leaving her staring after him, her feelings wavering between relief and fear. She might be safe for the moment, but what evil did he have in mind now?

As the next few weeks passed uneventfully, she began to think his words had merely been an empty threat. On the day of Master Oakley's suicide he sat in his study, writing late into the evening, and one of the servants had been dispatched with a letter at dawn the following morning, but apart from that, life lapsed back into its dull daily routine.

It was almost a month later when a rider clattered into the courtyard. Lucy watched from the window as Master Watkins went to meet him. The man tugged his forelock, handed over a sealed missive and was rewarded by a few coins for his pains.

When Master Watkins appeared at the breakfast table, he was looking remarkably pleased with himself. 'I shall have one of the men kill a calf for Sunday,' he announced.

'Why?' Lucy asked sarcastically. 'Are we expecting the Prodigal Son?'

'Very witty, my dear,' he smirked. 'No, Master Oakley is coming to dine with us.'

She gawped at him. Was age beginning to addle his wits? 'Are you mad?' she gasped. 'Master Oakley has been buried these four weeks past. Unless the grave is giving up its dead, how can he come to dine with us?' She shivered at the sudden image of his rotting corpse, risen from its suicide's grave to sit opposite her at table, with its neck askew and its tongue protruding from between blackened lips.

'Of course he has,' agreed Watkins, 'but his eldest son hasn't. He was a chaplain in the New Model army. I wrote to him regarding taking over his father's position here, and he has kindly agreed to come and succour us in our hour of need.'

Lucy stared at him. Ye Goddes Bones! Just what they needed; another sanctimonious prig! These Puritans were like weeds. Cut one down and another sprang up to take its place.

'Yes, very kind of him,' she agreed. 'Of course his acceptance has nothing to do with his father's fine house and estate, I am sure.' She smiled sweetly. 'And I am also sure your invitation was made from the goodness of your own heart and your concern for your neighbours' souls. Nothing at all to do with procuring an ally in the dispute over that land you have your eye on.'

Her words obviously hit a sore spot.

'Hold your tongue, young lady,' he snapped. 'These are men's matters and do not concern you. Stick to your household duties and do not stick your nose in where it is not wanted. Just make sure our guest is well-served on Sunday and leave the rest to me.'

He smiled unpleasantly. 'I have not forgotten our little conversation the other day, my dear, and you would do well to remember it, too. The moment you cease to be of use to me, you may find yourself at the stake.'

With that threat hanging over her head, Lucy had no choice but to do as she was told. Much to Mistress Blackstock's annoyance, she spent the rest of the week ordering in fresh supplies; standing over the maids as they cleaned and dusted, and hovering round the kitchens, checking that everything would be perfect for her unwelcome guest.

When Sunday meeting came round, she pulled her hair back and chose the drabbest of her drab gowns. Taking her place demurely beside her husband, she waited for their new preacher to appear.

She was not the only one. There was a buzz of expectancy from the congregation, which subsided into silence as the door opened and their new minister walked in.

As soon as Lucy saw him a cold finger touched her spine. Master Oakley had been a fat pompous fool, far too fond of the sound of his own voice, but at least there had been a faint flicker of humanity beneath the bombast. Why else would he have killed himself?

Young Master Oakley was a different kettle of fish entirely. He reminded Lucy of one of the village boys who had delighted in tearing the wings off flies and torturing small animals.

Not that it was his appearance that gave him away. He was nothing like his father in that, either. In fact, if Mistress Oakley had not been such a downtrodden creature one might suspect that Master Oakley had not fathered him at all! He was tall, where his father had been short. Good-looking where his father had been plain. Dark hair and blue-eyes enhanced his pale, finely boned features, and Lucy could feel the frisson of excitement spreading amongst the female members of the congregation.

No, it was something deeper. The beautiful blue eyes were cold and expressionless as he looked down on them from the pulpit. There was an emptiness to them too, as if a patch of blue sky were being reflected from a deep and dangerous tarn. And there was something about his mouth as well, as if those perfectly formed lips could twist as easily into cruelty as they could into a smile.

His eyes met hers and his brow creased in a slight frown, as if he knew what she was thinking. She shivered and dropped her gaze. When she looked up again he was smiling benevolently as he began his sermon.

'That was very satisfactory,' said Master Watkins on their way home. 'Very satisfactory indeed. Did you see how eager everyone was to greet him?'

She had. As they left, young Master Oakley was standing at the door of the meeting hall, besieged by members of the congregation crowding round their new minister to welcome him, shake his hand and either offer condolences on his father's death or congratulate him on the excellence of his sermon. She had been forced to shake his hand as they left, and his touch had set her skin crawling.

Unconscious of her reaction, Watkins continued to congratulate himself on the success of his move. 'He will have even more influence than his father did,' he predicted smugly. 'And with his influence to back me, I shall have no difficulty in obtaining that bit of land.'

'Don't you have land enough already?' sighed Lucy. 'Why should one more small piece be so important?'

He smiled at her naivety. 'Because, my dear wife, that's where the river rises. Once I have that land, I shall have complete control of this area.' He smiled rapaciously. 'I am sure my neighbours would pay sweetly to prevent the possibility of its drying up.'

She stared at him. 'Drying up? How could it dry up? That river has been there time out of mind.'

'Rivers have been diverted before,' he smirked. 'All it would take would be a few stout fellows with trenching tools to make sure it ran exclusively through my estate.'

'But... but you can't do that!' gasped Lucy. 'People depend on that water for their livestock. And for themselves, for that matter. Not everyone has a well.'

'I know,' he agreed, rubbing his hands together. 'And that is why Master Oakley's good will is so important.' His smile vanished and he glared at her. 'So you will do your utmost to make him welcome today, or you will pay dearly for it later.' He grabbed her wrist and twisted. 'Do you understand me?'

'Of course I do,' she snapped, shaking herself free. 'I understand you all too well.'

'Good,' he said as the carriage drew up. 'Oh, and one more thing.' She looked at him apprehensively. 'Now we are home, go and do your hair more becomingly. I do not wish Master Oakley to think I am married to a frump.'

She was in her chamber, shaking her hair free of its tight bun, when there was a nervous tap at the door. It opened to reveal a small maid, almost dwarfed by the long wooden box she carried. 'The master says you're to wear this, ma'am,' she said, attempting to bob a curtsy and almost toppling beneath the weight in the process.

'What is it?' asked Lucy, staring at the box in surprise.

'A new gown, ma'am,' said the girl, laying it on the bed. 'He had it ordered special.'

Her surprise turned to suspicion. What ulterior motive lay behind this unexpected gift? Curiosity overcame her. It would be lovely to have something new to wear. Lifting the lid she peered inside, and gasped in pleasure.

Like her others, this gown was black too, but there the resemblance ended. Instead of thick, coarse cloth, this was made of fine satin. She stroked the shining folds with a tentative finger, admiring the way the rich material caught the light. 'It's beautiful,' she sighed, smiling at the maidservant. 'Quick, help me put it on.'

'Me, miss... erm... ma'am?' gasped the girl. 'B-but I couldn't. I ain't a lady's maid. I just does the pots. They only sent me 'cos everyone else was busy getting ready for the master's guest.'

'What's your name?' demanded Lucy.

'Erm... it's Joanie, ma'am,' blushed the girl.

Lucy smiled. Thank goodness – a good honest English name for a change, instead of one of those damned Prudences and Chastitys. 'Well, Joanie,' she said, 'just for today you're my lady's maid. Come, help me dress.'

'Yes, ma'am,' said Joanie, her blush now one of pleasure. Together they shook out the new gown and, with a little fumbling, the girl helped Lucy undress and slip it on. Settling the folds of the skirt she went to look in the mirror, and stopped short in shock.

The gown was as high-necked and severe as her others, but instead of billowing loosely around her, it had been cut so that it clung to her like a second skin. The smooth satin pulled tautly across the swell of her breasts, showing the tight buds of her nipples beneath. The waist was so tight she could barely breathe, then the material flowed down to emphasise the curves of her hips. The effect was stunning, but she might as well have been naked! She took a step back and her breasts jounced beneath the tight material. In fact, this was worse than being naked!

She bit her lip. So that was Master Watkins' little game. It all made sense now. He was going to use her as bait to entangle young Master Oakley, the way he'd tried to entangle his father. She was to be the cheese in his rattrap. Well, he could go to hell! The very thought of that man touching her made her sick to her stomach.

'I'm not wearing this,' she said determinedly. 'Help me off with it.'

'I can't, ma'am,' whispered Joanie. 'The master were most insistent you wear it.' Her bottom lip quivered. 'If you don't, he'll have Mistress Blackstock beat me.'

Lucy looked at the girl and her heart sank. 'Don't cry,' she said. 'It's not your fault. I'll wear the damned thing.'

Joanie sighed with relief and gave her a watery smile. 'Thank'ee, ma'am,' she said gratefully. 'That Mistress

Blackstock's a right bitch when she gets a belt in her hand.' Her fingers flew to her mouth and she looked at Lucy with frightened eyes. 'Oh Lord, sorry ma'am, I didn't mean to say that.' She looked at Lucy beseechingly. 'You won't tell her will you, miss? Please?'

'Of course I won't,' smiled Lucy, and she winked at the girl. 'Mistress Blackstock and I are not the best of friends, either.' She glanced at herself in the mirror. 'Oh well, might as well be hung for a sheep as a lamb,' she muttered, sitting before the mirror and handing Joanie the comb. 'Help me do my hair before I go down.'

Fifteen minutes later she was ready. 'Thank you, Joanie,' she said, dismissing the girl.

Alone again, she bit her lips and pinched her cheeks to bring colour to her pale face, then dabbed rose water at her neck and wrists. She looked at her reflection and smiled grimly. Master Watkins should be well pleased. She didn't look like a respectable Puritan wife – she looked like a whore masquerading as one.

Downstairs she paused for a moment outside the hall. She could hear young Master Oakley's voice, followed by her husband's sycophantic laughter. Ignoring the quiver of fear in her belly, she took a deep breath, threw open the door and swept in.

Her husband and young Master Oakley were standing at the mullioned window, staring out at the rainy courtyard and talking in low voices. At her entry they turned, and she was conscious of both pairs of eyes on her as she walked the length of the hall.

When she reached them she ignored the discomfort of her constricting gown, and dropped into a deep curtsey. Rising, she fought down her instinctive reaction to flee and smiled at their guest instead. 'Master Oakley, how kind of you to grace our humble home,' she said, holding out her hand. 'And our commiserations on the death of your father. He will be much missed.' Though not by her!

He took her hand and raised it to his mouth in an unexpectedly gallant gesture. She shivered at the coldness of his lips, her nipples hardening at his touch. He nodded his acceptance of her condolences, but his eyes lingered hungrily on the front of her gown where her breasts were clearly outlined against the tight satin of her bodice. A quiver of perverse desire ran through her.

'A great loss,' he agreed. 'But life must go on, and it was kind of you to invite me to dinner. A hand offered in friendship is a great consolation in times of sorrow.'

His speaking voice was as warm and smooth as molten honey, lower and more intimate than his 'pulpit' one, and despite her revulsion against the man himself, she found herself responding to it. Heat began to blossom in the pit of her stomach, and she suppressed it firmly. What was wrong with her? She could sense evil in this man, yet she was both repelled and attracted by him. To cover her confusion she took refuge in her duties as hostess.

'Come now, Master Oakley,' she said briskly. 'You must seat yourself before the fire. The meeting house was cold and you will catch the ague if we stand in front of this drafty window much longer. I shall have Mistress Blackstock fetch something to warm you.'

Once they were seated she pulled the bell-rope. The housekeeper scurried in and stood in front of her, hands folded. 'Bring us mulled wine and three glasses,' she ordered, 'and as quickly as possible. Our guest is chilled after his ride.'

'Yes, m'm,' muttered Mistress Blackstock. She raised her eyes and regarded Lucy insolently, taking in the tightness of her new gown, then her lips set in a thin line and she hurried off to do her bidding.

Lucy stared after her with an odd feeling of apprehension. For a brief moment she had seen something else beneath that mask of disapproval. Something strange and twisted. Why, the woman's eyes had lingered on her breasts almost the same way Master Oakley's had! She shook herself and gave a nervous little laugh at her own stupidity. She was jumping at shadows now. Good heavens, to imagine that a *woman* lusted after her – whatever next?

Turning back, she forgot all about her sick fancy as she exerted herself to charm their guest. More wine was served with the meal, which thanks to her efforts was plentiful and tasty, and the evening passed quickly as they chatted about trivial matters.

When the candles had burnt low and nothing remained on the table but nutshells, crumbs and a few slivers of cheese, Mistress Blackstock brought in a decanter of claret. Lucy got to her feet.

'I trust you will excuse me, gentlemen,' she smiled, 'but I shall retire now and leave you to discuss more important matters.'

Master Watkins nodded his consent. 'You have done well, wife,' he said approvingly. 'A most satisfactory meal.'

'Yes, I thank you too, Mistress Watkins,' agreed Oakley, getting to his feet. 'It makes a pleasant change for a bachelor such as myself to enjoy a family meal,' he said. 'Particularly one presided over by such a delightful hostess.'

Lucy smiled her thanks, bobbed a curtsey and turned to leave. By the time she had reached the door they were already deep in conversation again, their voices lowered.

In her chamber her smile vanished and she breathed a sigh of relief. Every muscle in her body was aching with the effort of keeping up a front for the guest – and fighting the twisted desire she felt for him. All she wanted to do was get out of the ridiculously tight gown, slip beneath her sheets and fall into dreamless oblivion.

The door swung open and Mistress Blackstock walked in. Lucy whirled round to face her. 'What do you want?' she demanded. 'I did not ring for you.'

'I merely came to disrobe you, madam,' said the woman ingratiatingly. 'The maids are all busy clearing up in the kitchen.'

'Very well,' said Lucy. 'Unlace me and help me out of my gown, and then you may go.'

Mistress Blackstock hurried forward and did as she was told, her cold fingers fumbling at the knots in the laces. As she helped Lucy slip the gown over her head, her fingers lingered on the warm skin beneath. Lucy flinched from her, clutching the material to her breasts. She could have sworn the woman had touched her deliberately – but when she whirled round she was looking at her innocently.

'Will that be all, madam?' she said blandly.

'Yes it will,' said Lucy, through gritted teeth. 'And in future if I need any help, send that little girl... what's her name? Ah yes, Joanie. I have a mind to train her as my lady's maid.'

'But that's impossible!' exclaimed Mistress Blackstock, scandalised. 'She's only the pot-girl!'

'I don't care if she's the head gardener,' snapped Lucy. 'I am mistress here, not you, and if I say I want her as my maid then, by God, I shall have her as my maid.' Her eyes narrowed. 'Oh, and one more thing: I do not want you in my bedchamber again.' She glared at the woman.

'Have I made myself clear?'

'Perfectly, madam,' Mistress Blackstock said coldly, then head in the air she stalked out, leaving Lucy trembling with reaction.

It took her a long time to fall asleep. She lay tossing and turning, her cheeks hot against the pillow. The flame of perverse desire still burned in her belly, tormenting her, and she found herself imagining young Master Oakley lying beside her, his poisonously honeyed voice whispering obscenities in her ear as his hands roved over her feverish body.

With a groan she gave in to her needs. Parting her legs, she allowed one hand to stray down over her belly to the hot wetness beneath, while the other pulled and teased her swollen nipples.

Stroking the hard bud of her womanhood with her thumb, she slid two fingers inside herself, moving them slowly at first and then thrusting more and more frantically as her desire mounted. Her gasps and whimpers came faster and faster until finally her back arched in climax and she subsided in the aftermath of guilty pleasure. Desire sated, she was asleep in moments.

Thankfully her husband's discussions with young Master Oakley must have lasted late into the night. She did not even hear him come to bed, and when she awoke in the morning he was already gone. She was still yawning and stretching when Joanie appeared, tongue between her teeth as she concentrated on carrying in the hot water for Lucy's morning toilette.

Putting it down with a sigh of relief at not spilling it, she bobbed a curtsey and smiled shyly at Lucy. 'There's your water, ma'am. Is there anything else I can do for 'ee?'

Lucy smiled. 'Come back in a quarter of an hour and

you may help me dress and do my hair.'

Joanie bobbed another curtsey. 'Yes, m'm,' she said, and then at the door she hesitated, biting her lip.

'What is it, Joanie?' asked Lucy.

The girl looked down at the floor and shuffled her feet. 'I'd just like to thank'ee for taking me on as your maid, ma'am. 'Twill be an honour to serve you.' Her prepared speech over, she looked up at Lucy and grinned. 'You should've seen that old cow's face when she told me!' she burst out. 'She were that mad I thought she were going to bust her corsets!'

Lucy kept her face straight with extreme difficulty. 'You must not speak of Mistress Blackstock so,' she chided gently. 'She is the housekeeper and must be respected.'

'Yes, m'm,' muttered a crestfallen Joanie, bobbing yet again. 'Sorry, m'm.' Subdued by her scolding, she left, closing the door quietly behind her, and Lucy promptly burst into a paroxysm of giggles, holding her hands over her mouth to muffle the sounds of her amusement.

Once it was over she wiped the tears of laughter from her eyes and sighed. It hadn't been that funny really, but with the threat of the damning parchment hanging over father's head and now the possibility of an accusation of witchcraft hanging over her own, it was such a relief to have found an ally in this house full of enemies. Even if it was just a simple serving maid.

But it was not all sweetness and light, as Lucy found out when Joanie did her hair. Or attempted to. 'Goodness me, girl!' she exclaimed, wincing with pain as the comb caught in her curls yet again. 'Be a little gentler. You are not currying a horse!'

Joanie reddened with mortification. 'Yes m'm, sorry m'm,' she apologised, bobbing yet again.

'And that's another thing,' said Lucy crossly. 'For

heaven's sake, you don't need to curtsey every five minutes. Up, down! Up, down! You're making me feel dizzy!'

'Yes m'm,' said Joanie dutifully, starting to curtsey once more, then smiling sheepishly and stopping herself just in time.

'That's better,' grinned Lucy. 'Now let's see if you can finish my hair, and preferably without ripping it out by the roots this time.'

When she finally arrived downstairs, Master Watkins was just about to set forth on his morning ride round the estate. She looked at him cautiously to gauge his mood, and was surprised to receive a grudging smile. Good Lord, wonders would never cease!

'You did well yesterday,' he said approvingly. 'Dinner was excellent and Master Oakley was most impressed.'

'Why, thank you,' she said in astonishment. From her husband this was fulsome praise indeed. Emboldened, she went a little further. 'And your business about the land? Did it go well?'

He frowned. 'I thought it best not to broach the subject too soon,' he informed her. 'These matters are delicate. There will be time enough when I know the man better.' His frown vanished. 'But he is coming to dinner again this Sunday next.' He looked at Lucy warningly. 'I shall rely on you to do your best again.' He paused and smiled slyly. 'Oh, and wear that dress again,' he smirked. 'It was not just the food that impressed him…'

Over the next few weeks, Watkins extended himself to wheedle his way into young Master Oakley's good books. His standing invitation to dine after the Sunday meeting was accompanied by other invitations to hunt or to fish.

And he sent small gifts of wine or a haunch of venison.

'Goodness!' exclaimed Lucy, looking on in astonishment as yet another basket was being dispatched, this time containing a fine fruit cake and a dozen eggs, carefully wrapped in straw. 'You'd think you were going a-wooing, the way you're carrying on.'

'But I am, my dear,' smirked Watkins. 'Once I have won Master Oakley to my side, that land is as good as mine.' His smile broadened. 'And what is the cost of a few paltry gifts compared to what I shall gain then?'

'I see,' said Lucy. 'So you are attempting to bribe the man.' She smiled. 'And if he is not open to bribery, what will you do then?'

'They are not bribes,' he snapped. 'I would not stoop so low as to insult Master Oakley by offering him money. These are merely tokens of my regard and esteem.'

'Yes, and you would esteem him so much more if he were to take your side,' agreed Lucy. She shrugged. 'Well, I wish you luck in your endeavours.' She crossed her fingers behind her back to belie her words. The only luck she wished him was ill luck. The longer Master Oakley prevaricated, the better it would be for their unfortunate neighbours.

It seemed as if her wishes were coming true.

'God rot the man,' snarled Watkins, pacing back and forth in front of the fire as Lucy sewed. 'I have spent a fortune on gifts, yet one minute he agrees with my claim to the land and the next he sides with my opponent, Ridley. Will he never make up his damned mind?' He smacked his fist into his palm. 'This business will stretch out till doomsday at this rate!'

Lucy kept her head down over her embroidery to hide her smile. Perhaps she had underestimated young Master

Oakley. It seemed he was a man of principle, after all. Either that, or…

'Perhaps he has been accepting "tokens of regard and esteem" from Master Ridley as well?' she suggested.

'I wouldn't put it past him,' growled Watkins. 'The two-faced bastard!' His expression became self-pitying. 'And to think I was the one who persuaded the congregation to give him his father's place, as well.'

'How unjust,' agreed Lucy. 'At the very least, you'd think the man would show a bit of gratitude.'

Master Watkins looked at her suspiciously, but she managed to keep the mockery off her face. 'Indeed!' he snapped. 'Well, he need not think to gull me! Nobody crosses Ezekiel Watkins and gets away with it.' An unpleasant smile crossed his face. 'And there is more than one way to skin a cat.'

A cold premonition touched Lucy. 'What do you mean?' she asked apprehensively.

'Oh, you'll find out, my dear,' he said with a mocking smile. 'You'll find out.' The smile became a sneer. 'And so will that whoreson, Oakley.'

Despite his words, nothing untoward occurred in the following weeks. Spring was advancing, the early snowdrops giving way to yellow celandines and then to the tall green leaves of daffodils.

The house was in at state of dust and confusion with the annual ritual of spring-cleaning, with Mistress Blackstock using every excuse to cuff the female servants into even more strenuous efforts. Any attempt on Lucy's part to help with the proceedings was met with a cold, 'I have things well in hand, madam.' So finally she gave up and used the better weather as an excuse to escape from the chaos whenever possible.

Wrapped in her thickest cloak, she spent her afternoons wandering the grounds of the estate, her long skirts trailing through the damp grass. A feeling of brooding melancholy overwhelmed her as she sat on the stile, gazing out over the fields. New lambs gambolled and long-legged calves, still unsteady on their feet, nuzzled at their mothers.

She sighed bitterly. Everything in nature seemed to be fruitful and blooming with new life. If it hadn't been for the damned war, she too might have been married to the man she loved and suckling her firstborn. Instead she was cut off from her family and trapped in a barren, loveless marriage with a man she despised.

She shivered as the sun sank lower in the sky and the air became chill. Wearily she slipped down from the stile and trudged back towards the house and yet another evening of her husband's ranting, or – if she was lucky – oppressive silence.

At least by the time she got there some order had finally been imposed on the chaos. The hangings that had been taken down and beaten to remove the dust of winter had been put up again; the silver had been polished and replaced in the court cupboard; and every bit of wood in the house had been burnished with beeswax till it shone. The scent of dried lavender hung in the air, and there was even a huge bowl of spring flowers at each of the hall windows.

If she had not known better, she would have been impressed by the well-ordered, welcoming air the house exuded. As it was, she merely smiled wryly. Even a spider web could look pretty when it was rain-washed and caught by the sun – despite its bloated occupant.

As if conjured up by the thought, Master Watkins stalked into the hall as she was removing her cloak and handing it to Joanie. 'Where in God's name have you been?' he demanded. 'I have been looking everywhere for you.'

Lucy nodded her thanks to Joanie, who gave her master one apprehensive glance and scuttled off. Turning to her husband, Lucy smiled. 'Why, only for a walk,' she said. 'As Mistress Blackstock made perfectly clear, my services were not required here.' She raised an enquiring eyebrow. 'Why? What is so important that you required my presence?'

'Master Oakley is coming to dine again this Sunday,' he announced with satisfaction.

Lucy shivered. Apart from at meeting, it had been four weeks since she'd seen the man. Much to Watkins' fury, Master Oakley had refused his pressing invitations to dinner each week, insisting that as Minister of the Parish he must show no favouritism. Instead he chose to dine with each of his major parishioners in turn – including the detested Ridley.

Lucy hid a smile. It had been quite amusing, actually. Watkins spent the entire day almost apoplectic with impotent rage, imagining his rival cozening Master Oakley into supporting his claim to the disputed land.

Her smile vanished and a cold knot of fear formed in her tummy, as all that had done was put off the inevitable. She knew her husband's twisted mind, God help her! Her few weeks of grace were over. He had some devilish plan, and this Sunday he would put it into practice.

To add to her unease over the next few days, Mistress Blackstock seemed in remarkably good spirits, a constant mocking smile on her lips, as if she knew something that her mistress didn't. Lucy caught the woman looking at her when she thought herself unobserved, and her expression – an odd mixture of hatred and hunger – made her feel strangely ill-at-ease.

It was reflected elsewhere in the house, too. 'Dunno

whass got into that old bitch,' said Joanie, when she was helping Lucy dress. 'That Chastity dropped a bowl of cream in the kitchen this morning – a full one an' all, it were, straight from the dairy – and all she did were yell at her not to be so clumsy in future.'

Lucy stopped arranging the folds of her skirt and looked up at her maid in surprise. 'What's so strange about that?' she asked in bewilderment.

Joanie looked at her as if she were mad. '"Whass so strange about that?"' she repeated scornfully. 'I'll tell you whass strange about it. She didn't take the skin off her backside with that belt of hers, tha'ss what's strange.'

She paused thoughtfully. 'Maybe she's finally got herself a man?' she muttered, and then giggled. 'Though he'd have to be blind in both eyes and deaf into the bargain to take that one on. The scrawny old bitch looks more like a man than a woman! She ain't no beauty, tha'ss for sure. Nor no spring chicken, neither.'

A sly smile crossed her face and she lowered her voice. 'Though they do say as how she used to warm the master's bed, before he set his sights a bit higher and started courting you.' She giggled again. 'He ain't no beauty either, but it don't matter so much if you're a man an' you've got a bob or two in yer pocket, do it?'

Lucy knew she shouldn't encourage the girl, but the subject was too interesting to drop. 'Fiddlesticks, I'm sure that's just empty rumour,' she said loftily, knowing full well that Joanie would be unable to resist the temptation to prove her wrong.

'No it ain't,' she said. 'Tha'ss a fact.' She glanced over her shoulder and came closer. 'Purity – tha'ss Chastity's sister – she were taken short one night and had to go to the privy. And who did she see going into the master's bedchamber in her shift, but the old bitch herself.' She sniggered. 'You can't tell me she were there at that time o' night just to turn down his bed sheets.' She snorted. 'Climb in between 'em more like!'

'I don't believe it,' said Lucy.

'Iss true!' Joanie protested indignantly. 'On her road back from the privy, Purity said she heard 'er yowling like a cat in heat.' She rolled her eyes in disgust. 'Criminy! Can you imagine 'em at it? Be like two skeletons in a graveyard! Besides,' she went on, 'that sister of hers were over one day and I heard 'em with my own two ears.' She looked suddenly guilty. 'Just by chance, o' course,' she added hastily. 'I weren't listening at the door or nothing.' Lucy hid a smile. 'Anyways,' Joanie went on, 'she were telling her that she'd be mistress here iffen all went well.'

She chuckled gleefully. 'I wish I'd been there to see her face when she found out the master had no more intention of marryin' her than turning Papist! That'd've been a sight to see!' She grinned at Lucy. 'You put her nose out of joint an' no mistake. No wonder she hates yer guts.' Her hand flew to her mouth as she realised what she'd said. 'Sorry, madam, that all just sorter slipped out.' She stared at Lucy, wide-eyed with fright. 'You won't tell her what I said, will yer?'

'Of course not,' said Lucy ruefully. 'You didn't tell me anything I didn't know already.' She made herself scowl at the girl. 'But in future, keep that tattling tongue of yours under control lest it get you into trouble.'

'Yes, m'm,' said Joanie meekly, and hurried from the room before her mistress could change her mind.

Once she'd gone, Lucy walked to the window and stared out, seeing nothing. Before, she'd merely suspected the relationship between her husband and Mistress Blackstock. Now she knew for certain. No wonder the woman loathed her.

She sighed. Not that the knowledge was reassuring. Quite the contrary. Knowing why the woman hated her didn't make that hatred any less poisonous. Her unease intensified. Mistress Blackstock was not the kind of woman to take rejection lightly. If she saw the chance to take revenge on her rival, she would seize it, and gladly.

Her fears were not allayed by her own confirmation of Joanie's words. Mistress Blackstock was indeed in a good mood, and her constant smug smile grated on Lucy's nerves. When she gave the housekeeper her orders for the forthcoming dinner, the woman's expression became positively gloating. 'And what is so amusing, pray?' demanded Lucy.

Mistress Blackstock smirked. 'Why nothing, ma'am. Nothing at all.' Her eyelids lowered to hide a gleam of insolent amusement, and when she raised them again it was gone and she was the picture of innocence. 'I merely wish to serve you to the best of my ability, mistress,' she said, her lips twitching with secret amusement. 'That is all.'

'Well, see that you do then,' snapped Lucy.

'Oh I shall, madam, I shall,' said Mistress Blackstock. She curtsied then swept off about her duties, leaving Lucy fuming impotently. The woman was up to something, she could swear it!

She could not complain about the dinner, though. The housekeeper had excelled herself. From the thick soup that started the meal, through the freshly caught fish and the delicately flavoured meat course, to the baked apples drowned in thick cream, everything was delicious. Fine wines that had lain in the cellar since the days of Sir Roland

and Lady Mary accompanied each course.

To still her jangling nerves, Lucy had drunk more than she was accustomed to and her head was swimming pleasantly. As the conversation about cattle and prices droned on, she fell into a happy reverie about the past, when meals like this were everyday occurrences, and her mother and father presided over a table of friends and relatives. She smiled dreamily. There would be music and dancing afterwards, and…

'Are you listening to me, wife?' demanded Master Watkins, bringing her back to earth with a bump.

'I am sorry,' she said, collecting her scattered wits and smiling at him in placation. 'I am afraid I was off wool-gathering. What did you say?'

He glared at her. 'I said that I am having more work done on the house,' he repeated, 'and I invited Master Oakley to accompany us to see how it is progressing.'

She stared at him in confusion. What was he talking about? What work? To her certain knowledge, apart from their own bedchamber, nothing had been changed above stairs. Perhaps it had been started while the spring-cleaning was on, and in the turmoil she simply hadn't noticed. She shrugged. Oh well. No doubt she would find out.

'Why then, let us go and see indeed, husband,' she said, getting to her feet. 'I am sure Master Oakley will be vastly entertained.' She swayed slightly and giggled to herself. Oh dear, that last glass of wine had been a mistake.

Walking with tipsy carefulness she allowed Watkins to take her arm and lead their guest towards the staircase, and they were almost halfway up before caution set in.

'Perhaps I should stay below and supervise the servants as they clear dinner,' she said uneasily. 'I know nothing about pargetting, panelling and the like. I am sure you two gentlemen would prefer to discuss such fascinating subjects without me.' She attempted to pull away, but her husband's fingers fixed her arm in a grasp of iron.

'Not at all, my dear,' he said smoothly. 'Your advice will be invaluable. After all, it is a woman's touch that makes a home.' His fingers bit deeper and she was forced to continue upwards.

At the top of the stairs Master Watkins turned left and led his wife and guest along the gallery towards the west wing. Lucy relaxed a little. This part of the building was indeed in need of work, and it was so far away from the main body of the house that Master Watkins could have had an army of masons hammering away from morning to night and it would still have passed unnoticed.

They finally reached a heavy oaken door at the end of the passage, and Master Watkins let go of her arm long enough to fumble in his breeches for a rusty iron key. He inserted it in the lock, turned it with difficulty, pushed the door open and ushered his wife and guest inside.

Lucy stared round the chamber, and her mouth went dry with fear. There were no signs of workmen here. No piles of rubble or discarded tools awaiting their owners' return. There was almost nothing in the room at all, apart from a few dusty hangings on the wall, and an ancient four-poster bed in the centre.

But it was no ordinary bed. From each of the two head-posts ran a chain, which met in the middle, then divided into two again. At the ends of each length was a heavy iron shackle. A matching set of chains was attached to the posts at the bottom of the bed. It was like the rack out of some vile torture chamber.

Then she noticed the chairs. There was two of them, set slightly back so that whoever sat in them would have an uninterrupted view of the bed. Beside the chairs stood flagons of wine and a couple of glasses.

Lucy swallowed, suddenly reminded of the travelling theatres that had attended the fair once a year, before they were banned like everything else. This was no bed. It was a stage, and it was set for some unholy performance in which she would be the main player!

The sound of the key turning made her whirl round, instantly sober. Master Watkins was standing between her and the locked door, his face a mask of malicious delight. She turned again to face Master Oakley, but there was no help there. He was regarding the situation with the detached interest of a hunter watching a trapped animal futilely attempting to escape.

'Wh-what do you think you are doing?' she demanded, trying and failing to keep the quiver out of her voice. 'Let me out of this room at once or I shall scream.'

Master Watkins shrugged. 'Scream to your heart's content, my dear,' he said. 'This far from the main house no one will hear you.' His smile broadened. 'As to what I am doing, why, I am merely being a good host and providing amusement for our guest.' He nodded to the other man. 'Please be seated, Master Oakley, and let the entertainment begin.'

Lucy looked round wildly. There was no way out through the locked door, but perhaps there was another way? Hope flared up again. The house had been old even in Sir Roland and Lady Mary's day, and when she'd played there as a child the boys had shown the secret passageway in the old wing. She'd never dared enter the dark, cobwebbed tunnel then, but now she would brave anything to get away from these two evil men.

She fled across the room, pulled back the tattered hangings, and then recoiled in horror. She was looking straight into the grinning face of Mistress Blackstock!

'May I help you, madam?' she sniggered. 'You look

tired. Perhaps you should lie down. Pray, allow me to help you disrobe.' Her claw-like hand shot out and seized Lucy's tight bodice.

Lucy staggered backwards in an attempt to free herself from the woman's grip, but it was the worst thing she could have done for the thin satin, already under strain, ripped from neck to hem, revealing her firm breasts, smooth belly and curved hips. Lucy gasped and tried to hold the gaping gown together, but her feet caught in the sagging material and she went sprawling to the floor.

The woman was on her in a moment, and twisting Lucy's arms behind her back she ripped the torn gown off her struggling body, leaving her as naked as the day she was born.

Sobbing with shock and humiliation, Lucy curled into a ball to hide her shame, but all this served to do was present the smooth curve of her buttocks to her tormentor. There was a low swishing sound and fire exploded through her lower body. Her mouth opened in astonished agony and she straightened, her back arching as her body tried to escape the scorching pain.

Mistress Blackstock needed no further opportunity, and before Lucy could roll into a ball again she dropped the leather belt she had used, seized her victim by one arm, wrenched her to her feet and flung her facedown onto the bed.

Putting her bony knee in the small of Lucy's back to pin her down, she grabbed one of her flailing arms. There was an ominous click and to her horror Lucy found her right wrist shackled. Hampered by the chain she was unable to fight back, and it was an easy matter for the housekeeper to slip the other one over her left wrist and snap it into place.

Her legs were still free though, and when the woman

bent to grip her ankle she kicked out, almost sending her flying. For a few moments the housekeeper stood there, bent double and gasping, then she slowly straightened up, her eyes mad with rage. 'Oh, you will regret that, madam,' she vowed, advancing on her again. 'Be assured you will.'

Lucy kicked out again, but this time Mistress Blackstock was ready for her. She caught the girl's legs and threw all her weight across them, forcing them down. Lucy whimpered as the cold iron closed about first one ankle and then the other, leaving her helpless. Then Mistress Blackstock stepped back, panting from her exertions, to admire her handiwork.

Now chained at wrist and ankle, Lucy was spread-eagled naked across the bed, her slender white body vulnerable to whatever the vicious old harridan chose to inflict upon it. Head on one side, the woman considered for a moment, then pulled one of the pillows from beneath Lucy's head and thrust it beneath her belly, forcing her hips upward so that her buttocks jutted into the air, their peach-like curves presenting the perfect target for what was to come next.

Smiling with anticipation, the housekeeper retrieved the fallen belt and stood with it dangling loosely from one hand as she looked to her master for permission to continue.

'"A woman, a dog and a walnut tree. The more you beat them, the better they be". Isn't that what they say, Oakley?' Watkins smirked, nudging the other man in the ribs. 'And 'tis as true now as it was in my grandfather's day.' He rubbed his hands gleefully, nodding in agreement with his own words. 'Mistress Watkins has always been far too headstrong for her own good, but I vow she will be a damned sight less impudent after this.'

Lucy turned her head and gazed at Master Oakley, her eyes pleading. She held her breath, hoping against hope that he would leap to his feet and declare his disapproval – forbid this travesty of 'discipline' – but he merely sat, calmly sipping his wine and regarding the scene before him as if it were something from a puppet show. Her head sank back onto the pillow in despair. There would be no mercy. No last minute reprieve.

Master Watkins refilled his glass and that of his guest, and then nodded his approval to Mistress Blackstock. The woman smiled down at the trembling girl, and raised her arm.

'Think you're too good for the likes of me, do you, madam?' she sneered. 'Well, we'll soon see how fine you are by the time I've finished with you.' She brought her arm down and the broad leather belt bit into Lucy's bottom with a *Thwack*! that echoed with startling clarity in the bleak chamber. Her buttocks quivered beneath the blow.

For a moment the shock was so great that Lucy felt nothing – then a wave of agony engulfed her and she buried her head in the pillow to prevent herself crying out. She was damned if she'd give the bitch the satisfaction of hearing her scream.

'Enjoy that, did you?' taunted Mistress Blackstock. She trailed the belt slowly across Lucy's bottom, enjoying the way the girl flinched beneath its touch. 'Like the feel of leather on that delicate aristocratic skin?' Lucy's dogged silence infuriated her, so raising her arm she viciously swept the belt down again.

This time it was worse – much worse. Her soft skin, already tender from the previous two blows, was appallingly sensitive. There was no moment of blessed numbness before the pain shot through her, hot tongues of agony licking her bruised flesh. She whimpered and bit into the coarse material to muffle the sounds of her weakness.

'Oh my, a brave one, aren't we?' said Mistress Blackstock, and her lips drew back from her yellow teeth as she put even more effort into her next blow. Lucy's buttocks jounced beneath the fury of the onslaught and a high keening escaped from between her clenched teeth. The pale skin of her bottom was scarlet now, crisscrossed by broad welts where the belt had left its mark.

Mistress Blackstock paused, just long enough for Lucy to think her torment was over – then two more blows in swift succession put paid to that frail hope. This time the pain was beyond endurance and Lucy's will broke. Her mouth opened and shriek after shriek tore from her lips, mingling with the harsh sound of leather on flesh.

Then just when she thought she could bear no more, Master Oakley's voice rang out. 'Enough!' he barked. 'I do not wish her damaged beyond repair.' A look of disappointed rage flashed across Mistress Blackstock's face, then she nodded sulkily and let her arm fall to her side again.

Lucy sobbed with relief, thinking her ordeal over.

But she couldn't have been more wrong.

It had barely begun.

Before she realised what was happening, the housekeeper had flipped her over onto her back as easily as she flipped a fish in a frying pan. She lay there, naked body quivering as she looked up at the other woman. To her horror, Mistress Blackstock was disrobing, slipping off her dowdy black gown to reveal the scrawny body beneath. With her bony limbs and drooping teats she looked like the woodcut of a witch Lucy had seen once in a book.

Naked, she bent over the helpless girl and Lucy gasped in shock as she reached down and fondled each of her full breasts in turn, rolling the nipples between thumb and finger, smiling as they hardened beneath her touch.

Sick with loathing, Lucy cringed. Nothing – even her husband's sharing her with another man – had prepared her for this perversion. How could a woman touch another in such a way? It went against all the laws of nature!

But worse was to come. Bending lower, she continued to caress Lucy's left nipple while taking the right in her mouth, suckling it as her wet tongue rasped over the tender flesh. Lucy froze, her mind frantically rejecting what was happening, while her traitorous body responded.

The heat from her beaten bottom radiated through her lower belly, the pain throbbing with each beat of her heart, but now something else was throbbing, too. To her horror, she felt herself moistening.

'Nooooo,' she moaned, tossing her head from side to side in a fruitless effort to escape the tendrils of evil pleasure that coiled through her.

The woman's clammy mouth and tongue left her nipple, and kneeling on the bed she crouched over Lucy and rubbed her dangling tits against Lucy's pert young ones, groaning aloud at the touch of the soft skin.

Then turning her attention lower, she drew her nails down the insides of Lucy's thighs, making her shudder with sick desire. Lucy twisted and turned, trying to pull her legs together, but she was held in place by the damned shackles. The most private part of her body lay open to the woman's wicked attentions.

As Lucy watched in dismay the housekeeper parted the lips of her sex, revealing the glistening pinkness within. Then, unbelievably, she dipped her head and ran her tongue the entire length of Lucy's cleft, and finding the hard bud of her clitoris she circled the tip of it teasingly, her tongue flicking it till Lucy whimpered again... this time with unwilling pleasure.

She flung her head back, closing her eyes to shut out
the sight of Mistress Blackstock's bobbing head and the
gloating gaze of the watchers, but she could not shut out
the feelings engendered by the woman's touch. Despite
herself, she could not help raising her hips to allow that
busy tongue to continue its ministrations.

Suddenly Mistress Blackstock stopped and Lucy's eyes
flew open in a mixture of relief and disappointment – then
widened in shock as she saw what the woman held in her
hands. It was a piece of polished wood, carved into the
shape of two cocks, joined at the base and pointing in
opposite directions. As she watched in horrified fascination,
the woman bent her knees and slid one inside herself.

Lucy gasped. Now it looked as if Mistress Blackstock
was some bizarre combination of both man and woman.
Her heavy breasts hung above her waist, but between her
thighs thrust a monstrous phallus. She tried to writhe away
as the woman crept close again but the shackles bit into
her limbs, holding her helpless. She whimpered as the
cold, hard wood prodded its way between the lips of her
vulva. There was a momentary resistance, Lucy held her
breath incredulously, and then it slid inside, penetrating
the warm, living flesh.

Grinning down victoriously, Mistress Blackstock began
to move, her skinny buttocks clenching and unclenching
as she thrust the dildo deep inside both Lucy and herself.
'Like that, do you, my pretty?' she panted, and tears of
humiliation running down her cheeks, Lucy groaned in
unwilling response as the thick cock ploughed in and out,
her body writhing beneath the onslaught, her hips moving
in rhythm with the other woman's.

She was almost on the edge of release when Master
Watkins rose to his feet and crossed the chamber in two

quick strides, then grabbing the housekeeper by the hair he wrenched her aside and tossed her to the floor. 'Take your toys and get out of here, you raddled old whore,' he snarled, and with a last longing glance at Lucy's quivering body, the housekeeper grabbed her clothes and scuttled out.

Turning his attention back to Lucy, he fumbled with his breeches, pulled out his own cock, rigid and swollen with lust, and threw himself on her. Grunting, he shoved himself inside her hot wetness and brought himself off in a few quick strokes, then panting he pulled himself upright and tucked his wilting cock away, sauntered back across the chamber and slapped his guest on the back.

'Your turn now, man,' he said jovially, looking at the telltale bulge in Oakley's breeches, and winking. 'I can see you're eager to have a go at her.'

Lucy cringed as Master Oakley carefully put down his glass and stood up. But what followed surprised her, and shocked her husband.

'Oh, I think not, Watkins,' he said coolly. 'This has been a most... enlightening evening, but if you don't mind I would rather not participate. I shall bid you good evening. And too you, Mistress Watkins.' He nodded at Lucy with as much aplomb as if she had been fully dressed instead of chained naked to a bed, and then calmly walked out of the room.

It was Master Watkins' turn to gape, his trap sprung with no prize inside it.

Even as her body ached from her beating and tears of shame and humiliation ran down her cheeks, Lucy could not help but smile weakly at the look of shock and consternation on his face!

'Oh, madam, your poor arse!' exclaimed Joanie, gazing at the rainbow of bruises in horror, though she knew better than to ask her mistress how she had acquired them.

Facedown on the bed, with her skirts above her waist, Lucy grimaced in pain as the girl delicately applied marigold ointment to her bruised flesh. She smiled wryly. Her 'poor arse' indeed. It had been two days and she still had to sleep on her front. Every movement caused hurt and she could only sit for a few minutes at a time, and even then only if the chair were well padded with cushions.

Her only consolation was that on the few occasions she'd seen her husband, he had looked no happier than she was. Since the failure of his plan to entrap young Master Oakley, he had been skulking around the house like a bear with a sore head, muttering to himself under his breath and worrying his fingernails down to the quick.

'There, all done,' said Joanie, pulling down her mistress's skirts and wiping her hands. Lucy grimaced once more as the coarse material touched her sensitive skin. 'Can I do anything else for you, mistress?' the girl enquired anxiously. 'Bring you something to eat, or a hot posset?'

'No, thank you,' said Lucy, forcing a smile as she sat up stiffly. 'The only thing you can give me is news. I have barely been out of this chamber these past two days.'

'You haven't missed much,' said Joanie glumly. 'You'd think somebody'd died. The house is as quiet as a graveyard. The master has been locked in his study from morning till night.' And sleeping there too, thought Lucy. 'And Mistress Blackstock has been as quiet as a mouse.' Her eyes danced with mischief. 'Hardly surprising, since she's got a black eye the size of my fist! Says she walked into a door,' she added scornfully. 'As if anyone would believe that taradiddle!'

'Oh dear, what a shame,' said Lucy, her smile becoming

genuine. It was a pleasure to know she wasn't the only one to feel Master Watkins' wrath. No doubt he blamed the woman for the failure of his plan. Well, hell mend her! She had been mighty handy with that belt, so it would do her good to be on the receiving end for a change. Heartened by the news, she smiled at Joanie. 'You know, I think I might be able to eat something after all.'

It was still another couple of days before she could walk again without wincing at every step. At the breakfast table she seated herself carefully, looked across at her husband for the first time in several days, and gasped.

He was unshaven and the dark circles under his eyes gave mute witness to worry and lack of sleep. His clothes were crumpled and obviously hadn't been changed for days. Considering how fastidious he was normally, this was another sign of how worried he must be. Well, hell mend him, too. He deserved everything he got!

'I trust I find you well, husband?' she said sarcastically. 'Not too tired by your exertions of the other night?' She shook her head. 'What a shame Master Oakley did not seem to enjoy the "entertainment" as much as you had hoped.'

'Damn the man,' he muttered, lifting his glass of wine with a shaky hand. She watched as he drained it in one gulp; another bad sign this early in the morning. He looked at Lucy with haunted eyes. 'Why haven't I heard from him?' he demanded petulantly. 'What is he doing?' Fear flickered in his eyes. 'You don't think he has reported me, do you?' She looked at him in astonishment. The very fact he had asked her opinion at all was proof of how far gone he was.

A warm sense of satisfaction spread through her as she watched him squirm. 'I have no idea,' she said lightly.

'But no doubt if he has, you will find out soon enough.'
She helped herself to bread and cold beef and smiled again.
'I know the penalty for adultery is death,' she went on
conversationally. 'But I am not sure what it is for
whoremongering one's wife against her will.'

He gave her one horrified glance, leapt to his feet and
fled with his hand clapped over his mouth. Lucy smiled
and took another slice of meat. Oh dear, he seemed to
have lost his appetite!

From then on he spent most days watching anxiously
from the window of his study, desperately hoping for
some reassuring letter from Master Oakley, not daring to
attend meetings for fear of his reception. There was none.
By the time Mayday had come and gone – uncelebrated –
and there was still no word, his fear had turned to rage.

His behaviour became even more erratic. He paced
endlessly back and forth, like the caged lions at the Tower,
pounding his fist into his hand and cursing. He barely
came to her bed, and when he did, much to her relief, he
did not lay a finger on her. On the few occasions he ceased
his restless pacing he sat slumped before the hearth, staring
into the fire in grim silence, the veins in his forehead
throbbing as he ground his teeth in impotent fury.

Finally the endless monotony was broken by the sound
of a horseman galloping into the courtyard. 'A message
at last,' he muttered, relief suffusing his features. He leapt
to his feet and hurried down the stairs, with Lucy hastening
after him.

Grabbing the sealed parchment he tore it open and
scanned the contents anxiously. Then his brow creased
in confusion. ''Tis not from Master Oakley at all,' he
muttered.

'So who is it from, then?' demanded Lucy, a sudden

frightening thought striking her. 'It… it isn't from my parents, is it? They are not ill?'

'Not them,' he groaned. 'I wish it were. 'Tis Master Cromwell. He has been taken with a grave sickness after news of his daughter's death.'

Lucy's mind raced as she considered the possibilities raised by the death of the Lord Protector. His son, Richard, was so useless that he was better known as 'Tumbledown Dick'. He could never take his father's place, and if he couldn't, why then, anything might happen.

'How unfortunate,' she said. 'Let us hope he recovers soon. I hate to think what might become of you if the king were to return to power.' She smiled at him mockingly. 'For who would be the traitor then?'

As her words sank in his already pale face whitened even further. He raised his hand as if to slap her words away, then groaned and bent double, clutching his head. Lucy's arms went out automatically to steady him before he fell, for much though she might like to, she could hardly leave him lying in the courtyard.

'Help me get him into the house,' she ordered the messenger. 'Then you may go to the kitchens for some food and drink before you leave. I will see that there's a coin or two in it for your trouble.' Between them they got him, stumbling, back into the house, where he collapsed on the settle before the fire.

Revived by hot wine he recovered his spirits. 'I warrant 'tis but some passing sickness,' he said. 'He will recover and all will be well.' He smiled and took another sip of wine, his confidence growing. 'You mark my words, wife, 'twill take more than some paltry fit of the ague to carry off a man like Master Cromwell.'

It seemed he was right. Word came barely a week later that the Lord Protector had rallied a little, had even announced that he was not dying yet. The effect on Master Watkins was almost as miraculous. The good news, together with the fact that Master Oakley had obviously held his tongue regarding that disastrous evening, combined to restore him to his former self.

'Oakley daren't get on his high horse with me,' he sneered, his confidence returning with every passing day. 'He might not have enjoyed the use of your body, but he watched. And what did he do about it? Nothing!' He smirked. 'Gutless bastard! Not man enough, I warrant. No doubt he went home to pleasure himself in his solitary bed instead.'

Convinced that all was well, he began to eat more and drink less, though thankfully he did not resume his demands that she perform her marital duties.

So secure did he feel that he thought nothing of it when Master Oakley's servant finally did arrive with a message as he was standing in the courtyard watching his new stallion being put through its paces. Waving the man away, he stuffed it carelessly into his breeches pocket and forgot all about it.

It was only the crackling of the parchment as he sat down to dinner that reminded him, and pulling it out, he looked at it without interest. 'Some trifling parish business he needs my advice on, no doubt,' he shrugged, breaking the seal and beginning to read.

As Lucy watched, the colour drained from his face then surged back again until he was scarlet with fury. His knuckles turned white, his fingers gripping the parchment so tightly she thought it would tear.

'Wh-what is it?' she pressed anxiously.

'That… that treacherous little whoreson!' he snarled,

crushing the paper and flinging it onto the table. He leapt to his feet, sending his food and drink flying. 'How dare he?' he spluttered, froth forming at the corners of his lips. His eyes bulged as he banged his fist repeatedly on the table, his rage making her tremble. 'I'll see him rot in hell for this!' he spat. 'I'll be damned if I don't!'

'But… but what has he done?' cried Lucy.

'"What has he done?",' he mimicked, and she recoiled as he pushed his face into hers, spattering her with spittle. 'I'll tell you what the misbegotten get has done. He's bought the disputed land himself!'

Grabbing the letter from the table he shook it under her nose. 'And what's more, he has the temerity to say that unless *I* pay *him*, *he* will divert the river from my land! I am ruined. Ruined!'

Lucy stared at him, fighting back a bubble of hysterical laughter. How ironic. He'd been hoist by his own petard. The very plan he'd intended to use himself used against him, and he was squealing like an outraged virgin! Still, it would be best to try and placate him lest he vent his rage on her.

But it was too late.

'This is all your fault,' he snarled, giving her a look that chilled her bowels. 'I have had nothing but ill luck since I wed you. Witch!' he spat. 'The sooner I am rid of you the better. I shall have my horse readied and lay charges against you this very moment.' Whirling on his heel he turned and stalked towards the door - but he never reached it.

Barely halfway there he spun on his heel again, and clutching his throbbing temples he gaped at her with a look of dull astonishment on his face, gave a gurgling moan, and collapsed slowly to the floor.

For a moment she stood there, frozen, waiting for him

to rise again, but he simply lay there, eyes closed, making a strange snoring sound, a thin line of drool dribbling from his slack mouth. She flew across the hall and knelt beside him.

'Master Watkins!' she cried, shaking him by the shoulder. 'Master Watkins!' It was no use. She might as well have been shaking a waterlogged corpse for all the response she got. Getting to her feet she ran to the door. 'Come quickly!' she shouted. 'The master is ill!'

'I have bled him and administered a clyster, madam, but to no avail,' said the doctor. 'He is conscious again, but there is little more I can do.' He regarded his patient with a professional eye. 'I have seen this kind of thing before. If the attack is slight then the patient may recover, the functions returning of their own accord, though there is always a weakness left. But if not…' he shrugged.

'And is my husband's attack a slight one?' asked Lucy.

The doctor shook his head and sighed. 'I am afraid not, madam.'

'So what will become of him, then?' she persisted.

The doctor removed his eyeglasses and polished them, avoiding her gaze. 'That is out of my hands now,' he informed her. 'He could last for years in this condition – or die within the week.'

He put his glasses back on. 'Now, as to his care, mistress, he must be put on a simple diet,' he announced, on safer ground again. 'Bread and milk, egg custards, that kind of thing. No red meat or wine to inflame the blood, and above all, no excitement. None whatsoever. The smallest shock to his system could be enough to kill him.' He gathered his equipment. 'I shall call again next week – if he is spared. In the meantime, madam, I shall bid you good day.' And he was gone, leaving Lucy alone with Master Watkins.

He was not a pretty sight. His face was as white as the pillows he was propped against, and one side of it looked as if some demon had clawed the flesh downward. His left eye glittered from beneath the half-closed lid and the left side of his mouth drooped open, a weak trickle of saliva running down his chin. A bowl of blood sat to one side of the bed and a foul stench arose from the sheets, which were splattered with the results of the clyster. Lucy shuddered and rang for the servants.

'Get him cleaned up immediately,' she ordered. 'Change his soiled nightshirt and put new sheets on the bed.' She wrinkled her nose. 'Faugh! I am going to wash myself. He stinks worse than the shambles.'

When she returned, all was fresh again. Someone had brought in a small brazier and flung a handful of herbs on it, to sweeten the air. But despite this, the air was heavy with the scent of sickness. Pulling up a chair Lucy seated herself beside the bed. Master Watkins struggled to speak, but all that came out of his mouth was a string of unintelligible grunts.

'Oh dear,' she said softly. 'I am sorry, my love. What were you trying to say? Is there something you desire? A drink of water? The chamber pot? No?' She smiled. 'Then maybe you wished to threaten me with the stake again? To tell me how much you would enjoy seeing me burn?' Her smile widened. 'Perhaps you were right, my dear,' she whispered. 'Perhaps I am a witch. After all, aren't witches known for their ability to strike men down?'

He was frozen now, his good eye fixed on her in fear, and his terror sent a pleasurable quiver running through her as she realised her own power. The boot was on the other foot now. He was the one who would live in dread of what the morrow might bring.

'But who needs witchcraft?' she smiled. 'If I chose, I could take those pillows you're lying on and hold them over your mouth till the last flicker of life is crushed out of you. You wouldn't be able to stop me, would you, sweetheart?'

The stench of fresh urine filled the room, overpowering the scent of burning herbs, and she looked at the spreading pool of dampness on the clean bedding. 'Oh dear,' she cooed, revelling in his humiliation after the many times he'd humiliated her. 'What a shame. You've had another little accident.' She got to her feet. 'I had best send the servants to change you, again.'

At the door she turned and looked back. For a moment she almost felt sorry for him. Almost, but not quite. Now it was his turn to be trapped and helpless in the hands of someone who could use him as they pleased. She smiled. 'Oh, don't worry, husband,' she said lightly, 'I have no intention of murdering you in your sleep. That would be doing you a kindness. I intend to make sure you live to enjoy your circumstances as long as possible.'

She was halfway down the stairs when she heard the shrieking.

Her first startled thought was that Master Watkins had realised the full horror of his fate and was howling like a trapped animal, then it dawned on her that the sound was coming from below stairs, not above. Picking up her skirts she ran down the rest of the steps towards the sound.

Bursting into the kitchen she found a pretty scene. Mistress Blackstock, her face flushed with anger, had Joanie bent over the edge of the table with her skirts flung up and was applying a belt with vigour to the girl's rosy buttocks. The other girls looked on, cowering, lest

Mistress Blackstock's wrath descend on them as well.

Her own anger rising, Lucy strode across the kitchen and seized the woman's arm, wrenched the belt away from her and dropped it on the floor. 'What do you think you are doing?' she demanded. 'How dare you? This girl is my personal maid, not some kitchen servant. You have no right to beat her.'

Mistress Blackstock glared at her. 'I am housekeeper here and shall chastise whoever deserves it,' she sneered. 'I return from visiting my sister and what do I find? This idle girl playing cards, if you please!' She drew herself up to her full height. 'This is a God-fearing house,' she informed Lucy. 'We'll have none of the Devil's picture books here.'

''Twas only a game of patience to pass the time till you needed me, mistress,' complained Joanie. 'I weren't gambling nor nothing.'

'And there have been worse things in this house than a pack of cards,' said Lucy grimly. She snapped her fingers and pointed at two of the tallest maids. 'You! And you! Take Mistress Blackstock's arms.'

The two girls looked at one another, their fear of the housekeeper warring with their fear of being sent packing if they did not obey their mistress. Finally the latter won, and reluctantly they came forward and did as they were told.

'And what do you think you are playing at?' snorted Mistress Blackstock.

'Oh, I am not playing,' smiled Lucy, picking up the belt. She doubled it between her hands and snapped it viciously. 'You are so fond of beatings, I thought you might appreciate one of your own.'

Mistress Blackstock stared at her in disbelief as it dawned on her what was going to happen. She glared at the two maids and struggled to break free, and when that proved useless she attempted to browbeat them into releasing her. 'Unhand me this minute, you good-for-nothing trollops!' she snarled. 'Or it will be the worse for you.'

It did not work. For once her bullying tactics failed. Mistress Blackstock looked round for help, but saw nothing but a sea of loathing faces. The maids had all suffered from her temper at one time or another, and now it was time to pay the price. Far from taking her side, they were enjoying themselves hugely at the prospect of their former tormentor receiving a taste of her own medicine.

'Bend her over the table,' ordered Lucy. 'And pull up her skirts.'

The maids obeyed with alacrity and in a trice, Mistress Blackstock found herself facedown with her scrawny buttocks exposed in the humiliating position Joanie had occupied when Lucy first walked in. Head twisted to the side, she glared up at Lucy. 'Oh, you will pay for this, madam,' she spat.

'I think not,' countered Lucy. 'My paying days are done. It's your turn now.' She let the leather belt uncoil, then raised her arm and brought it down with all the strength she possessed.

As the thick belt bit into her backside with a dull *thwap*! Mistress Blackstock stiffened with shock and outrage, then let out a howl of pain. Her fingernails clawed at the table and she redoubled her efforts to break free, but the maids tightened their grip. Lucy brought down the belt again… and again on the woman's writhing buttocks, and then dropped it, sickened, for much as she hated the woman, she could not do this.

But if Mistress Blackstock thought she was going to get off that easily, she was wrong. As Lucy turned away one of the other maids darted forward, picked up the belt and walloped the housekeeper's wriggling backside. 'Tha'ss for the time you beat me for dropping them eggs,' she crowed.

Then in front of Lucy's astonished eyes, there was a mad rush to take possession of the belt, the servants almost coming to blows in their eagerness to pay back old scores. They took a turn each, dispensing retribution with a heavy hand, until Mistress Blackstock's bottom was a mass of scarlet weals and she was reduced to a whimpering, snivelling wretch.

It was only when the pot-girl picked up a carrot and advanced on the helpless woman with the express intention of shoving it up her backside that Lucy stepped in.

'Enough!' she said sharply. 'You have had justice, now let that be an end to it. Let her go.' Reluctantly the two maids did as they were bidden and Mistress Blackstock got shakily to her feet, shaking her skirts down to hide her shame. The pot-girl beat a hasty retreat.

The housekeeper dragged the tattered remnants of her pride together and glared round at them. 'You will all regret this day.' She spat on the floor in front of Lucy. 'And you in particular, my lady. By the time I have finished with you, you will rue the very day you were born.'

'I doubt it,' said Lucy. 'How convenient that your bag is still packed from your visit to your sister. I am sure she will be delighted at your unexpected return.' Her expression grew sterner. 'Now pick up your things and get out. I do not want to see you in my house again.'

Mistress Blackstock smirked. 'You cannot tell me to go,' she said confidently. 'Only the master can.' She turned and hobbled towards the door. 'I shall speak to him right now, and then we shall see who holds the upper hand, madam.'

'But…' began Joanie.

'Hold your tongue and get out of my way, girl,' snapped Mistress Blackstock, pushing her aside. Joanie looked towards Lucy for guidance, but Lucy just shrugged.

'Let her go,' she said. 'She'll find out by herself.'

Cursing and snivelling the housekeeper struggled up the stairs, clinging to the banister. Bitch! Bitch! Bitch! She'd show her! Once Ezekiel heard of the way she'd been treated, he'd teach the little slut a lesson! Oh, she'd pay. They'd all pay! Just wait! They'd soon be smiling on the other side of their faces.

Still muttering, she threw open the door of Master Watkins' chamber. 'Ezekiel…' she began, then stopped with her mouth open as she stared in horror at the drooling wreck of her erstwhile lover and master.

Throwing back her head, she howled like a wolf. 'Noooooooooooo!!!'

'Oh yes,' said Lucy from behind her. 'It's over now, for both of you.' She sauntered into the room. 'Now get your bag and leave, before I have you beaten again and thrown out.' Still sobbing, Mistress Blackstock stumbled from the room.

Lucy smiled. She held the upper hand now, and there were going to be changes.

She began first thing the next morning.

'Fetch me my cloak,' she told Joanie, after she had dressed and eaten.

'Yes, ma'am,' said Joanie, bobbing a curtsey. 'Are you going riding?'

'I am indeed,' Lucy confirmed. 'I am going to visit my parents.' Her heart lifted at the very words. It had been months since she had seen them and she could imagine

161

the expression on their faces when she rode in. 'Bring your own cloak, too,' she told the girl. 'You will accompany me.'

'Me?' said Joanie in horror. 'The only 'oss I ever been on were the one me dad used ter pull the plough. I can't ride!'

'Fiddlesticks,' said Lucy. 'I cannot go by myself. It wouldn't be fitting. Anyway, you won't be doing it yourself. You'll be riding pillion with one of the grooms. Now do as you're told and fetch those cloaks.'

Ten minutes later, Lucy was standing in the stable yard, with an extremely nervous Joanie hiding behind her, eyeing the horses with apprehension.

And she wasn't the only one who was apprehensive. Word of the master's condition and Mistress Blackstock's fate had already gone through the servants' quarters like wildfire, and the speedy dispatch of the stable boy who had tried to press his attentions on her had merely confirmed who held the reins now. The head stableman was almost obsequious in his attentions to his suddenly powerful mistress.

'The bay, ma'am?' he muttered, nodding his head and twirling his cap between his hands. 'Of course, ma'am. Whatever you say, ma'am.'

Lucy hid a smile. Good heavens, the man was so frightened of losing his post he was practically tugging his forelock. 'Thank you,' she said graciously as he helped her up into the saddle, and as she waited Joanie was hauled up behind the new stable lad, squeaking and trembling, where she perched like a bundle of laundry, hanging on to him like grim death. She gave a final shriek when they started moving, and they were off.

It was and hour and a half before they finally reached the familiar road leading to Lucy's former home, and she enjoyed every minute of it, though the same could not be said for Joanie. Leaving the other two to make their way more sedately, she dug her heels into the bay's sides and galloped up the tree-lined drive, threw herself down from the saddle and ran inside.

'Whaτ...?' began her mother, looking up as Lucy burst into the hall, then her sewing tumbled to the floor as she leapt to her feet and ran to embrace her daughter. 'Jeffrey! Jeffrey!' she shouted, clutching Lucy as if she might vanish again as suddenly as she'd appeared.

'What's all the pother,' grumbled Sir Jeffrey, striding into the hall. 'Can't a man get a little peace in his own home?' He stopped dead at the sight of his womenfolk laughing and crying in each other's arms. 'Good God, Lucy!' he gasped, clearing his throat to get rid of the unaccountable lump that seemed to have formed there. 'What brings you here? Has that damned husband of yours finally seen sense?'

'Not quite,' smiled Lucy, hugging him. 'It's a long story.'

She told it over wine and cakes, while Joanie and the stable lad were entertained in the kitchens. 'So you see, I am my own mistress once more,' she concluded.

'Serves the bastard right,' gloated Sir Jeffrey. 'Detestable toad of a man!' He looked at Lucy shrewdly. 'So what will you do now, my dear?'

'That's rather up to you,' she said. 'I wondered... could you spare Martha and perhaps one or two of our own servants?'

'Of course, my dear,' he beamed, and then paused thoughtfully. 'How about Jack and Harry; good Royalists both.'

'And Phyllis to give Martha a hand,' chimed in her

mother. 'She may be young, but she has a light hand in the kitchen, and a tongue that could clip cloth if needs be. Between them they should soon knock your household into shape.'

'That would be wonderful,' said Lucy. 'Where is Martha now? I'd like to tell her the news myself.'

Martha was in the linen press, putting away clean sheets, but at the sight of Lucy the sheets were left to their own fate. Scattering them to the four winds, she swooped on Lucy like a mother hen reunited with her chick.

'Oh, my pet,' she wept. 'I thought I'd never see you again.'

Disentangling herself Lucy was forced to tell her story all over again, and at the end of it Martha gave a satisfied smile. 'God rot the Puritan turd,' she said gleefully. 'Just what he deserves.' She patted Lucy's shoulder. 'And of course I'll come with 'ee, my love. Who else should take care of you but old Martha?'

By the end of the day everything was organised. Martha and Phyllis would come over the following afternoon with a baggage cart, with Jack and Harry accompanying them on horseback. 'And your father and I will visit on Sunday afternoon to see that all is settled,' added Lettice, kissing her daughter farewell. 'Take care, my love. Safe journey.'

She and Sir Jeffrey stood waving until Lucy and her tiny entourage disappeared.

Lucy was smiling as they cantered back through the dusk. It had been wonderful seeing her parents again, and everything was working out beautifully. Her smile widened as she heard the sound of female giggles interspersed with the stable lad's chuckles, coming from behind her. Hmmm, it seemed as if Joanie had got over her fear of riding, too!

There was an initial flurry of resentment as Martha established herself, but under her benevolent rule the household became more relaxed and homely. There was the occasional boxed ear in the kitchens, but no more savage beatings.

And so the long slow summer passed. Lucy felt as if she were in limbo, waiting endlessly for something to happen. Gradually she fell into a routine. Each morning she paid a wifely visit to her bed-bound husband, visited her parents once a week and dutifully attended meeting each Sunday.

There was one consolation to the latter. Master Oakley was gone, following his father to the grave in another brief moment of scandal. As he stood, overseeing his men as they dug the diversion to the river, the undermined bank had crumbled beneath his feet, pitching him headfirst into the swirling water. It was three days before they found the body, bloated and waterlogged, and hurried it into the grave.

He'd made few friends and there had been mutterings that he'd been 'about the Devil's work' and 'the devil reclaiming his own', but it was a nine-days' wonder. His replacement was an innocuous little man who's only vice was a fondness for the sound of his own voice, so there was little change there. It was as if Lucy was living in a little corner of her own, untouched by the hurly-burly of the world outside.

But things were changing.

In September the Lord Protector died, and his son, 'Tumbledown Dick', took over, amid much grumbling. England was sick of being 'protected'. Sick of being good. She wanted singing and dancing and revelry. She wanted the good old days back.

Lucy sighed and stabbed her needle viciously into her embroidery. A fat lot of use grumbling was. That had been a year ago now and nothing had happened. She could see her life stretching endlessly out before her, every day the same as the one before, as alike as beads on a string. She would be dead of old age before she'd ever lived!

The sound of hoof beats brought a brief flicker of excitement, which died almost as soon as it was born. She sagged back in her chair and sighed again. No doubt it was simply the reeve she had taken on to run the estate bringing exciting news of a pig farrowing or the quarterly accounts to be examined. She glanced up at the door, expecting him to enter, and was surprised to see Sir Jeffrey instead.

'Father,' she gasped, getting to her feet and hurrying to him. 'What brings you here so unexpectedly? Nothing is wrong, is it?'

'Wrong?' he grinned. 'Far from it. Everything is right again, at last.' He grabbed her and whirled her round, finally depositing her back on her feet, laughing and giddy. 'It's the king, my dear,' he informed her, barely able to contain his excitement. 'His majesty is coming home!'

'What?' gasped Lucy.

'It's true,' he said gleefully. 'He is on his way to reclaim his country even as we speak, and Roddy is with him. Thank God I lived to see this day.' He chuckled. 'Your mother is beside herself. She is cleaning the house from top to bottom, and every beast on the farm is in fear of its life lest it be part of the homecoming feast!' He rubbed his hands. 'Now what about a toast to his majesty and his safe journey home?'

By the time he had gone Lucy was half drunk with wine and joy. The king home again! And Roddy! And Jamie, her betrothed, the man she loved! Smiling, she performed a few dance steps in the empty hall.

Then suddenly she stopped short, her smile vanishing. How could Jamie be her betrothed when she was married already? And to a traitor, now that the tables were turned again. Master Watkins hung round her neck like a dead weight, dragging her down.

Her eyes narrowed as the doctor's words came back to her: 'The slightest shock could be fatal.'

For a moment she was stunned by the sheer enormity of what she was considering, then her mouth tightened. The man had blackmailed her into marriage, taken her innocence and, if fate had not intervened at the last minute, would cheerfully have watched her burn at the stake. The world would be a better place without him.

Making up her mind, she set off for the stairs.

When she entered his chamber he was slumped against the pillows, where his attendants had propped him. Time had not been kind to him. Although he had recovered enough use in his left side to feed himself, his hand lay on the coverlet like a claw. His speech was still unintelligible and his face still slack. She gazed at him, her nose wrinkling in disgust at the rank smell of his chamber. Lacking exercise and fed only on pap he had become massively bloated. It was like looking at a squatting toad. Horrifically, his mind was still intact, and his good eye glittered with hatred as he glared back at her, the other half-hidden beneath the drooping lid.

'Good morrow, husband,' she said, pulling up a chair beside the bed. He grunted something, drool spilling from his lips. 'Not pleased to see me? Fie upon you! And when I bring such good news, too,' she went on, smiling. He continued to glare at her in silence.

She leaned over and patted his hand. 'Come now,' she

said. 'Do you not wish to hear it? No? Well, I shall tell you anyway.' She leaned over and smiled into his face. 'The king is returning,' she informed him.

For a moment he continued to stare blankly and she thought he had not understood, then a slow tide of blood suffused his ruined features. His mouth opened and shut, but nothing came out.

'Yes, I thought you would be excited,' she said. 'After all, it concerns you deeply.' She examined her fingernails. 'So, husband, what do you think he will do to traitors like you?' she asked conversationally. 'D'you think he will have you hung, drawn and quartered? Or do you think he will be merciful and merely have you beheaded?'

He emitted a strange gargling noise, but she ignored it and widened her eyes innocently. 'Oh, how silly of me. I forgot; you are not of noble blood. I expect it will just be the gallows for the likes of you.' She looked at him thoughtfully. 'Though 'twill be a pother getting you up the gallows' steps in your condition.' She smiled again. 'Still, no doubt they'll find a couple of stout fellows to carry you to the gibbet,' she added cheerfully.

For a few seconds he stared at her in horror, then his eyes rolled up in his head and his entire body stiffened. He thrashed like a stranded fish, his head twisting back and forth on the pillows, but it did not last long. There was one long moaning susurration as the last breath left his lungs, his body voided itself in the final humiliation and he sagged back, his lifeless eyes staring blindly up at the bed canopy.

It was over. She had not laid a finger on him, but she had murdered him as surely as if she had stuck a knife in his black heart.

Closing her eyes she wrapped her arms around herself to still her trembling, her breath coming in shuddering gasps. Finally under control, she got shakily to her feet. There were arrangements to be made. At the chamber door she did not even pause to look back.

His life might be over – but hers was just beginning.

'Is there no sign of them yet?' asked Lettice, fretfully.

'No, mother,' said Lucy, peering out of the window and down at the empty drive, where her father was pacing back and forth impatiently. She turned back to her mother and rolled her eyes. 'And it's hardly surprising, since you asked me exactly the same question not two minutes ago. And two minutes before that as well.' Despite her sensible words, she couldn't help the feeling of excited anticipation bubbling up in her own tummy.

Her mother wasn't listening anyway. Instead she was looking around anxiously. 'Is everything ready, do you think? Is there anything I have forgotten?'

'Marry come up!' laughed Lucy. 'How could there be? You have spent the last two weeks preparing for Roddy's homecoming, and checked the house from top to bottom at least twice this morning already. There is not a speck of dust nor a cobweb to be found anywhere. The very mice are packing their bags and leaving, and there is enough food prepared to feed the king himself and his entire court!'

'I just want everything to be perfect,' said Lettice quietly. 'It has been so long.'

'I know,' agreed Lucy. 'And you have worked wonders.' She took her mother's hands. 'You look beautiful, too,' she added impulsively. 'Your gown is lovely. Roddy will think he is greeting some grand court lady instead of his mother.'

Lettice giggled girlishly. 'Get away with you,' she said, waving her hand. '*You* look beautiful. I look exactly what

I am; an old lady in an even older gown.' She ran a complacent hand over her dark blue satin. 'But I must say, the dressmaker has excelled herself in refurbishing it.' She pulled a face. 'And 'tis such a pleasure to be out of that never-ending black.'

Lucy smiled her agreement. Her own gown was of amber satin, and cut low enough to reveal the tops of her breasts and with a touch of lace at the sleeves, it made her feel the equal of any woman in the land. She had discarded her cheap wedding ring and replaced it with Jamie's emerald betrothal one, and the matching pendant nestled in the swell of her bosom.

A brief flicker of unease crossed her face. Master Watkins was barely two weeks in the ground and by rights, as a widow, she should wear black for at least a year. She shook it off. Damn convention! He had forced her into the marriage and she wasn't such a hypocrite as to put on mourning for him. She'd wear what she liked, and if that shocked society, then so be it.

Her thoughts were interrupted by a triumphant bellow from outside. Picking up their skirts, both women ran to the window. Sir Jeffrey waved up at them, grinning. 'They're here,' he called, pointing down the drive.

In the distance they could see a group of horsemen. As they watched one broke away and galloped headlong towards them. Reaching the top of the drive he flung himself off his horse and took Sir Jeffrey in his arms, pounding him on the back.

Laughing, Lucy ran down the stairs and out into the sunshine, her mother following more sedately behind.

'Roddy!' she squealed, throwing herself at him. Her brother lifted her off her feet, spun her round, bussed her soundly on both cheeks and deposited her back on her feet.

'Lucy,' he grinned. 'And so grown-up as well! Whatever happened to the tomboy I left behind?' Before she had time to answer her mother flew past her, and embraced her son as if she would never let him go, her head buried in his chest as she sobbed out her thankfulness at having him home again.

The rest of the group had arrived, but held back in deference to the family reunion. Instead they dismounted, talking quietly amongst themselves. Lucy's eye was caught by a thickset figure, whose dusty green velvet cloak made him stand out amongst the more muted colours of the servants' clothes.

'Who is that?' she whispered.

Roddy gawped at her in surprise. 'Good Lord, Lucy!' he exclaimed. 'I know we've been away for some time, but I'd have thought you would recognise your own betrothed. It's Jamie!'

It was her turn to gawp. She peered surreptitiously at the man, trying to see in him the lithe boy she remembered, but it was impossible. It couldn't be him! This man was stocky, his doublet straining over an incipient belly; his fine features slightly blurred by the signs of too much food and drink. He turned, caught her eye and smiled – and her doubts vanished as she recognised him at last.

'Jamie!' she gasped, running towards him. 'I barely knew you!' She stopped short in front of him, shyness overwhelming her. But he had no such compunction, and grabbing her he kissed her until she was breathless.

'But I'd have recognised you anywhere, sweetheart,' he said, letting her go. He looked her over. 'There's only one change.'

'What's that?' she asked apprehensively. Was he going to say she looked old? After all, she was over twenty now and almost past her prime.

'You look prettier than ever,' he said. She blushed and lowered her eyes, wondering how on earth she hadn't recognised him immediately. He hadn't changed a bit!

'Enough of all this mawkishness,' chuckled Sir Jeffrey, clapping his hands. 'What are we standing around here for? We have time enough and plenty to catch up with all the news over some decent food and drink.' He winked and clapped his son on the back. 'I hope you have an appetite, boy. Your mother has made enough meat to feed an army, and a good job too, since she has invited everyone in the county to share it.'

'It's been a long journey,' said Roddy, and he held out his arm to Lettice. 'Come, mother, lead on. I think we can do justice to all your hard work.'

In the event, he had to wait. The guests began to arrive, their carriages rolling up the long drive and disgorging them at the door, and each new arrival had to express their congratulations at Roddy and Jamie's safe return and in turn be regaled by tales of their exploits in the king's service. By the time they finally sat down to their meal it was almost ten at night.

But it was well worth waiting for. Lettice had excelled herself. Fresh salmon from their own river was followed by platter after platter of roast meats. Just when the guests thought they could eat no more, the servants staggered in under the weight of an enormous serving dish bearing a whole suckling pig, and after that came the sweetmeats: puddings and syllabubs, each richer and creamier than the last. And all of it washed down by the wines Sir Jeffrey had concealed in the depths of his cellars, waiting on the day his son would come home.

It was well after midnight by the time the meal finally ended, but the festivities had only just begun. The table was cleared and pulled aside, fresh candles lit, the fiddlers tuned up and the dancing began, led off by Lettice and Roddy and Lucy and Jamie, while Sir Jeffrey looked on, beaming proudly.

'No more!' Lucy protested after several dances. She pushed Jamie away, laughing. 'I am exhausted! And you have trodden on my poor feet more times than I care to think of!' She looked at him with mock reproach. 'I do believe you are tipsy, sirrah.'

'Never,' he grinned. 'Or if I am, it is your fault, for I am drunk on your beauty.' He bowed and led her from the floor. 'There, my love, you take your ease and I shall fetch you another glass of wine.' For a few moments she watched as he wove his way unsteadily through the other guests, then the fiddlers began again and she was distracted by the scene in front of her.

After years of Puritan drabness it was a riot of colour, though most of the women were wearing gowns whose style had gone out of fashion before the war. Some, like herself and her mother, had attempted to refurbish them in honour of the occasion, but many had not bothered. Here and there was the occasional lucky woman, whose men-folk had returned from abroad bringing the gift of one of the latest gowns from Paris, though these were few and far between. The candlelight flickered off earrings and necklaces and rings and brooches, released from their long incarceration in hidden jewellery boxes.

Even the men had been transformed from dull crows into gorgeous peacocks. Jackets and breeches in jewelled colours of rich ruby and scarlet and green had replaced the never-ending black, and like peacocks, they strutted and capered and preened before their womenfolk, celebrating the end of Cromwell's long reign and welcoming a new era of pleasure and indulgence.

She smiled up as Sir Roger, one of her father's oldest

friends, approached her, his wrinkled face rosy with drink and exertion. 'What's this?' he said gruffly. 'One of the prettiest women here, left sitting all alone? Can't have that, m'dear.' He bowed stiffly. 'May I have the pleasure of this dance?'

She glanced round. There was still no sign of Jamie. He must have got trapped in conversation with someone. So smiling back at Sir Roger, she got to her feet. 'T'would be my pleasure, kind sir,' she agreed, curtseying and dimpling up at him, and then she was swept back into the throng and forgot all about Jamie for the moment.

It was four in the morning before the weary fiddlers finally put down their bows. Sir Jeffrey took Lucy by the hand and led her to the front of the hall, where he tapped on the side of his glass with his ring until the laughing and chattering stopped and silence fell.

'Ladies and gentlemen, neighbours and friends,' he began, smiling round. 'As you know, my daughter had the misfortune to be wed – against my will, I might add – to that jumped-up jackanapes, Ezekiel Watkins.' There were mutterings of agreement from the assembled company, who knew the reason behind the marriage. 'Well, her sacrifice is over now,' he went on. 'And Master Watkins has gone to pay his dues in hell.' There was a muffled cheer. 'I know it is customary for a widow to wait at least a year before remarrying, but in this case I feel we can dispense with the formalities.' He held out his hand and Jamie came forward, swaying slightly. Sir Jeffrey clapped him on the back. 'My son and this young man must return to court, but I am sure the king will release them from their duties at Christmas, so I have great pleasure in announcing that the wedding of my daughter and Lord James Happington will take place on Christmas

174

Eve.' He grinned widely. 'And you're all invited to help us celebrate!'

Lucy stared from her father to Jamie in shock and joy, then as the guests applauded Jamie pulled her into his arms and kissed her soundly.

The next few months were a whirl of activity as Lucy attempted to get her affairs in order, and she was delighted to find that Master Watkins' penny-pinching had resulted in her becoming a very rich woman. And if she sold his shop – as no member of the aristocracy would wish to be tainted by 'being in trade' – then she would become even more so.

Ironically, whilst going through his papers she finally found the damning parchment that had resulted in her marrying him in the first place, though now it was no longer a symbol of treachery, but one of loyalty to the king. She smiled and laid it aside. One day she could show it to her grandchildren.

There were other, more exciting things to be seen, too. Her wedding dress, for a start. Lettice had found her old dressmaker and there were silks and satins to be chosen and fittings to be made. 'You look beautiful, my dear,' said Lettice, dabbing a tear from her eye as she looked at her daughter.

'Well, I feel like a pincushion!' said Lucy crossly. She glared at the seamstress kneeling at her feet. 'Will you never be done?'

'Almost finished, mistress,' mumbled the woman through a mouthful of pins. She put the last one in the hem and leaned back on her heels. 'There,' she said in satisfaction, 'and pretty as a picture you look, too.'

Lucy regarded herself in the cheval glass and laughed with pleasure. At the risk of sounding vain, she *did* look beautiful. As a token gesture to her widowed status the gown was of violet satin, inset with a V-shaped panel of white, embroidered in tiny silver roses. The full sleeves, caught at the elbow with ribbons, frothed out into a cascade of lace and when she whirled in front of the mirror, the full skirt belled out around her.

'If this doesn't put Jamie's eye out, nothing will,' she crowed.

'I should think so, too,' said Lettice smugly. 'Now come along. Take it off. 'Tis barely a fortnight till your wedding and there is work to be done.' Reluctantly Lucy allowed the seamstress and her assistants to slip the gown from her shoulders and they bustled out, promising that it, and the others, would be ready before the week was out.

The time flew by in an orgy of preparation. The wedding feast was to make Roddy's homecoming one look like a pauper's by comparison. Lettice rushed from one place to another overseeing it all, while Lucy was so busy she didn't have time to feel nervous.

Finally Christmas Eve and the hour of her wedding arrived. All was done: the great hall decked with holly and ivy; the food and drink readied; the servants dressed in their best. Her stomach fluttered with nerves as Joanie dressed her hair and fastened the ornate sapphire necklace – Jamie's wedding gift – around her neck.

'You look lovely, mistress,' beamed Joanie, stepping back to admire the effect of the glittering blue gems against the violet satin. 'I never seen a prettier bride.'

'Let's hope the groom thinks so, too,' said Lucy, nervously fingering the necklace.

'Of course he will,' said her father, coming into the room. 'He'd be blind if he didn't.' He stooped and kissed her cheek. 'You look ravishing, my dear.' He held out his arm. 'Now come along. Let's not keep the poor boy – and your mother – on tenterhooks.'

Smiling, she placed her hand on his arm and together they walked from the chamber.

At the door of the chapel she paused for a moment, taking in the scene before her. The ancient stones, which had witnessed so many christenings, weddings and funerals, glowed softly in the flickering light from the candles. Great swags of winter greenery and Christmas roses filled the air with their piercingly sweet scent. It was beautiful – and so different from the stark austerity of her first wedding.

At her entrance the low hum of voices fell silent and Jamie, standing at the altar with Roddy, turned to smile at her. She took her place beside him, repeating her vows in a clear voice as the vicar spoke the ancient words of the wedding ceremony. Finally they exchanged rings and were pronounced man and wife.

Solemnity past, they led the procession of guests to the hall and the celebrations began. Smiling servants staggered in with course after course of food – all of it washed down with massive quantities of wine – until not another morsel could be consumed. Then the real festivities started.

Laughing, Jamie whisked Lucy to her feet to lead off the first measure. After that she lost sight of him. In fact she hardly had time to draw breath as one guest after another seized the privilege of dancing with the bride. Dizzy with happiness and exhilaration, she barely felt her aching feet.

By the time she and Jamie were reunited and the pair of them were escorted to the bridal chamber – with many a saucy jest along the way – the first fingers of dawn light were beginning to streak the sky. And as she finally slipped beneath the covers with her new husband, a cock crew in the distance.

Alone at last, she turned to him – and was greeted by a resounding drunken snore. She smiled ruefully. Somehow this wasn't exactly how she'd envisioned her wedding night!

Propped on one elbow she looked down at his sleeping face and smiled indulgently. Ah well, if a man couldn't get drunk at his own wedding, when could he?

Snuggling down beside his warm body, she sighed in contentment. Anyway, what did one night matter? They had days and months and years – a whole lifetime – ahead of them to make love.

In her dreams she was back in the family chapel, walking down the aisle again. As she reached the altar her groom turned to her and she gasped in horror. It was not Jamie who turned to smile her – but the rotting corpse of Master Watkins, his grey and tattered lips parting in a demonic grin.

She tried to turn and flee, but her feet felt as if they were made of lead and she could not move. She tried to scream, but though her mouth opened nothing came out. As she stood rooted to the spot, the vicar repeated the age-old ceremony binding her irrevocably to the travesty of humanity beside her.

The final words spoken, one skeletal hand reached out and tore the wedding gown from her trembling body, then he threw her onto the altar, parted her legs and thrust himself upon her…

'Nooo!' she wailed, struggling to break free.

'Hell's teeth, you little bitch, stop your damned wriggling,' came Jamie's irritated voice. Her eyes flew open and she found herself looking up into his bloodshot ones. His breath was foul from stale wine and it was obvious he was still half-drunk.

'No Jamie, wait!' she begged, continuing her attempts to break free. 'Please! Not like this!'

'I've waited long enough, madam,' he snarled. 'Besides, you are no virgin, so you can spare me these maidenly vapours. You are my wife now, so perform your marital duties. Spread your damned legs!' Gripping her wrists to stop her arms flailing, he held them above her head while his free hand pulled up her nightgown and plundered the softness between her thighs.

Groaning with pleasure he pushed his swollen cock inside her, ignoring her whimpers of pain. She gave up the unequal struggle and lay there motionless, slow tears leaking from beneath her eyelids as he thrust and grunted his way to his own release. He gave one final shudder and his sweaty body collapsed on hers.

'God's truth, but you're a cold fish,' he complained as he finally rolled off her. 'That Puritan bastard's ruined you for a real man. I've had tuppenny whores who showed more enthusiasm.' Within moments he was asleep again, his drunken snores escaping from his slack lips.

Lying beside him with her romantic dreams in tatters, she tried to muffle her tears. God only knew what hardships he and Roddy had experienced during their long exile that had changed him so, but the Jamie she knew was gone, replaced by this heartless stranger. Even from the grave, Master Watkins and his ilk had stretched out their cold fingers to ruin her life. Would there be no escape?

Gritting her teeth against the stabbing pain between her thighs, she eased herself out of bed, careful not to disturb her sleeping husband. Dipping a cloth into the cold water from the basin, she dabbed her eyes to remove the redness from her weeping, then washed herself, carefully wiping away all traces of their lovemaking. She smiled bitterly. Lovemaking? Hah! He had used her like a cheap whore. The only difference was that at least a whore got paid!

Still, it was Christmas Day, and there were twelve more days of festivities to get through. After so many years without celebrations she did not wish to spoil this first one for everyone else. There was nothing do but put on a brave face and pretend she was happy with her lot.

Dressed in red satin to mark the season – though she felt far from celebrating – she went down to the hall. Her mother was already there, lighting candles to fend off the darkness of the day. At the sight of her daughter she stopped and came to her.

'A merry Christmas, darling,' she beamed, hugging her. 'Or should I say "my lady", now that you are Jamie's wife?' She glanced over her daughter's shoulder. 'And where is that handsome new husband of yours?'

'Still sleeping, I am afraid,' said Lucy, forcing a smile. 'I think he celebrated our marriage rather too well.'

'Men,' tutted Lettice, shaking her head. 'They're all the same. Your father is just as bad. He's like a bear with a sore head this morning.' She smiled indulgently at the foibles of the superior sex. 'Not that it has anything to do with the quantities of wine he drank last night. Oh no.' She winked at Lucy. ''Tis merely a megrim brought on by the poor weather. And even Roddy has gone out for a ride to clear his head.'

Lucy brightened at her mother's light-hearted comments, conveniently forgetting Jamie's cruel words. She smiled. Of course, what was she thinking of? No doubt every man in the county was feeling the results of her wedding celebrations this morning.

'Perhaps we should take a glass ourselves,' she said,

smiling at her mother. 'And drink a toast to their swift recovery.'

It was almost noon before any of the men-folk made an appearance, still looking rather the worse for wear. Lucy's last doubts were wiped away by the apologetic look Jamie flung her, before collapsing at the dinner table with his head in his hands. 'Never again,' he moaned.

'I should hope not,' she laughed. 'After all that wine, you snored fit to wake the dead.'

'Well, perhaps just *one* glass to settle my stomach,' he grinned, reaching for the bottle. 'A hair of the dog that bit me.'

Christmas Day was a muted celebration after the wedding. They ate lightly at midday, and then exchanged their own gifts. Afterwards the servants lined up to receive theirs, and then retired to the servants' hall to their own celebrations.

While the men remained at home, talking of horses and hunting in front of the fire, Lucy and her mother took the carriage and went round the estate, handing out baskets of food to the poorer families. When they returned they dined quietly *en famille*, attended church in the evening then sat around the candlelit table, playing cards.

It would have been a pleasant day if it had not been for one thing. Jamie's 'one glass' of wine had become two, then three, until finally all pretence of abstention was gone. By the time ten o'clock came round he was as drunk as he'd been the night before.

'Well, I am for my bed,' said Sir Jeffrey, throwing down his cards and yawning. 'We are invited to the Montague's tomorrow. I had best save my strength for the dancing.'

'And I,' agreed Lettice.

'One more hand,' protested Jamie, reaching for his glass

and almost knocking it flying. 'The night is young yet.'

'But we are not,' smiled Lettice, getting to her feet. 'I can hardly read my cards any longer.'

'Neither can Jamie,' said Roddy, with a wink. He grinned at his friend and nodded pointedly at the half dozen coins left lying in front of him. 'God's truth, man, if we were playing for gold instead of pennies, I would own you body and soul by this time.'

'Then give me a chance to win some of it back,' said Jamie sulkily. 'It's damned bad form to leave the table when you're winning.'

'Not a problem you're ever likely to have,' joked Roddy. 'Oh, all right then, since it's Christmas. Just a couple more games though.' He glanced up at Lucy as he gathered in the cards and began to shuffle them again. 'What about you, sister? Are you in?'

'No, thank you,' said Lucy, smiling through stiff lips. 'You two stay and enjoy yourselves. I think I shall retire as well.' As she left the hall, the last thing she heard was Jamie calling for one of the manservants to bring in a fresh bottle.

In the wedding chamber she lay unsleeping, rigid as a board, waiting for him to come to bed. It must have been one in the morning before she finally dozed off, and there was still no sign of her errant husband.

She awoke with a jerk, to find the winter sun beating full in her bedroom window, and the bed beside her still empty. She smiled with relief. She had misjudged him. He couldn't have been as drunk as she thought. He must have come to bed soon after she fell asleep, then got up at the crack of dawn to go riding with Roddy.

But she was wrong. When she entered the hall the first thing she saw was Jamie, sitting slumped over the table with his head in a pool of spilt wine. The cards were scattered round him and an empty bottle lay toppled beside the burnt-out candles. Her nose wrinkled in distaste at the string of drool trickling from his half-open mouth.

The sound of footsteps made her turn. It was Roddy. 'Hell's teeth,' he muttered ruefully. 'He told me he was going to bed after he'd finished his last glass.'

'Well obviously he didn't,' snapped Lucy. 'Help me get him upstairs before mother and father come down.'

'Leave it to me,' said Roddy cheerfully. He shook Jamie's shoulder. 'Come on, old chap. Time for bed.'

'Eh, wha...?' slurred Jamie, looking at them blearily and getting slowly to his feet. Roddy stooped, flung his friend over his shoulder, stamped upstairs and deposited him on the bed, where he grunted, rolled over and promptly fell asleep again.

'Don't look so glum,' said Roddy, clapping Lucy on the shoulder. 'He's not always like this. When he's sober there's not a better man in the country.'

'How very comforting,' Lucy said tartly. 'Well, I shall not hold my breath. Two days we have been married and he hasn't drawn a sober breath yet.'

Roddy took her by the shoulders and shook her gently. 'Be a little more understanding, sister,' he chided. 'You don't know what it was like in exile. The frustration of being able to do nothing but drink and wench and gamble to pass the time. It saps a man.' He smiled reassuringly. 'But we are home now. The responsibilities of court will soon put him back on the straight and narrow. You'll see.'

Lucy regarded her comatose husband doubtfully. 'I do hope so,' she sighed.

Roddy was right. By the time they set off for the Montague's, Jamie had woken, washed, shaved and changed into clean clothes and was perfectly presentable.

Although his hands shook and he was a trifle green about the gills, he was perfectly sober – and stayed that way.

He accepted a glass of wine from their host, but it remained untouched at his elbow, while he spent the evening dancing attendance on his new bride. When they reached home and the privacy of their bedchamber he made slow, sweet love to her, gently caressing her breasts and thighs until she whimpered with lust and begged him to take her. And when he finally entered her and drove her to the pinnacle of desire, the memory of her abortive wedding night was washed away by a wave of exquisite pleasure.

He remained sober, too. The remaining days of his stay were spent riding whenever the weather permitted; visiting friends and relations and spending pleasant evenings playing cards and forfeits with Roddy, her parents and whatever guests they had. It was the happiest she had been since she was a child.

All too soon the twelve days of Christmas passed and it was almost time for Roddy and Jamie to go back to court. Before that she and Jamie left Lucy's parent's house to spend their last few days at their own.

'Are you all right?' she asked anxiously as their carriage jolted over the rough track. He was sitting tight-lipped and scowling, and had barely spoken a word to her since they waved goodbye to her family.

'Of course,' he snapped. 'Why should I not be?'

'I don't know,' she said helplessly. 'But you seem displeased.'

'What have I to be displeased about?' he muttered. 'I married a rich woman, didn't I?'

She stared at him in bewilderment. Was he resentful of

the land and money she had inherited from Master Watkins? Surely not. Legally it was his now, not hers, and most men were grateful to wed an heiress. Even the most boss-eyed, crook-toothed simpleton could be guaranteed a husband if her dowry were great enough. It was just the way of the world.

Her puzzled thoughts were interrupted by their arrival at the house. Leaving her to get down by herself he climbed out and stood, staring up at it with his arms folded and a twisted smile on his lips.

'Not bad,' he sneered, spitting on the ground. 'Not bad at all. In fact, I'd say you got a pretty fair reward for your whoring.'

She stared at him open-mouthed. So that was it. It wasn't the land and money at all. It was male jealousy, pure and simple. She smiled, for it was quite flattering really.

But the smile was a mistake. He turned and glared at her. 'I am glad you find the subject so amusing.' His eyes narrowed. 'Perhaps you'd have preferred if I had remained abroad and allowed you to continue in your sluttish ways.' Turning his back on her he stalked inside, leaving her to hurry after him.

Despite its lack of a mistress over the Christmas season, the house was looking its best. If the servants had been remiss in their duties while she was away, there was no sign of it. Martha had returned two days before and any traces of the servants' own celebrations had been swiftly removed.

If Jamie was impressed, he did not show it. As he strode from room to room, taking in the improvements Master Watkins had made, his scowl became blacker and blacker. He looked more like a man who'd had his last penny stolen, rather than one who had come into a fortune. Lucy trailed along in his wake, watching him anxiously.

'Well?' she asked eventually.

'The house looks better now than it did when it belonged to Sir Roland,' he said grudgingly, but her relief was short-lived. 'Of course, he wasn't a profiteering Puritan bastard like your first husband, was he?' he went on bitterly. 'Living off the fat of the land while better men went without.'

Lucy did not answer; the mood he was in, whatever she said would be wrong.

'Anyway, I have seen enough,' he snapped. 'I am going to the library. Send in the grieve and I shall go over the books.' He smiled unpleasantly. 'Since I am married to a whore, I might as well see what else she has earned me.' He paused at the door. 'And one more thing. Have one of the servants bring wine. I seem to have a foul taste in my mouth.'

'Pour it into a jug and water it well,' she ordered one of the maids, watching anxiously as the girl obeyed her. 'A little more water,' she said. 'There, that should do it. Off you go.' At least this way he would not get drunk quite so easily.

But she was wrong yet again. The girl was back in five minutes, clutching the shards of the jug and with her apron splattered with wine stains. 'He flung it at me, ma'am,' she sulked. 'Told me not to serve 'im such muck and to fetch 'im a couple of bottles. Swore at me, too,' she added tearfully.

'Never mind,' sighed Lucy. 'Go and change your apron and I'll send one of the men.' So much for that little subterfuge.

He was closeted with the grieve for most of the day, calling only for more wine at regular intervals. Lucy had a tray of food sent in at midday, but it was returned untouched. Her heart sank, but she busied herself about the house, pointlessly overseeing small tasks to keep her mind off the situation.

Even when the grieve left he did not appear for dinner, and she sat in solitary splendour, barely able to eat herself. When the candles burned low she resigned herself to going to bed alone as well. It was probably for the best. With any luck he had drunk himself into a stupor as he had done on Christmas night.

In her chamber she sat in front of her mirror and allowed Joanie to brush out her hair. Her head ached abominably, as if she'd been the one drinking too much wine, she thought wryly. Then as she stood up to allow Joanie to slip her gown from her shoulders, the door swung open.

'Well, well, well,' slurred Jamie. 'If it isn't my little wife, preparing for her innocent slumbers.'

'You may leave, Joanie,' said Lucy, keeping her voice steady. 'I can manage now.'

'But…' began Joanie, looking doubtfully at the swaying figure in the doorway.

'I said leave,' repeated Lucy. 'Now.'

With one last nervous glance at her master, Joanie fled.

Jamie stepped into the room and banged the door shut behind her. 'Very nice,' he grinned, looking round the chamber. 'So this is where you did your whoring, is it?' His bloodshot eyes glittered in the candlelight and he took a lurching step towards her. She moved quickly aside and he stumbled and sat down heavily on the bed. He patted the coverlet. 'Spread your legs for him here, did you?' he smirked. 'Beg him to fuck you?' The smirk vanished. 'I'll wager you did, you little trollop. I'll bet you couldn't get enough of his big Puritan prick.'

She edged slowly towards the door. If she could get out now he would probably fall into a drunken sleep and remember nothing of this by morning.

Unfortunately she had misjudged him. Before she could make good her escape he lunged to his feet and seized her by the scruff of her neck. 'Well, we'll soon see who's the better man,' he hissed, shaking her. 'Get that dress off, you treacherous bitch. I'm going to give you a taste of Cavalier cock to compare it with.'

'Take your hands off me,' she squealed, struggling in his grip. A kick in the shins made him relax his hold, but as she started for the door he caught her hair and hauled her back. Then still holding her he locked the door and pocketed the key.

'Get it off, I said,' he spat, twisting her hair in his fist till she whimpered. 'Or I'll rip the damned thing off your back.'

'All right, all right,' she whimpered, and with a final shake he released her and sat back down on the bed. As slowly as she dared, she slipped the scarlet gown from her shoulders and allowed it to fall to the floor. Her silken undergarments followed until she stood before him, her naked body gleaming in the firelight.

He licked his lips, gloating over her full breasts, the sweet curve of hip and belly and the soft V of curls that concealed her private parts. 'As pretty a little traitor as I've ever seen,' he leered.

It was too much. Before she realised what she was about to do, her hand swung up and she slapped him so hard her breasts quivered. His head rocked with the force of the blow. 'How dare you?' she said. 'I am no traitor, and well you know it. I was forced into that damned marriage to protect my father.'

He stared at her in shock, rubbing his unshaven cheek, and then he began to grin again. 'So you like it rough, do you, madam?' he said, with a lascivious leer. 'Then who am I to deny you?'

His hand flew out and caught her by the wrist. Biting her lip she dug her bare feet in and tried to pull away, but even in his drunken state he was too strong for her. He jerked and she lost her balance and toppled forward into his lap.

'Let me go!' she panted.

'What, so you can slap me again?' he chuckled. 'I think not, madam. The boot is on the other foot now.' Hauling her over his knee he eyed her wriggling bottom with gleeful anticipation, and raised his arm. 'You asked for this, my fine lady, and now you're going to get it.'

His hand was broad, and hard from years of riding. When he brought it down on her squirming backside the noise was like a pistol shot. The blow left a perfect scarlet imprint of his hand on the pale skin of her buttocks and she shrieked in pain and indignation. Tears of rage and humiliation trickled down her cheeks. How dare he spank her like an ill-behaved child?

His hand came down again, and again, making the plump globes of her bottom jerk and quiver. The pain redoubled as the blows rained down on her already tender flesh, and all conscious thought was lost in a mist of agony.

Her entire backside was scarlet now, in shocking contrast to the rest of her pale body, but that did not deter him. Quite the reverse, in fact. Her struggles served only to incite him to punish her further, and even worse, she was horrified to feel his manhood swelling and digging into her tummy.

'Nooooo!' she wailed.

'Oh yes, my sweet,' he panted, then twisting he rolled

her off his lap onto the bed, pulled her legs apart and knelt between them. Slowly he began to unbuckle his breeches. His erect cock sprang free, swelling even further as he gloated over his helpless victim. His breath came faster as his eyes lingered over her heaving breasts, then his gaze drifted down to the parted lips of her vulva that revealed the moist pinkness within.

'Methinks the lady doth protest too much,' he smirked, and she whimpered as he leaned over and fondled her breasts, tweaking the nipples into hardness, then ran his down hand down over her belly to investigate the soft cleft below. His fingers slid smoothly into her hot wetness, and when he withdrew them they were glistening with her juices. 'By God, I was right,' he gloated. 'You *are* a whore. You are as ready as a bitch in heat.'

She closed her eyes to shut out the sight of his leering face, but she could not shut out the sensations his exploring fingers sent racing through her. Each touch was one of exquisite torture as the throbbing pain of her spanking blended seamlessly with the heat of her arousal, until she no longer knew where agony ended and pleasure began.

She whimpered again, this time with desire. Seizing her, he pulled her legs upward until her ankles were on his shoulders, his swollen penis pressing tantalisingly against the entrance to her body. She raised her hips and pressed against him like a cat, feeling the delicious heat radiating from him.

He took his cock in his hand and rubbed the swollen head up and down between the lips of her sex, until she thought she would go mad with frustration, then her eyes opened in shock as he plunged forward, burying the full length of his cock inside her.

She groaned as he began to move, withdrawing then thrusting again, each stroke carrying her further towards the pinnacle of pleasure. The sight of his thick shaft sliding in and out of her served only to inflame her more and she lifted her hips to meet each thrust, taking him deeper and deeper until she thought she might split in half.

Panting, he thrust faster and faster until he stiffened, and the jerk and shudder of his cock and the hot splatter of his seed sent her over the edge to spiral into the exquisite explosion of her own release. They collapsed against each other, sticky with sweat, struggling to regain their breath... and within moments Jamie was snoring.

As her senses slowly returned, Lucy was overwhelmed with shame at her own behaviour, but even worse, with doubts for the future. She was married to a drunkard who treated her like a whore. Had she escaped from one foul beast only to fall into the hands of another?

She bit back her tears in the darkness. Thank God he was going back to court. Perhaps by the time she joined him he would have come to his senses.

It was another two months before the roads were fit enough to travel on by coach, and Lucy could finally follow him to court. Despite this, it seemed little enough time to arrange everything.

The days passed in a whirl of organising and packing. Shoes and petticoats and stomachers and gowns and ribbons draped every available surface of her chamber. Great iron-bound wooden chests lay around, their contents spilling out as she tried to decide what must be taken and what must be left behind, driving her maidservants mad as she changed her mind half a dozen times a day.

More gowns had to be ordered, too. The king's coronation was to be in May, and it would not do for my Lady Happington to attend wearing anything less than befitted her station. The latest fashion books were ordered from London, pored over and her dressmakers almost worked their fingers to the bone copying them. 'Thank goodness, that's the last one,' groaned Lucy as they left. 'I have stood rigid for so many fittings I feel like a tailor's dummy, and if I'd had to look at one more bolt of cloth I should have run mad.'

'How can you say that, ma'am?' protested Joanie. She smoothed her own new russet silk skirts with a possessive hand, and there were another two, just as pretty, already packed away. She could hardly believe her luck. She sighed with contentment. 'I never had so many beautiful gowns in my life.'

'Well, I can hardly have my lady's maid looking like a scarecrow,' said Lucy. 'We may be country boobies, come up to town, but let's try our best not to look it.'

'You could never look like a country booby,' said Joanie, outraged at the very thought. 'You'll be the prettiest lady at court. You jus' wait an' see.'

'I wish I had your confidence,' said Lucy wryly. 'Still, fine feathers make fine birds, so they say, and heaven knows we have fine feathers in plenty.' She rolled her eyes. 'I swear I shall need another chest just to put those new gowns in.'

They were delivered the following week, along with the account. Lucy looked at the sum and gave an unladylike whistle. Good Lord, being fashionable didn't exactly come cheap! She shrugged. Still, no doubt it would be worth it to hold her head high at court.

'Go and see the grieve and have him give you a hundred pounds from the strongbox,' she told Joanie. 'I shall settle this debt now.'

'Thank you, ma'am,' said the dressmaker, smiling in grateful relief. Thank goodness the Carstairs belonged to the old school and believed in paying their bills on time. So many of her new clients tended to pay in promises, and she had her living to make.

Joanie was back in five minutes, empty-handed. She twisted a fold of her apron nervously in her fingers. 'Sorry, Miss Lucy,' she quavered. 'He says there ain't no money left.'

Lucy stared at her, incredulous. 'Is he mad?' she demanded. 'What about the autumn rents? And the money from the sale of Master Watkins' shop? There was nigh on fourteen thousand pounds in that strongbox.' She nodded at the dressmaker. 'Excuse me one moment,' she said grimly. 'I shall see to this matter myself.' Picking up her skirts she stalked from the room, her high heels clacking on the floor.

'I don't believe it,' Lucy gasped, staring at the strongbox. It was bare except for a few small coins lying forlornly on the bottom.

'The master emptied it before he left,' the grieve informed her.

She stared at him. 'And you did not think to inform me?' she said cuttingly. She looked at the man's crestfallen face and relented slightly. 'No, of course not, why should you?' she said bitterly. 'After all, he is master now.'

She thought rapidly for a few moments. 'Does Master Hawkins still wish to buy those fields on the south pasture?' she demanded.

'Why yes, ma'am,' said the grieve, in surprise. 'But I thought you didn't want to sell.'

'I don't,' she confirmed, 'but his lordship has left me no option. Ride across immediately. I want cash in hand, and bring the money to me as soon as you return.' In the meantime, thank God, there was still some fifty pounds hidden in the bottom of her old cedar chest. That would do on account for the moment. She would settle the balance when Master Hawkins paid her.

And when she got to London, she would settle the reckoning with her husband as well!

'Criminy!' gasped Joanie, peering out of the coach window. ''Tis not a town, 'tis a bloomin' fair!'

Lucy smiled and leaned back, trying to look unimpressed, but it was difficult. There was so much to look at she was hard pressed not to gawk like a bumpkin herself. She'd never seen so many people in her life.

The place teemed like an anthill: whores and hawkers; street vendors crying their wares; lavender sellers; milkmaids with yokes on their shoulders; beggars rubbing shoulders with baronets; urchins running in and out amongst the carriage wheels; fine ladies strolling with their gallants.

The noise was appalling – and as for the stench! It beggared belief. Which was hardly surprising when the very streets ran with raw filth tipped from chamber pots into the gutters. Catching sight of the bloated body of a dead cat, she shuddered and buried her nose in her pomander, blessing Martha for insisting she carry the clove-studded orange 'to ward off evil airs'.

They bumped to a halt for the hundredth time as a cartload of cheeses blocked the road. Lucy sighed and fanned herself against the formidable heat. There was a scraping noise as someone scrambled up the side of her carriage and thrust a grubby hand in the window. Lucy recoiled at the sight of its owner's face, almost eaten away by a suppurating sore.

'Spare a copper, my lady,' whined the beggar.

Eyes averted, she fumbled in her bag for a few pennies

and flung them at him, which was a mistake. The next minute they were surrounded by a mob of ragged figures, scrambling over each other to reach them. The coach rocked alarmingly and Lucy had visions of them being toppled out into the reeking gutter and set upon.

'Get out of it,' snarled the coachman, flicking at them with his whip. The beggars fell back cursing, the cheese cart finally lumbered out of the way and they lurched forward again. Lucy sighed, every bone in her body aching with exhaustion. At this rate they would never reach Whitehall!

But if she thought her troubles would be over by the time they got there, she was sadly mistaken. The palace was as much a warren as the city itself. There was no sign of Jamie eagerly awaiting his bride's arrival, and it took her coachman half an hour – and a hefty bribe – to locate his apartments and find one of the palace servants to escort her there.

Footsore and weary, she and Joanie followed the footman's liveried back through the maze of passages and reception rooms, too tired even to appreciate the luxury of their new surroundings. Their progress was followed by groups of chatting courtiers. The men casually assessed her charms while the women eyed her country dress with barely hidden amusement. Lucy smarted beneath their contemptuous gaze, wishing she'd worn some of her new finery to travel in, instead of her oldest gown.

Finally he led them up a flight of stairs, along a corridor and stopped in front of a carved door. 'Lord Happington's apartments, my lady,' he announced.

'Thank you,' she smiled, and he hovered expectantly until it dawned on her and she fumbled in her bag and pressed a shilling into his waiting hand. Good Lord, her remaining money wouldn't last long at this rate.

He pocketed it with a look of contempt. 'I believe his lordship is abed... er... resting, madam,' he said with an insolent smirk, before walking off. She stared after him. What was so damned amusing about that?

Pushing the door open she walked inside, to find herself in an ornate anteroom. There was another door at the far end. Ah, that must be the bedchamber. Leaving Joanie to admire her new surroundings, she walked across to investigate. Pushing that door open too she stepped through – and her jaw dropped in horror as the sight of her husband's bobbing buttocks greeted her.

No wonder the footman had smirked. Jamie was abed all right – but he was not alone!

With a squawk the unknown woman leapt from Jamie's bed, grabbed her clothes from the floor and clutched them to her bosom to hide her nakedness. Casting one last horrified glance at Lucy, she fled past her.

Lucy ignored her and concentrated on her erring husband. 'So this is what you spend my money on,' she hissed. 'Cheap trollops!'

If she'd expected him to cringe and apologise, she was disappointed. He simply rolled on his back, put his hands behind his head and grinned up at her. 'Two things, my dear wife,' he smirked. 'First, it is *my* money now that we are wed, and second, that was no whore, that was Lady Edmont. And damned expensive she was too! I had to buy her a diamond bracelet before she would condescend to share her favours.'

Lucy gawped at him, her rage warring with her hurt and bewilderment. 'But... but we are barely married two months!' she gasped. 'How could you betray me so?'

'That's rich coming from a woman who married another while she was still betrothed to me,' he sneered, and ignoring his nakedness he swung his legs out of bed and began to dress. 'And besides, my love, you are at court now. You must forget your provincial ways. Faithfulness is considered frightfully old-fashioned nowadays.' Dressed, he picked up a gold-topped cane and sauntered towards the door.

'Wh-where are you going?' she stammered.

'I have an appointment to dine, my dear,' he said. 'But no doubt I shall see you later. *Au revoir.*' Blowing her a mocking kiss, he disappeared, leaving her standing dumbfounded.

Not for long. She was here now – and she was damned if she'd allow his behaviour to ruin her life. If that was the way he wanted things, then so be it, but he would find it a lot harder to carry on his whoring with a wife in residence. And those sheets could go for a start! Rolling up her sleeves she set about establishing her presence. Going to the door she collared the first footman who passed, tipped him five pounds and began issuing orders. Within fifteen minutes a stream of servants began arriving, staggering beneath the weight of her chests.

It took longer than she thought with only herself and Joanie to do the unpacking, but at last she was finished. She looked round in satisfaction. That was better. She had stamped her presence on the apartments. Her gowns hung in the garderobe. Her brush, comb and jewel box lay on the table in front of the mirror. The very air was redolent of her scent.

The small ormolu clock on the mantle-shelf chimed the hour. Ten o'clock. Where had the time gone? She stretched and pressed her hands to the small of her aching back. She was exhausted, and Joanie was drooping too.

'That's enough,' she told the girl. 'I am for my bed. You may sleep with me tonight. We shall find a truckle

197

bed for you tomorrow.'

'But what about the master?' asked Joanie. 'Where will he sleep?'

'Wherever he pleases,' said Lucy, with a toss of her head. 'He need not think he can share a bed with some trull then come crawling back to mine – and if he tries, he will find the door locked against him.'

When they woke late next morning there was still no sign of him. Lucy smiled bitterly. No doubt he had unfinished business with my Lady Edmont. After all, he still had to get his money's worth for that diamond bracelet.

Pushing the thought aside, she sent a timorous Joanie down to try and find the kitchens. It was almost two hours before she returned, bearing a plate of cold food.

'Criminy, ma'am, 'tis like a rabbit warren here,' she gasped. 'Lord knows how many times I got lost before one of the footmen showed me the way.' Her blush suggested that that was not all he had shown her!

'Ugh,' muttered Lucy, taking a bite. 'If this is the best the king's kitchen has to offer, I think we should have brought Martha with us as well.' Taking a slice of meat in her hand, she wandered over to the window and looked out over the gardens and walks.

Down below she could see a tall, dark-haired man, surrounded by courtiers and a pack of yapping spaniels, walking towards the palace – and almost dropped her food. 'My God!' she gasped. ''Tis the king himself!' Pushing the casement open she leaned out to get a better look.

'Where?' demanded Joanie, rushing to her side, her eyes widening. 'And a fine, handsome fellow he is too!' she exclaimed, and forgetting her place in her excitement, she nudged Lucy in the ribs and winked. 'I wouldn't mind a taste of his rod and sceptre, would you?'

'Joanie!' gasped Lucy, and then they both dissolved in giggles.

Hearing the sound, the king looked up, to see two pretty new faces. His own broke into an answering smile, his teeth startlingly white against his swarthy skin, and he lifted his hand and waved. Plucking up their courage they waved back, then disappeared inside.

'Wait'll they hear this back home,' gloated Joanie. 'The king hisself! And he waved at *me*!' Her face fell. 'I'll bet none of 'em believe it.'

'Well, you'll have me to vouch for it,' smiled Lucy.

A rap on the door made them look at each other in surprise. 'Who can that be?' asked Lucy. 'I doubt if my dear husband would bother to knock. Quick Joanie, go and answer it.' Smoothing her skirts, she seated herself in front of the mirror and waited for her unexpected visitor to be ushered in.

And what a visitor it was. The woman who entered was both beautiful and arrogant. Gorgeously dressed, she swept in as if she owned the place, and stood in the centre of the room taking everything in, before finally taking a seat. Lucy disliked her instinctively.

'My... my Lady Castlemaine,' squeaked Joanie.

Lucy suppressed the desire to gawp at the woman. Even in the country they had heard of this tempestuous female, who'd become his majesty's mistress at Breda, when she'd been plain Mistress Palmer. Instead she nodded graciously. 'My Lady Castlemaine,' she smiled. 'To what do I owe the pleasure of your visit?'

'Call me Barbara,' drawled the woman, fanning herself languidly. She ran her eyes over Lucy and smiled. 'I have come to welcome you to court, and invite you to an intimate little supper this evening. It will give you a chance to meet people before you are formally presented to Charles.' She smirked. 'I mean, his majesty.'

'Th-that's very kind of you,' said Lucy.

'Not at all, my dear,' the woman said patronisingly. 'All this must seem very confusing to someone fresh from the country.' She got to her feet again. 'Well, I must be off. Charles and James are taking me to the play this afternoon. I shall see you this evening.' In a rustle of silk and satin, she took her leave.

'Bitch!' snapped Lucy, once she'd gone. '"Welcome you to court" indeed! The only reason she came was to look me over.' Unfortunately, what smarted most was the fact that she'd obviously been dismissed out of hand as no rival.

Lucy sighed. The trouble was that she was right. So much for all her preparations. Her gowns, the very epitome of style in the country, were already hopelessly outdated and dowdy here. Even the low-cut necklines that had seemed so daring at home were positively Puritan at court. Why, Lady Castlemaine's bodice had barely covered her voluptuous breasts! Lucy had expected them to spill out every time the woman took a breath!

There was nothing for it. She would have to find a seamstress here at court and begin all over again. Her lips set. The little she had left from the sale of those fields to Hawkins would not last long. It was time to have a little word with her husband.

'What do you mean, there's nothing left?' she shrieked. 'There must be! Even you cannot have drunk fourteen thousand pounds away in only two months!'

'I had debts to pay,' he said sulkily. 'That's where it went.' A self-pitying expression crossed his face. 'And must you screech like a fishwife?' he went on, putting a hand to his brow. 'My head is splitting.'

She stared at him in disgust. Hardly surprising when he'd arrived back at his apartments befuddled with drink. Again. Still, there was no point antagonising him. If she was to wheedle some money out of him, she would do better to cozen him than give vent to her true feelings. Forcing herself to smile, she stroked his forehead.

'Poor sweeting,' she cooed. 'Why don't you lie down? When Joanie comes back from the kitchens I shall have her make you a posset.' He nodded in agreement and she put her arm round his waist and led him to the bedchamber, helped him remove his coat and knelt to slip off his shoes. He slumped onto the bed and was asleep in moments.

Shocked at how low she'd sunk, she emptied the pockets of his coat. Nothing but a few shillings. She was about to give up when he grunted and rolled over to lie fully splayed out on the coverlet, and hearing a soft chinking sound she looked more closely and saw a bulky bulge in his breeches. She began to smile.

Slowly and carefully she reached over and slid her hand into the tight pocket. She felt his cock harden at her touch and she froze until he grunted and relaxed once more, allowing her to continue her investigations. Finally her fingers closed round a leather bag and she drew it out.

Back in the anteroom she spilled the contents onto the table, her eyes widening. There must be at least four hundred sovereigns there! She began to count them, putting them in small piles of ten. When she had finished she had forty-five stacks in front of her. It was an even better haul than she'd expected. Of course she couldn't take it all, so she made up her mind to take three hundred and replace the rest. He was so drunk he probably wouldn't even notice it had gone.

She tapped her lips. But what should she do now? No doubt if she left it where he could find it, it would vanish as quickly as the rest of her money had, and the remains of the sale money too.

It was Joanie who inadvertently provided the answer on her return, by tripping and almost sending her tray flying. 'Bloody floor,' she grumbled, kicking at the bump in the turkey carpet. 'Think in the king's ruddy palace they'd manage to fix things proper, wouldn't you?'

Lucy stared at her with her mouth open. 'You're a genius,' she cried, leaping to her feet and kissing the bewildered girl. 'Quick, help me roll up the carpet.'

Within moments the loose floorboard had been prised up, the money secreted safely beneath it and the carpet rolled back into place. Lucy sat back on her heels and smiled. There, let him try and get his hands on it now.

Getting to her feet, she dusted her hands and smiled at Joanie. 'Now we have dealt with that, there is only one problem left. And a pressing one it is, too.'

'What's that, ma'am?' asked Joanie.

'Isn't it obvious?' said Lucy with mock innocence. 'Whatever am I going to wear to Lady Castlemaine's dinner?'

By the time the gathering drew near Lucy's panic was mounting. She had already tried on and discarded almost every gown she possessed. Finally she settled on a midnight-blue velvet with silver lace at neck and sleeves.

A visit to the Royal Exchange that afternoon had provided more of the essentials that no court lady worth the name could possibly manage without. Lucy reached for one now, an ornately scrolled silver patch-box, and applied one of the patches slightly to the lower left of her lips and glowered at her reflection. 'God's truth!' she wailed. 'I look as if I have the pox!'

'Nonsense, Miss Lucy,' smiled Joanie. ''Tis the very height of fashion. I swear that every man there will want to kiss it.'

'More fool them, then,' muttered Lucy. 'The damned thing will probably fall off.' She applied rose-coloured lip salve, coloured her eyelids and dipped a rabbit's foot in powder to dust her face and shoulders. That done, she allowed Joanie to brush her hair and pin it into ravishing bunches of curls at her temples. Sapphire earrings and her magnificent wedding necklace completed her toilette. Lucy regarded herself again, and this time she smiled. The girl staring back from the mirror looked the very epitome of a fine court lady. Her confidence returned. She would give Lady Castlemaine a run for her money, yet.

She stood up, reached for her fan and was halfway towards the door when it opened and Jamie strolled in – sober for once. His eyes widened at the sight of her. 'Odds bodkins, madam,' he drawled, 'but you look fine this evening.'

Too pleased with herself to hold a grudge, she swept him a deep curtsey and smiled up at him from beneath her lashes. 'Thank you, kind sir,' she dimpled. 'We are invited to dinner by Lady Castlemaine.'

'I fear not,' he said. 'We have an appointment elsewhere with some friends of mine.'

Her smile vanished. 'Then cancel it,' she snapped. 'Your friends can wait. The king's mistress cannot.'

They glared at each other for a long moment, and then Jamie shrugged. 'No doubt you are right, my love,' he agreed, giving her his most charming smile. 'I shall send word that we shall attend tomorrow night instead.' He bowed. 'Now, if you will give me time to change, I shall escort you myself.'

'Thank you,' she said, pleased with her victory. She smiled magnanimously, 'And I shall be glad to meet your friends tomorrow.'

For some reason she found his answering smile unsettling. There seemed to be something unpleasantly amused about it. As if he knew something that she did not. With a shrug she dismissed this foolish idea. Now that she was almost ready to go her nerves had returned with a vengeance. That was all it was.

She paced the floor until Jamie appeared again, this time in a rich brocade coat and dark-green satin breeches. Lace foamed at his throat and cuffs. They made a fine couple.

An ornately written invitation had followed the verbal one, informing Lucy that the dinner would be held in the Queen's Presence Chamber. She had no idea where that was, but Jamie obviously did. Offering her his arm, he led her through the winding corridors till they reached the vast double doors, where a liveried usher waited to announce the guests.

'Lord and Lady Happington,' he bellowed. There was a sudden lull in the conversation and all eyes turned to assess the new arrivals. Lucy gripped her husband's arm as another pang of nerves hit her at the sight before her.

Lady Castlemaine's idea of 'an intimate little supper' was on a rather grander scale than Lucy's. The huge chamber was thronged with people, the light from a thousand candles reflected back from a thousand glittering jewels. A vast buffet, groaning with food and drink, lined almost the whole of one wall. Musicians, sweating with effort and heat, played in the background, the sound almost drowned out by the constant chatter. Gaming tables were set out round the edges of the floor for those who wished to play cards or dice, while yet more provided for those who chose merely to eat and drink.

In the midst of all this splendour, like a gorgeous spider at the centre of a gilded web, was their hostess, Lady Castlemaine, and Lucy's heart thudded as she recognised the tall man she was talking to as his majesty, King Charles II of England. As she watched, Barbara poked him unceremoniously in the belly and said something that made him throw back his head and laugh uproariously.

Another pang, this time of envy, ran through Lucy. She felt like a pauper outside a window, peering in at something she would never be part of. How could she possibly fit in with all these confident, self-assured people?

Barbara glanced up and saw the new arrivals. Picking up her skirts, she turned and swept towards them, the other guests parting like the Red Sea to allow her through. 'Jamie,' she said, kissing him so thoroughly that Lucy suspected Lady Edmont was not the only one who had shared his bed. She turned to Lucy and smiled condescendingly. 'And Lady Happington, too. How kind of you to accept my invitation.' Linking her arm with Lucy's, she pulled her towards the other guests. 'Come, my dear, let me introduce you to everyone.'

Tugged along by her hostess, with Jamie following in their wake, Lucy was utterly bewildered. There were so many faces and so many names. She'd never remember them all. Buckingham and Buckhurst. Jermyn and Sedley. Hamilton and Denham. The Duke and Duchess of York and of Monmouth. She recognised the names of all the great families of England, but their faces were nothing but a blur.

Finally Barbara halted in front of the king. Lucy's legs gave way and she almost fell into a trembling curtsey at his feet, her head bowed so low it practically touched her knee. Reaching down, he raised her up and smiled at her.

'So this is the young lady who waved to me from her window,' he said in amusement. 'You were not quite so shy then, if I recall.'

Lucy began to stammer apologies, but he merely laughed and waved them aside. 'Nonsense, my dear. The day I cannot be moved by a pretty face, I shall know I am ready for my grave.' He nodded to the floor and bowed. 'Perhaps you will do me the honour of dancing with me?'

Lucy moved through the stately measure of a pavane, scarcely believing what was happening to her. To think that she was dancing with the king!

The rest of the evening was a blur of pleasure. As soon as the king relinquished her hand she was swept away by yet another of the courtiers, her success underlined by the hostile looks of Castlemaine, who was obviously regretting her invitation.

The only sour note of the entire evening was her worry about Jamie. Even as she whirled by on the arm of some new admirer, she caught glimpses of him seated at one of the gaming tables with a glass at his hand – and going by his black expression, his luck was not running well. By the time the evening ended, he was drunk again.

'Damned cheats,' he mumbled as they returned to their apartments. 'The cards must've been marked.'

'Don't be ridiculous,' said Lucy crossly. 'I do not know why you gamble when you are so bad at it. What are you going to do if you fall into debt again? You have already squandered my marriage portion.'

He leered at her drunkenly and tapped the side of his nose. 'Don't you worry, my lady. I have my ways.' He attempted to remove his breeches and toppled sideways onto the chaise longue, where he promptly began to snore.

'Sorry, ma'am, I fell asleep,' muttered Joanie, coming

through yawning. She stopped and stared. 'Is the master all right?' she asked.

'Of course he's all right,' said Lucy bitterly. 'He has the constitution of an ox and will no doubt outlive us all. God knows he's well enough pickled.' She sighed with weariness. 'Now come and help me undress. I am exhausted.'

'What was it like?' asked Joanie eagerly as she helped her mistress off with her gown. 'Did you see the king?'

'See him? I danced with him!' exclaimed Lucy, her tiredness forgotten as she relived her triumph. Her eyes sparkled with mischief. 'And you should have seen Lady Castlemaine's face! I vow and swear, if looks could kill I would have dropped dead on the spot.' She sighed rapturously. 'It was wonderful. And you should have seen the dresses and the jewels and…'

Restored to good humour by the memory of her success, Lucy finally climbed into bed. Her last thought before she fell into a contented slumber was the hope that the dinner party with Jamie's friends would go as well as it had that evening.

It was noon before she woke, and Jamie was already gone. She started out of bed, horrified she had slept so late. At home, by this time, she would have been up for hours, gone riding and begun her daily tasks. 'The day's half done!' she snapped at Joanie. 'Why did you not wake me sooner?'

Joanie giggled. 'But we are at court now, ma'am. This *is* early. Most of the other ladies are still abed.' She plumped the pillows. 'Now lie back while I fetch you a dish of tea.' Her eyes sparkled with excitement. 'And oh, madam, just wait till you see what has come for you.'

'What do you mean?' asked Lucy, but Joanie had already vanished.

When she returned she was bearing a small black lacquered tray. On it sat a bowl of tea, giving off wisps of fragrant steam, and beside the bowl lay a heaped pile of stiff white envelopes, and a long velvet box. Lucy stared at them in amazement.

'Well, don't just sit there gawking at 'em,' scolded Joanie, whose nosiness had been driving her mad all morning. 'What are they and who're they from?'

'You must learn to read,' grinned Lucy. 'That way you can satisfy your curiosity without having to wait for me to wake.'

'Get on with you!' scoffed Joanie. 'Me, read? That'll be the day. Now come on. Open 'em before I burst.'

'We can't have that, can we?' teased Lucy. She patted the edge of the bed and Joanie plonked herself down beside her mistress and smiled expectantly, like a small child waiting to be told a fairytale.

It was like a fairytale to Lucy, too. 'An invitation to a ball next Sunday week, given by the Duke and Duchess of York!' she gasped, reading the first one. She threw it down and reached for the next. 'One to an evening party on the Thames from my Lady Rochester!' And the next. 'Buckhurst and Sedley have invited me to the play!'

The one after that made her gasp. 'What? What?' demanded Joanie, almost beside herself.

''Tis an invitation to an assignation – from Buckingham himself,' she giggled, partly shocked and partly flattered by his effrontery. She tore it neatly in half. 'Well, he'll have a long wait. I am a respectable married woman.'

She had saved the gift until last. When all the invitations had been read she turned to it, fumbling at the clasp with nervous fingers. What could it be? The box finally fell open and she gazed at the contents in awe.

'It's lovely!' she gasped, holding the pearl-encrusted pendant up, so that the stone caught the sun, sending coruscations of rosy light over the coverlet. 'Why, it is the prettiest garnet I've ever seen.'

'That's no garnet, ma'am,' said Joanie, looking at it shrewdly. ''Tis a ruby, I'd stake my life on it.'

'Who's it from?' gasped Lucy. She picked up the box again and a small square of card fluttered out. She pounced on it and read it eagerly. 'Welcome to court. Charles, R.' She stared at it in confusion. 'Who on earth is "Charles, R"?'

Joanie's hand flew to her mouth and she stared at her mistress in awe. 'Why, 'tis the king hisself, Miss Lucy,' she whispered, then looked at the pile of cards and smiled proudly, basking in her mistress's reflected glory. 'Just look at 'em all,' she gloated. 'You must be the most popular lady at court!'

'I suspect these invitations come more from malice than generosity,' Lucy said with a wry smile. 'Not to welcome me to court, but to cock a snook at Lady Castlemaine.' She shook her head. 'You should have heard some of the things they were saying about her last night. The devil himself could not have a worse reputation if you were to believe them all.'

''Tis the same below stairs,' declared Joanie. She leaned forward and lowered her voice. 'Why, Thomas was just telling me—'

The door flew open and the lady in question burst in, like an evil genie conjured from a bottle. Her face was purple with barely suppressed rage.

'You jumped-up little country strumpet!' she snarled, glaring down at Lucy and tapping her fan against her palm in fury. 'How dare you? To think I took pity on you, and this is how you repay my kindness!'

Lucy sat up straight and glared back. 'I may be from the country, my lady,' she snapped. 'But at least there it is considered good manners to knock before one enters.'

'You have the temerity to lecture *me* on the rules of good breeding, miss?' Castlemaine fumed. 'Well what about the one about poaching on another woman's property?'

Lucy stared at her, bemused. 'What in God's name are you talking about?' she demanded.

'Don't play the innocent with me,' snapped Barbara. 'I saw you last night making cow's eyes at the king.' She tossed her head. 'Well if you think he'd ever take notice of a puling little milksop like you, I'm afraid you're sadly mistaken.'

'You're the one who's mistaken, my lady,' said Lucy triumphantly. 'He already has!' She picked up the ruby pendant and held it out tauntingly before her rival. 'He sent me this gift, this morning.' She smiled. 'And somehow I don't think that he regards himself as your "property".'

Lady Castlemaine's lips curled in a sneer. 'I would not value myself quite so high, if I were you,' she snorted. 'That paltry bauble means nothing. Why, his majesty would think no more of giving you that than he would of tossing sixpence to a passing beggar.' Her eyes narrowed. 'But I suggest you keep well clear of him from now on, if you value your hide, that is.'

Satisfied she'd put Lucy properly in her place, she swept out as dramatically as she'd arrived, though she might not have felt quite so pleased had she heard the outburst of giggles which followed her exit.

The rest of the day was equally exciting. Dressed – and wearing the king's pendant – Lucy spent it gradually finding her feet in the day to day round of court. God knew how, but word of her quarrel with Castlemaine had already travelled from mouth to mouth like wildfire. Barbara's arrogance had made her many enemies and malicious pleasure at seeing her put at a disadvantage guaranteed Lucy a warm welcome.

Her crowning moment came when the king entered the long gallery and singled her out. 'Thank you for your gift, sire,' she breathed. 'It is beautiful.'

'Not half as beautiful as the lady wearing it,' he smiled, kissing her hand before walking on. Oblivious of the envious glances, she stared after him, her skin tingling where his lips had touched it.

'Criminy!' exclaimed Joanie when they finally returned to their apartments. 'What a day! I was right, you are the toast of court.'

'Until the next new face appears,' said Lucy. She smiled cynically. 'No doubt I'd get much the same reception were I the new whore in a brothel.'

'Madam!' exclaimed Joanie. 'How can you say that?'

'Easily,' said Lucy. 'They are all bored stiff with one another. All I have is novelty value. That will soon wear off and they will be as used to my face as they are to their own.' Her smile became mischievous. 'But that doesn't mean we can't enjoy it while it lasts.'

She tapped her lips thoughtfully with her fan. 'Anyway, enough of that. What shall I wear to this supper of Jamie's tonight? Something not too formal, but still pretty enough to make a good impression on his friends.'

'What about the green silk?' suggested Joanie. 'With the matching gold clocked stockings? You could wear your emeralds with it, too.'

'Excellent,' agreed Lucy. 'Now come and unlace me. I

211

shall lie down for half an hour before I have to dress again.'

Despite taking a catnap and almost two hours to finish her toilet, there was still no sign of Jamie. 'Hell's teeth,' snapped Lucy, pacing up and down and glancing at the clock impatiently. 'Where is the man? And what time does this damned supper take place at, anyway? ''Tis almost ten already. 'It will be time for breakfast before we get there.'

As if conjured by her words, the door opened and Jamie finally sauntered in.

'Ah, good, you are ready, my dear,' he smiled. 'I appreciate punctuality.'

'As do I,' said Lucy tartly. She stared at his wine-stained waistcoat. 'Do you not intend to change?'

'Oh, I will do as I am,' he shrugged. 'These are old friends. They will take me as they find me.' He offered his arm. 'Shall we go?' With a word to Joanie not to wait up, Lucy accepted it and allowed her husband to lead her out.

They had been walking for five minutes before Lucy became uneasy. 'Where are we going?' she asked anxiously. 'Surely the reception rooms are in the other direction?'

'Ah, but this is a private supper,' he smiled, and the smile increased Lucy's unease. She would have pulled away, but Jamie's grip on her arm made that impossible. Though every instinct warned her to run, she was forced to continue walking.

At last they reached a narrow doorway at the end of a particularly shabby corridor. Jamie pushed it open without knocking and tugged her inside. A few flickering candles barely lit the room and Lucy blinked as her eyes adjusted to the semi-darkness.

What she saw did not reassure her. A fire guttered low in the grate, its light revealing only a single table holding the remains of a gargantuan meal and several empty wine bottles. Were they too late? Had the supper already finished? Where was everyone?

She whirled round as the door closed behind her and she heard the key turn in the lock. 'Wh-what are you doing?' she quavered.

'You'll see,' leered Jamie. Taking a taper he lit several more candles, and Lucy's hand flew to her mouth. The room was not empty at all! Beyond the supper table sat a grotesquely fat man, his lips still smeared with grease from his meal. Flanking his chair stood his two servants. Lucy gasped. No wonder she had not seen them in the darkness. Their skin was as black as sea-coal!

A wave of horror ran through her as she recognised the seated man – not by acquaintance, but by reputation. Lord Crockettford – rumoured to be the most debauched man in England. If she had not recognised him by his enormous girth, she would have known him by his attendants. One of his affectations was to drive nothing but white horses and be attended by Castor and Pollux, his twin black servants, for whom he had paid an enormous sum.

Ignoring the man, she glared at her husband. 'Why have you brought me here?' she demanded, with a bravery she did not feel.

'Simple, my dear,' said Jamie, with a twisted smile. 'Gambling debts. As I seem to lack the money to pay my Lord Crockettford, he has kindly agreed to accept payment in another coin.'

'Wh-what do you mean?' she stammered. Surely he didn't intend to…

He did. 'It is quite simple, my sweet,' he went on. 'In exchange for the use of you for a single evening, he will wipe my slate clean.'

Turning she bolted for the door, tugging frantically on the handle with both hands. But her efforts elicited merely a rumble of amusement from the bloated figure in the corner, and when Jamie grabbed her by the shoulders and she whirled round and kicked him viciously in the shins, his amusement increased.

'Egads, but you have your hands full there, man!' he chuckled, as tight-lipped, Jamie marched her across until she stood directly in front of Lord Crockettford. 'Well, my lord,' he smirked, 'is it a fair bargain?'

Taking up his quizzing glass, Crockettford inspected her as if he were examining a piece of horseflesh. Close up, Lucy could see his face wore a superficial expression of joviality – until you reached the eyes, which were as cold and hard as shards of ice. She shivered beneath his scrutiny.

'It seems so,' he concluded. 'Of course, I should have to examine her more closely. For all I know she could be pocked or crooked beneath those clothes.' His greasy lips twisted in a smile and he clicked his fingers at his attendants. 'Strip her!'

'What?' Lucy gasped in outrage. She wriggled her shoulders and briefly managed to free herself from Jamie's grip, only to be seized again by the two servants. As one held her the other proceeded to divest her of her garments. Her green silk gown slid to the floor, followed by the froth of petticoats until she stood naked before the loathsome beast.

Unable to hide herself, she felt a hot flush of shame suffuse her entire body as he eyed her with unconcealed lust. In the dimness her skin had an opalescent sheen.

The candlelight gleamed off the proud swell of her breasts, while shadows pooled at the juncture of her smooth thighs, providing her with a spurious modesty.

Lord Crockettford leaned back and gave a sigh of pleasure, as if he was regarding a work of art. 'Darkness and light, evil and innocence,' he murmured. 'Delightful.' He gestured at Jamie with his quizzing glass. 'Doesn't the contrast between the lady's delicate white flesh and the blackness of those brutes' hands simply make one's mouth water?'

In answer, Lucy gathered the water in her own mouth, and spat full in his face.

His expression remained unchanged, despite the spittle trickling down his cheek. 'Oh dear,' he said softly. 'It seems the lady must be taught a few manners before we begin.'

He nodded to his servants again, and before Lucy could do anything she found herself spun round and bent over, her arms pulled back and to the side so that the slightest movement resulted in excruciating pain in her shoulders. In this humiliating position her bottom was presented fully to her tormentor, who took full advantage of her helplessness. She bit her lip as his hands explored the soft fullness of her buttocks, then winced as his fat fingers explored the warm cleft between her thighs, prodding and fondling.

As her captors avidly watched their master's lewd probings, she felt their grip slacken a fraction and used it to lift her foot and kick backwards. It connected with a pleasingly solid thud, there was a muffled 'Oof!' and the intruding hand fell away.

But her satisfaction did not last long.

'Oh dear, I see my little lecture on manners has fallen on stony ground,' tutted Lord Crockettford, with mock regret. 'It seems we must resort to stronger measures to tame the lady.' He shook his head. 'Though it seems a pity to spoil such a sweet derriere, needs must when the devil drives.'

Straining her neck, Lucy saw to her horror that he had reached down beside his chair and produced a thin malacca cane. Bending it between his hands, he smiled genially. 'Perhaps this will teach you a little civility.'

There was a whistling sound as he raised his arm and brought the cane down sharply across her buttocks. A thin red weal painted itself across her pale skin and she stiffened and gasped as pain flowed through her. He lifted his arm again and this time she screamed as the cane connected and a second, then a third weal rose, parallel to the first.

There was a brief pause as he gathered his breath from his efforts. She whimpered as his hand explored the damage he had done. He licked his lips as he ran his fingers almost tenderly over the bruised flesh, relishing the way her buttocks clenched defensively beneath his touch. His hand strayed lower and he thrust two fingers viciously inside her. She shrieked and tried to kick him again.

'Not yet learned, my pretty one?' he said, shaking his head at her stubbornness. 'Ah, well.' He lifted the cane again.

This time there was no respite. He lay on with an expert hand, each blow eliciting a shriek of agony. Her backside was a mass of red stripes now, the flesh jerking and quivering each time the cane descended. By the time he finished her legs had given way, her shrieks had faded to whimpers and she hung between the two black servants with all resistance gone.

This time she did not even attempt to evade his probing fingers. Then unbuttoning his breeches he rummaged beneath his vast belly till he found his cock, and continued to fumble at her with one hand while stroking himself with the other. Fondling her clitoris with his thumb he continued to ram his fingers in and out of her, and she was horrified to find herself moistening in response, the tips of her swaying breasts beginning to harden.

As his hand moved faster she moaned, this time in twisted pleasure. Grunting in satisfaction at her response, he tugged harder on his erection until he gave one last groan and she felt his seed splatter weakly onto her welted buttocks. The servants let her go as their master sagged back in his chair, his vast bulk heaving with the effort of his release. His hand fell away from her vulva, leaving her both relieved and disappointed. Desire still throbbed and burned between her thighs, but she could pleasure herself at leisure later. At least her ordeal was over.

But no, it was only just beginning.

Her tormentor poured himself a glass of wine and offered one to Jamie, who had stood lounging against the wall, watching his wife's degradation with cynical eyes. 'Not bad for a trifling amusement,' he commented, his eyes narrowing. 'But hardly amusing enough to warrant the sum you owe me. What say you to a little further entertainment?'

'Whatever your lordship desires,' said Jamie, raising his glass in a toast. 'I am sure my good lady wife will be more than happy to oblige you, now that she has been taught her place.'

Fear gripped Lucy's bowels. They had already debased her – what more could they do to her? Her answer was not long in coming. Lord Crockettford clapped his hands. 'Take off your clothes,' he ordered, and Lucy stared at him as if he had run mad. What was he talking about? She was naked already. Did he intend to strip her to her very bones? Then movement caught her attention and she turned her head, to see the two black servants impassively removing their livery. Lips parted, she watched in horrified fascination as they shed the last of their garments. In the flickering flames of the fire their bodies gleamed like statues carved from ebony – but statues did not normally sport such massive members!

Her knuckles flew to her mouth to hold back her squeal of terror. Surely even Lord Crockettford would not hand her over to these creatures? But even as her mind quailed at the very thought, her body betrayed her. The tingling between her thighs intensified as her eyes ran the length of their thick dark cocks. She had heard whispers that some of the ladies of the court employed their black servants to pleasure them, and now she could see why! In this case the rumours about the enormity of their endowment was utterly true!

'Well, don't just stand there, boys,' Lord Crockettford wheezed jovially. 'Have at her!'

Their white teeth gleaming, Castor and Pollux advanced, trapping her between them. Reaching out, one began to fondle her breasts, his fingers shockingly black against her flesh and nipples. The other approached her from behind, slipping his hands around her waist then down over her flat tummy, where his fingers parted the lips of her sex and stroked the bud of her clitoris. She moaned in reluctant pleasure as she felt one throbbing erection pressing against her buttocks and the other against her belly.

Her moan became a gasp as the first lowered his mouth to her breasts and his tongue flicked her nipples, hardening them even more, while the other thrust strong fingers inside her, to continue where Lord Crockettford lay off. The first pushed her to her knees and thrust his cock in her face, and lost to everything but the lust pounding through her, she reached for it, stroking the velvety black skin before parting her lips and allowing him to push himself inside. It was his turn to groan as he was engulfed in the warm wetness. He was so huge, she almost gagged as his cock filled her mouth, and then she relaxed and allowed her tongue to trace the satin smoothness and hard rim of it before beginning to suck greedily.

Following his twin's example, the other knelt behind her, anointing the swollen head of his own cock with the juices from her cunny, before parting her thighs and plunging between them. She whimpered as she felt the enormous length of his yard sliding slowly inside her, his hands continuing to fondle her swaying breasts as he began to thrust. Groaning, she pushed her hips back to impale herself further on his massive weapon as she continued to lick and suck his brother's.

The two white men watched lustfully, as the twins went about their work with vigour, their huge black cocks pounding in and out of Lucy's mouth and sex as she writhed and moaned and sucked.

'By God!' gasped Lord Crockettford. 'This is worth all your debt – and more!'

Lucy didn't even hear him. She was almost there now, every inch of her body straining towards release. Then she felt the cock inside her swell and spasm as it gushed its hot seed, while the one between her lips jerked, filling her mouth with viscous, salty liquid – and her own insides dissolved. She stiffened, shuddered and everything went black as *la petite mort* overwhelmed her.

When she came to, it was to find Jamie kneeling beside her. Her first emotion was gratitude at his concern – then she realised his breeches were round his knees and his cock was jutting out like an iron bar.

'On your hands and knees, bitch,' he said thickly. ''Tis my turn now.'

She tried to roll away, but he was too strong for her. Sliding his arm round her waist he hauled her into position and fell to his knees behind her. Taking his erection in one hand, he spat in the other and wet its bulbous head. Satisfied, he pulled her buttocks apart to reveal the soft, pink pucker of her anus.

Realising his intent she wailed and tried to pull away. But he wrenched her back, his swollen cock pushing against the forbidden entrance, each jab sending a new spasm of pain through her weary body. He was going to split her in half!

Cursing at the resistance he pushed harder, then gave a grunt of satisfaction as he felt it give way. She shrieked as the tip of his cock slid slowly inside her, and grinning cruelly, he pressed on until he was buried to the hilt. Then digging his fingers into her hips he began to thrust, his balls smacking against her vulva at every stroke.

She whimpered as she felt the rigid length of him sinking into her rear passage, and the rhythmic slapping of his sack against the tender lips of her sex, and she groaned with dismay as once again her treacherous body betrayed her. Heat washed through her as pain twisted into perverse pleasure. She reached down between her legs and began to stroke herself in time to his thrusts. Her fingers, sticky with the spend from her previous fucking, slid in and out faster and faster as her shameful excitement mounted.

Jamie gave one last massive thrust, his hips bucking as his seed spurted and she sobbed as it triggered her own release. Then as he withdrew she collapsed, semen trickling from her violated orifices.

As her mind cleared humiliation overwhelmed her. She

staggered to her feet, unable to look any of her leering tormentors in the face as she hurriedly dragged her clothes on over her exhausted body. The full horror slowly dawned on her. If word of this ever got out, she would never be able to look *anyone* in the face ever again.

Her cheeks flamed scarlet with shame as she imagined the scandal if it was ever found out. The knowing glances. The spiteful tittering as the other ladies gossiped about her behind their fans. Castlemaine's delight at her downfall.

Lost in despair she barely heard Lord Crockettford's lewd comments on her 'performance', or the roars of laughter that greeted them. All she wanted was to escape.

When Jamie finally took his leave she followed him dully from the room with her head still hung in humiliation and fear.

Back at their apartments Joanie was waiting. 'Did you enjoy the supper party, madam?' she asked eagerly, then gawped in astonishment as her mistress fled to her chamber, weeping as if her heart would break.

Next day, it was long after noon before Lucy opened her eyes, and her first waking thought was that the events of the night before had been merely some terrible nightmare, the result of too much cheese at suppertime.

As she struggled to sit up she realised, with a sinking stomach, that it had been all too real. Her body ached in a thousand places; her hips and thighs were marked with tiny bruises made by the cruel fingers of her tormentors, and her bottom still throbbed from the beating administered by Lord Crockettford. With a groan of shame she collapsed back on her pillows.

'About time, too,' said Joanie, bustling in and pulling the curtains. 'I thought you were going to sleep till the crack of doom.'

'I wish I could,' moaned Lucy, burying her face in her hands.

Joanie stared anxiously at her mistress's pallid face and reddened eyelids. 'Whass wrong, madam?' she asked in alarm. 'Are you ill?' Her face whitened. 'Thomas was just saying yesterday there's plague in the town.'

Lucy forced a merry laugh. 'Fiddlesticks,' she cried, trying not to wince as she swung her legs out of bed. 'There's always plague at this time of year, and only among the poorer sort. It will go as soon as it came, and besides, it will never touch us here at court.' She shook her head. 'There's nothing wrong with me but a heavy head from an excess of wine at supper last night.'

Joanie smiled with relief. That would account for the tears last night as well. It was common enough. Why, old Simon back home had been exactly the same. One tankard too many and he'd spend the rest of the night weeping into his beer and bewailing the loss of his poor wife. 'So what would you like to do this afternoon then, madam?' she asked.

Lucy thought for a moment. All she really wanted to do was take to her heels and flee back to the country with her tail between her legs, but that was not possible. Here she was and here she would have to stay – but at least she could get out of this place for a few hours. 'We'll go to the Royal Exchange,' she announced. 'The walk will do us good, and besides, I need new ribbons to trim my shifts.'

'Oh good!' exclaimed Joanie, then she lowered her eyes. 'Er… I mean, very well, madam.' She flushed slightly. 'Shall I ask Thomas to accompany us?'

Lucy smiled, forgetting her aches and pains for a moment. 'Hmm, and would this Thomas be the same young footman who keeps hovering round the apartments, by any chance?' she teased. 'The one you keep mentioning?'

'Yes, m'm,' Joanie admitted, blushing even more and fiddling with the folds of her skirt.

'I see,' said Lucy, with mock severity. 'All this time I thought he was hanging round in hopes of earning a tip, and now it turns out he was only hoping for a stolen kiss.' A thought struck her. 'Who does he serve?' she enquired.

'My Lady Castlemaine,' said Joanie, who sighed. 'But he is just one of many. He has little hope of advancement, tha'ss why he hangs around trying to make a bob or two on the side.' She looked at her mistress. 'Why?'

Lucy smiled wickedly. She could kill two birds with one stone; steal him from Barbara and make Joanie happy. 'Then ask him if he would consider leaving her service and joining mine,' she said casually. 'I'll pay a guinea a year more than she's giving him.'

'Oh, madam!' gasped Joanie. 'That'd be marvellous. May I go and ask him now?'

'Of course you can,' smiled Lucy.

As soon as Joanie had gone, almost tripping over her skirts in her eagerness, Lucy's smile vanished. Easing herself up from the bed she took off her nightgown. The stale scent of sex hit her like a blow and her face twisted in a grimace of disgust. She stank like a whore after a busy night's work.

Reaching for the washcloth she scrubbed herself till her skin was as red as her beaten bottom, sluicing between her legs until she was certain she was clean. She sighed bitterly. That was a jest. She would never be clean again. After drying herself gingerly to avoid her bruises, she barely had time to slip into her concealing shift before

223

Joanie burst back in, wreathed in smiles.

'He says thank you very much, mistress,' she announced happily. 'He'd be honoured to serve such a fine lady.'

'Excellent,' said Lucy. 'We shall bespeak his new livery while we are out.' She clapped her hands. 'Now don't just stand there, grinning like a halfwit. Make haste and fetch my turquoise satin, then come and do my hair. If we do not hurry, the booths will be closing by the time we get to the 'Change.'

The fresh air cleared Lucy's head and the hustle and bustle of the 'Change proved a pleasant distraction from her unpleasant thoughts. Escorted by Thomas she wandered from booth to booth, nodding to acquaintances and picking over the latest trinkets. She ordered a dress length of cloth-of-gold, and bought herself an ostrich-feather fan and several yards of ribbon in assorted colours. By the time they left to go back to the palace her spirits had been much raised by her outing. Joanie's happiness was contagious too, so much so that Lucy actually found herself laughing when they paused to watch the antics of a trained monkey, dancing for coppers. Fishing in her bag she threw a sixpence to its master, who caught it in midair and gave her a flashing grin.

As she turned away the rumble of wheels over the cobbles caught her attention. She looked up and the colour drained from her face as she saw the two black servants riding postilion on the huge gilded coach. And behind the horn windows she thought she could make out the bloated face of her tormentor from the night before.

Joanie confirmed her worst fears. 'Oh, look!' she exclaimed. ''Tis wicked Lord Crockettford!' She lowered her voice. ''Tis said he's sold his soul to the devil hisself!'

Lucy bit her lip. She could quite believe it.

'He's off to take the waters at Buxton,' Thomas informed them, and Lucy stared at her new footman and had to resist the urge to kiss him. He couldn't have given her better news if he'd brought a proposal of marriage from the king himself!

She began to smile. With Lord Crockettford out of the way and Jamie's gambling debts paid in full, she could afford to relax again.

Relieved of her worries, Lucy threw herself into her new life with fresh vigour, attending everything to which she was invited: balls; card parties; plays. Her initial diffidence wore off as she became more accustomed to the hectic pace of court, until it seemed she'd been there forever. Her awe of his majesty had worn off too and she bantered as merrily with him and his brother James, as any of the other gallants.

Even her life with Jamie settled into an uneasy truce. He came and went as he pleased, but despite his continued drinking his luck seemed to have turned and for once the cards were running his way.

'Here,' he announced one day, tossing a leather bag into her lap as she sat before her mirror, powdering her cheeks with a hare's foot. She picked it up and hefted it, feeling the coins inside clink.

'Where did you get this?' she asked suspiciously.

'A wager with my Lord Rochester,' he smirked. 'Two thousand guineas on whether my bay was faster than his chestnut. I won.' His mouth twitched unpleasantly. 'Shall we say this is your share – for services rendered?'

She flushed at his reference to *that* evening. She had tried to thrust it from her mind and forget about it. Then another thought struck her. 'But where did you get two thousand guineas to make the wager in the first place?'

she demanded.

His face darkened. 'None of your damned business,' he snapped, turning on his heel and stalking out. 'Just take it and be grateful.'

Once he had gone she hoisted her skirts, pulled back the carpet and knelt to deposit the unexpected gift in the hidey-hole along with the rest. Then dusting her hands, she returned to her seat and smiled at her reflection. At least with her secret hoard she need not fear being carted off to Newgate for debt.

So life went on pleasantly. His majesty's coronation took place in May to much rejoicing. Bells rang out; wine ran from the public fountains; and the streets were hung with banners as the whole of London celebrated too.

Lucy dipped into her hoard for new gowns for herself and Joanie, and joined the revelry with the rest of the court. In fact, the only one not smiling was Lady Castlemaine as negotiations for a royal bride threatened to push her from her place.

'I don't know why she's so worried,' scoffed Joanie. 'His majesty'll never change now, wife or no wife.' She winked. 'You know what they said about him and his mistresses, when he came back from his travels and they changed the names of half the pubs in London?' Lucy looked blank and Joanie giggled. '"The *King's Head* might be empty but the *King's Arms* is full.'

She was proved right, too. Meek, virginal, little Catherine of Braganza, with her sallow skin, old-fashioned clothes and staid Spanish upbringing, was no match for the king's flamboyant mistress and before long he was back in her bed again, making her more arrogant than ever.

'God's bones!' snorted Lucy, fluttering her fan in annoyance as she and Joanie walked back from Castlemaine's parties at which the king had been as attentive

226

as ever. 'I don't know what he sees in her. The woman's a bitch.'

'No doubt she has hidden talents,' grinned Joanie, holding open the door to the apartments for her mistress. ''Tis said she's insatiable in bed.'

'She would need to be,' said Lucy dryly. 'Her charm outside it leaves a lot to be desire—'

Both women stopped short on the threshold, their jaws dropping as they stared in dismay at the state of the anteroom. Every drawer had been turned out; books and clothes lay scattered over the floor; even the furniture had been tumbled.

'Thieves!' gasped Joanie. 'My God! We could have been murdered in our beds!'

A crash from the bedchamber made them cling together. 'Oh, criminy!' quavered Joanie. 'They're still here!'

'Run and fetch Thomas! Quickly now,' hissed Lucy, reaching for a heavy glass vase.

'B-but you c-could be killed!' protested Joanie.

'I might well be if you don't get a move on,' snapped Lucy. 'Now do as you're told.' Picking up her skirts, Joanie took to her heels.

Holding her breath and clutching her makeshift weapon, Lucy tiptoed to the bedchamber door, peered in, then let out a sigh of relief and let the vase fall. 'Good God, Jamie, what on earth are you about?' she demanded, walking into the chamber and regarding him with her arms folded.

He stood there swaying, still holding one of her petticoats in his hand from where he'd been ransacking her garderobe. 'Where ish it?' he slurred, focussing on her blearily.

'Where's what?' she asked. 'What are you talking about?'

Despite his drunkenness he moved fast. 'Where'sh my

money, you bitch?' he snarled, stalking across the chamber and seizing her by the throat. He shook her like a terrier shaking a rat and her vision began to blur. 'What've you done with it?' he demanded.

Defiantly she prised his fingers from her throat and pushed him away, gasping for breath. 'What are you talking about?' she rasped, rubbing her throat. 'What money?' She glared at him rebelliously. She'd be damned if she meekly handed over her hard-won gold. She'd earned that!

He stared at her for a long moment and she braced herself for a blow, but it never came. Instead he muttered something incomprehensible and pushed past her, almost knocking over Joanie and Thomas as they rushed in. The door banged behind him.

For a moment they all stared at one another, then Joanie rushed to her mistress's side. 'Are you all right?' she asked anxiously.

'Of course I am,' said Lucy. ''Twas a false alarm. The master was merely... um... looking for something.' She looked round at the devastation, realised how ridiculous that sounded, and shrugged. It was a feeble excuse, but it would have to do. She forced a smile. 'Come, let us put this to rights before we go to bed. 'Twill all be forgotten about tomorrow.'

It was Joanie's turn to shrug – if her mistress didn't want to confide in her, that was her business. So rolling up her sleeves she set to. It just went to show that a lord was no better than any other man. In his cups, her own father had been wont to turn the cottage upside down 'looking for something'. She suppressed a wry smile. Usually a bottle that didn't exist!

Much to Lucy's surprise, Jamie appeared the following day, bearing a gift of a box of sweetmeats and full of remorse for his behaviour of the night before. 'I have treated you shamefully, sweetheart,' he apologised.

'Indeed you have, sir,' Lucy said tartly, and flung the beribboned box on the bed. 'And a few candied violets are hardly likely to change it.'

'But *I* will change,' he said. 'I swear to God I will.' He looked at her pleadingly. 'Just give me one more chance.'

Lucy eyed him doubtfully. She'd heard it all before. Still, he *was* her husband. She was stuck with him and might as well try and make the best of it. 'Oh, all right then,' she muttered.

'Oh, thank you, darling, thank you,' he beamed. 'You won't regret it.'

Much to her surprise, she didn't. For the next few weeks his behaviour was exemplary. His gambling ceased. He slept in his own bed every night. Barely a drop of wine passed his lips and he escorted her to every ball and card party, where he danced attendance on her, hardly leaving her side. Lucy finally began to believe he had reformed.

'What's this for?' she asked in surprise when he entered their chambers one morning, bearing a nosegay of yellow roses, which he presented to her with a flourish.

'Do I need a reason?' he asked, with a hurt expression. ''Tis a beautiful summer's day, that's all.' He smiled. 'In fact, let us make the best of it and play truant. We could take a barge up the river and go to this little country tavern I know. Blow the cobwebs away.'

'But we are invited to Lady Denham's this afternoon to hear that new tenor,' she pointed out.

Jamie rolled his eyes. 'Do you really want to spend a day like this cooped up inside, listening to some squawking

Italian?'

'I don't suppose she'd miss us,' agreed Lucy, smiling wistfully. 'And it would be nice to get out into the country again. Town does stink abominably at this time of year.'

'Then it's settled,' he confirmed. 'You go and dress and I'll get Thomas to order the carriage.'

Giggling, Lucy rushed to do as she was told.

'A day in the country,' said Joanie excitedly, as she helped her mistress to dress in a simple blue silk gown. 'Why, 'twill be quite like old times. Shall I fetch some cold meat and ale from the kitchens?'

'No need,' smiled Lucy. 'We are to dine at some inn Jamie knows.' She tapped her foot impatiently. 'Now let us hurry. We don't want to keep him waiting.'

He had returned by the time they were both ready, and when he saw Joanie his smile faded for a moment, then returned so quickly that Lucy thought she'd imagined it.

'What need of a lady's maid on a day like this?' he asked lightly. 'If we are to play truant, why not let Joanie do the same?' He fished in his breech's pocket and produced a half-sovereign. 'Here, why don't you and that young man of yours go off and enjoy yourselves, too?'

'Oooh, thank you, sir,' cried Joanie, bobbing a curtsey and beaming at her master. Her disappointment at not being taken along had vanished instantly at the thought of an unexpected holiday, and with money to spend as well!

'That was kind,' smiled Lucy, as they made their way to the waiting coach.

'Not at all,' he said. 'It was pure selfishness.' He took her arm and helped her in. 'Just for once I shall enjoy having you all to myself.'

Seated in the barge, with a wide-brimmed hat to protect her delicate skin from the sun, Lucy thoroughly enjoyed her trip. As they drifted along, the bustling docks and wharfs gradually gave way to the salad gardens and then to open fields. At this distance the grazing sheep and cattle looked like toys: freshly painted animals, unpacked from some wooden Noah's Ark and dotted artistically round the countryside to make it look picturesque.

She half-closed her eyes and sighed with sheer pleasure. At long last things were beginning to go well. She could put the past behind her and look forward to a happy future. Lulled by the sun, the birds singing and her own pleasant thoughts, she fell into a contented doze.

'Wake up, sleepyhead,' grinned Jamie, shaking her. 'You've been snoring for the past half-hour.'

'I don't snore,' she protested indignantly.

'Of course you don't, my sweet,' he teased. 'It must have been some farmer driving his pigs to market I heard.' He ignored her glare of outrage. 'Anyway, we're here now. What d'you think?'

Lucy stared at the little country inn, with its thatched roof and roses growing round the doorway, and smiled in pleasure. 'It's lovely,' she breathed. Her belly gave a sudden growl and it was her turn to grin. 'But I just hope the food is as good.'

'I'm sure it will be,' he assured her as the barge glided into the jetty and he helped her out. Paying the bargeman, he took her elbow and led her up the little path and pushed open the door of the inn.

The landlord bustled towards them, rubbing his hands and bowing obsequiously. 'My Lord Happington,' he gushed, 'what a pleasure to see your lordship again.' He bowed again, even deeper. 'The upper room is yours for as long as you want it.'

'Thank you, Hodges,' said Jamie, throwing a couple of sovereigns onto the scrubbed deal table. He winked at the man. 'Make sure we remain undisturbed.'

'But of course, my lord,' beamed the man. 'You know me. I am the very soul of discretion.'

'Is this an assignation, my lord?' giggled Lucy, as she went up the winding stairs.

Jamie slid his hand beneath her petticoats. 'Why don't you wait and see?' he said enigmatically, and at the top of the stairs he threw open the door and she walked through, smiling at him flirtatiously over her shoulder. Then turning back to look at the room, she froze in disbelief at the sight of the stout rope hanging from the bed canopy – and the two men lounging on the window seat, their faces concealed by vizards.

Oh no! How could she have been such a fool? To have been duped once was forgivable – to allow herself to be duped again was sheer idiocy.

Whirling round she slapped her husband's face with as much strength as she could muster. 'You bastard!' she hissed. 'Your fine words of remorse meant nothing, did they? It was all an act.'

He grabbed her flailing arm and flung her backwards onto the bed. 'And a damned hard one it was, too.' He smiled unpleasantly down at her, reached for the brandy bottle and raised it to his lips. Swallowing, he continued. 'All that moping and mowing: "Yes, my love. No, my love. Three bags full, my love". And not even a decent drink to wash the taste of it out of my mouth.'

He shrugged. 'Anyway, 'tis your own fault,' he went on. 'If you'd given me my money when I asked you, I would not have needed your sweet body to pay my debts.'

Lucy grasped at the straw. 'You can have the money,'

she promised. 'All of it. We could go back and get it now.'

'Too late, my sweet,' he said with mocking regret, and waved towards the two onlookers. 'These gentlemen are eager to sample your charms. You would not have me break my word, now would you?'

'Why not?' she said bitterly. 'You broke your vows to me.'

'Enough of your whining,' snapped Jamie, reaching for her. 'You brought this on your own head. Get up and get your clothes off.' He grabbed her by the arm, then yelped as she bent and sank her teeth into his wrist. 'Bitch!' he snarled, his temper not improved by the laughter of his audience.

Ignoring the blood staining his cuff he hauled her to her feet, seized her other wrist and bound them with the dangling rope so that she was forced to stand on tiptoe to keep her balance. 'Not quite so clever now, my love,' he sneered.

Reaching out he gripped her bodice and tore it away, to reveal her quivering white breasts. Panting, he wrenched at the waistband till it gave too, and dragged the tattered gown and petticoats down over her hips until she hung there naked and helpless. There was an appreciative whistle from the watching men.

Lucy glanced at them in apprehension, and then gasped in horror as Jamie produced a black velvet hood. Grinning evilly, he slipped it over her head and she was plunged into musty darkness.

For a long, long moment she hung there in an agony of suspense. Despite the muffling hood, fear made her senses unnaturally sharp. She could hear each whisper and rustle as if it were magnified a thousand times. What were they doing?

At first the strange hissing sound made her think of an adder slithering through grass, then she shrieked in agony as the lash curled round her hips. 'That's for slapping me,' snarled Jamie. The hissing came again and another tongue of flame licked at her pale skin, leaving a fiery weal in its wake. 'And that's for all those weeks of bowing and scraping.' As he continued to curse and whip her she moaned and jerked at the end of the rope, her backside aflame.

When he had finished she was sobbing and the smooth curves of her bottom were scarlet. Pain throbbed through her, but even worse were the tendrils of heat that coiled insidiously through her lower tummy, the pain mingling with vile pleasure. She moaned, her muscles trembling involuntarily as Jamie ran the handle of the whip mockingly up between her legs, the harsh leather scraping the silken flesh of her thighs.

'She's all yours, gentlemen,' he announced.

Lucy heard the sound of movement, and then jerked again as anonymous hands began to fondle her breasts and explore the secret place between her thighs. Humid breath wafted over her skin and a slobbering mouth replaced the fingers at her breast. A tongue rasped across her nipples and she shuddered shamefully as she felt the little traitors harden.

She groaned as a finger skewered into her anus – then the groan became a squeal of dismay as it retreated and a rigid penis took its place. At the same time her legs were pulled apart and she felt another erection push its way roughly between the lips of her sex. Oh, they would tear her apart!

She struggled helplessly at the end of the rope as both men forced their way, inch by slow inch, inside her trembling body until she felt she could take no more. One pair of hands gripped her hips, another hand continued to maul her breasts, while yet another thumbed the bud of her clitoris.

Darkness and heat engulfed her and she spiralled out of control. As they began to thrust in unison, their cocks plunging in and out, her eyelids flickered shut and her mouth opened as she gave way to the incredible sensations rushing through her.

She could hear nothing but the savage grunting of her tormentors, the slap of flesh on flesh and the sound of her own moaning. Each thrust brought her closer to release, and when their seed erupted inside her even the hood was not enough to muffle her shrieks of pleasure.

They withdrew, and as she slumped on the end of the rope and regained her breath she heard muffled voices, the rustling of clothing and finally the sound of the door opening and closing. When Jamie tore the hood from her head, they were alone.

'You filthy little trollop,' he snarled as he freed her. 'You disgust me!'

Pulling on her tattered clothing she followed him out, head bowed. Lost in a welter of shame and misery she huddled in the barge, barely aware of the trip back to Whitehall. She had no need of Jamie's words of condemnation.

She disgusted herself.

'Won't you get up, madam?' begged Joanie. 'Just for a little while? You've been lying in bed for nearly a week.'

'Leave me alone,' Lucy murmured, rolling over. What reason was there to rise? So that her husband – husband, hah! Her whoremonger, more like! – could use her body as coinage to pay his debts again?

Misery washed over her. She was nothing more than a

pawn to be used however her masters pleased. First Master Watkins and now Jamie, and she could not even console herself that he was old and might die and free her. He would use her till her youth and beauty were gone and she was nothing but a raddled old whore.

''Tis Lady Castlemaine's ball tonight,' coaxed Joanie.

'Then she will have to do without me,' muttered Lucy. 'For I am not going.'

'Oh well,' sighed Joanie. 'Tha'ss that, then. Le'ss hope your absence does not give credence to her rumour that you have been so long abed because you're poxed and dare not show your face.'

'What?' gasped Lucy, sitting bolt upright in outrage. 'How dare she?' She swung her legs out of bed. 'Well, I'll show the bitch if I'm poxed or not! Fetch me my robe.'

'Yes, m'm, right away, m'm,' said Joanie, bobbing a curtsey to hide her smile at the success of her subterfuge.

'Do I look all right?' she asked, staring anxiously at her reflection and smoothing her satin skirts.

'Beautiful, madam,' said Joanie. 'You'll show that Castlemaine a thing or two tonight.' She handed her mistress her fan. 'Now, shall I fetch Thomas to escort you?'

Lucy nodded.

At the door of the Queen's Reception Chamber she paused, took a deep breath, walked in – then froze in horror. Joanie had not said it was a *masked* ball! Her stomach lurched as she looked from one hidden face to another. Any of these men could have been her ravishers. Her head spun and the merry laughter turned to jeers. Whirling on her heel she fled, sobbing.

236

Blinded by tears she did not even see the man until she almost sent him flying. He held out a hand to steady her. 'Come now, why so sad?' he asked. He was masked, too, but the eyes that looked down at her were kind. Then slipping his arms around her he patted her back as if she were a skittish horse.

Gradually her sobs faded and she became aware that his hand was caressing rather than patting, and that her body was responding. Her breasts were pressed against his chest, and under his breeches she could feel his manhood swelling.

When he tenderly wiped away the last of her tears she smiled and put up her face to be kissed – and when he took her hand and led her towards one of the private rooms she followed.

Naked beneath her anonymous lover's body, she gave herself to him completely. What did it matter that she didn't know his name or rank? He was kind and gentle and that was enough. His impressive cock moved slowly inside her, then faster until her back arched, her breath caught in her throat and the last of her tension released itself in her final cry of satisfied desire.

'A most unexpected pleasure, my dear,' he said, kissing her breasts. 'I must congratulate Lady Castlemaine on the success of her ball.' He peeled off his vizard and Lucy's mouth opened in speechless shock.

When Jamie next deigned to show his face in their apartments, it was his turn to be shocked. It was a shambles and Lucy stood in the middle of it all, supervising the packing of her travelling chests.

'What the hell's going on?' he demanded, pushing past the porters who were carrying out her things.

'What does it look like?' smiled Lucy. 'I am moving to

apartments of my own.'

'B-but… you can't!' he said in outrage. 'You are my wife!' He lowered his voice. 'Besides, I have arranged another little "supper party" for you to attend. I owe my Lord Randall almost two thousand guineas.'

'What a shame,' purred Lucy. 'Still, never mind, my love; I have heard that he is fond of gentlemen as well as ladies. This time you can pay with your own arse, instead of mine.'

He gawped at her for a moment, and then rallied. 'I know what this is about, you little strumpet,' he sneered. 'You've taken a lover.' His lips twisted. 'My God! You really are a slut!'

'Yes, I am,' agreed Lucy equably. 'And who made me so? Why, my two loving husbands.'

'I knew it!' he snarled. 'But just wait! You'll come running back to me soon enough, when he casts you off.'

'Oh, I doubt it,' smiled Lucy, walking towards the door that led to freedom. She might have a taste for pain as well as pleasure, but from now on she would choose where and with whom she would satisfy it. She would never be anyone's pawn again.

'Once a whore, always a whore,' he jeered, flinging his final barb.

'True,' she agreed, and paused on the threshold of her glittering future to smile triumphantly, and blow him a last, mocking kiss.

'But now I am the king's whore!'

All **Chimera** titles are available from your local bookshop or newsagent, or direct from our mail order department. Please send your order with your credit card details, a cheque or postal order (made payable to *Chimera Publishing Ltd*) to: **Chimera Publishing Ltd., Readers' Services, PO Box 152, Waterlooville, Hants, PO8 9FS**. Or call our **24 hour telephone/fax credit card hotline: +44 (0)23 92 646062** (Visa, Mastercard, Switch, JCB and Solo only).

To order, send: Title, author, ISBN number and price for each book ordered, your full name and address, cheque or postal order for the total amount, and include the following for postage and packing:
UK and BFPO: £1.00 for the first book, and 50p for each additional book to a maximum of £3.50.
Overseas and Eire: £2.00 for the first book, £1.00 for the second and 50p for each additional book.

*Titles £5.99. **All others (latest releases) £6.99**

For a copy of our free catalogue please write to:

Chimera Publishing Ltd
Readers' Services
PO Box 152
Waterlooville
Hants
PO8 9FS

or email us at:
chimera@chimerabooks.co.uk

or purchase from our range of superb titles at:
www.chimerabooks.co.uk

Chimera Publishing Ltd

PO Box 152
Waterlooville
Hants
PO8 9FS

www.chimerabooks.co.uk

chimera@chimerabooks.co.uk

***

Sales and Distribution in the USA and Canada

Client Distribution Services, Inc
193 Edwards Drive
Jackson
TN 38301
USA

***

Sales and Distribution in Australia

Dennis Jones & Associates Pty Ltd
19a Michellan Ct
Bayswater
Victoria
Australia 3153